A House to Die For

A DARBY FARR MYSTERY

A House to Die For

Vicki Doudera

WHEELER
CHIVERS

This Large Print edition is published by Wheeler Publishing, Waterville, Maine, USA and by BBC Audiobooks Ltd, Bath, England.
Wheeler Publishing, a part of Gale, Cengage Learning.
The text of this Large Print edition is unabridged.
Other aspects of the book may vary from the original edition.
Set in 16 pt. Plantin.

LIBRARY OF CONGRESS CATALOGING-IN-PUBLICATION DATA

Doudera, Victoria, 1961–
    A house to die for : a Darby Farr mystery / by Victoria
Doudera.
      p. cm. — (Wheeler Publishing large print cozy mystery)
    ISBN-13: 978-1-4104-2746-5 (pbk.)
    ISBN-10: 1-4104-2746-3 (pbk.)
    1. Women real estate agents—Fiction. 2. Murder—Investigation—Fiction. 3. Real estate business—Fiction. 4. Maine—Fiction. 5. Large type books. I. Title.
    PS3604.O895H68 2010b
    813'.6—dc22   2010013125

BRITISH LIBRARY CATALOGUING-IN-PUBLICATION DATA AVAILABLE
Published in 2010 in the U.S. by arrangement with Midnight Ink, an imprint of Llewellyn Publications, Woodbury, MN 55125–2989 USA.
Published in 2010 in the U.K. by arrangement with Llewellyn Worldwide Ltd.

U.K. Hardcover: 978 1 408 49164 5 (Chivers Large Print)
U.K. Softcover: 978 1 408 49165 2 (Camden Large Print)

Printed in the United States of America
1 2 3 4 5 6 7 14 13 12 11 10

Dedicated to my family, and in particular, my husband Ed, for his unflagging help, love, encouragement, and countless dinner preparations; and to Scott Horty, with grateful thanks for giving me my start in real estate.

PROLOGUE

The ring of the hospital pager ripped through the quiet night like a gunshot. Dr. Emerson Phipps woke instantly, his body tuned to the sound from years of interrupted slumber. He reached for his watch and swore. *Three A.M. So much for a decent night's sleep.*

Phipps pulled himself out of his king-sized bed, unable to suppress a groan. Fumbling in the dark for his cell phone, he hit the speed dial for Boston Memorial Hospital. "Phipps. What is it?"

A hesitant voice on the other end described an accident in West Roxbury and the badly damaged spine of the victim. "The patient fell off a rooftop deck during a party. I know Dr. Masterson is on call, but he's in the neonatal ICU with a spina bifida delivery. I thought . . ."

"You thought correctly." The nurse calling was new to the hospital, but Phipps could picture her ponytailed hair and ready smile. "It's Amanda, isn't it? I really appreciate your diligence and quick thinking."

"Thank you, Doctor." She was flattered, he could tell, and as he hung up the phone he allowed himself to imagine Amanda in his penthouse. A little wine, a look at his fabulous view of the skyline, a few questions about her work at the hospital . . . He yanked off his silk pajamas and tossed them on the bed.

Once dressed, Phipps padded on the plush carpet down the hallway, his powerful body tensing as he thought about the patient awaiting his skilled hands. No telling how long the operation would take. Depending on the spinal cord injury, he could be in surgery for hours. He stopped before the hall closet and frowned. He'd planned to drive up the coast today, and now he'd have to change his plans. Dick Masterson was a fairly decent surgeon, but he was notoriously slow. It might take all day before the plodding doctor stepped in to relieve him.

Phipps pulled a butter-soft leather jacket from a hanger, inhaling its rich scent. For a few seconds he was transported back to Milan and the posh store where he'd purchased it. He saw the clerk's appreciative nod of approval when he chose the highest grained leather without regard to the cost, the admiring glances the women on the street had thrown his way. There's a man who knows fine things, their faces said. A man who can afford life's greatest luxuries . . .

And one of those luxuries was waiting for him on an island in Maine: Fairview, a magnificent estate overlooking the Atlantic, a place that spoke of privilege, prestige, and power. He'd wanted it since the first time he saw it, and now, a dozen years later, it would finally be his. He glanced at his overnight bag, already packed for the trip. Why not throw it in the car and leave straight from the hospital? That way, no matter how long Dick Masterson took with his surgery, Phipps would be ready to blow out of town and head north.

The bag felt light in Phipps' confident grasp, but he knew without looking that he'd packed all that he needed: a few polo shirts, a sailing jacket, and shorts, attire suitable to the yachting haven of Hurricane Harbor. *A little different than Haiti,* he thought wryly. On his frequent trips to volunteer for the non-profit group Surgeons Who Serve, he lugged a large duffel bag crammed with malaria medication and clothing appropriate for mosquito-infested jungles and Third-

World accommodations. It was a different world, and one in which the surgeon found himself oddly at home. A place where money, looks, prestige, and power paled in comparison to medical training and talent.

Taking one final opportunity to glance in the hall mirror, Phipps made a minute adjustment to the jacket's collar. He grabbed his car's key fob from the antique chest beneath the mirror, where a framed photo of one of his Haitian patients, a toddler named Celina, leaned against the wall. She smiled crookedly at him, her dark hair covered with tiny plastic barrettes, and he remembered the sobs of her mother outside the makeshift operating room in Trou du Nord. Eight hours of surgery to correct the little two-year-old's scoliosis: eight hours cutting gaps between vertebrae, grafting bone from her pelvis, and installing metal rods to hold the spine still while the vertebrae fused correctly, all under a weak 60-watt lightbulb dangling from a piece of jute. The conditions had been atrocious, and yet the little girl could now run normally through the village, a testament to his skill and her tenacious spirit.

He sighed and willed himself not to wonder whether Celina was still robust and healthy. Instead, he made sure his door was locked and stepped into a waiting elevator.

The parking garage was eerily quiet and Emerson Phipps' footsteps echoed sharply in the darkness. He strode purposefully to his space and popped open the back of his BMW 760Li, tossing in his overnight bag and closing it securely. Once inside the rich leather interior, he wasted no time in pushing the start button and speeding into the night. Behind him, the garage echoed with the sound of the twin turbocharged engines.

The streets were vacant and dark, unusually quiet for the tail end of a Saturday. Phipps noted an oily slickness coating the pavement; it had obviously rained while he slept. Despite the slippery surface, he drove the sedan a good twenty miles over the limit. He'd been stopped several times for speeding, but so far had not received a ticket, or a warning for that matter. In fact, the cops who'd approached him and asked for his license and registration had been embarrassed when he explained his haste. *Officer, I'm a surgeon, on my way to save a life . . .*

Minutes later he was inside the brightly lit corridors of Boston Memorial's Emergency Room. The sights and sounds of the ER — haggard relatives slumped on plastic chairs, the drone of CNN on the television, the smell of bitter coffee and hand sanitizer — no longer registered. Oblivious to the banality around him, Emerson Phipps made his way to the trauma rooms, pausing to peer at the charts to find his patient. He felt a light touch on his arm and turned sharply. Amanda's round face quickly colored.

"Dr. Phipps — I didn't mean to startle you . . ."

"No problem," he said smoothly, giving her a dazzling smile. "So where's this SCI you interrupted my beauty sleep for?"

She giggled softly and pointed at an adjoining room. "In 3. Dr. Chan checked his vitals and she said to tell you she'd be back. The patient's on a backboard — the paramedics did that — but Dr. Chan didn't want him moved until you had a look."

Emerson Phipps nodded. *As it should be,* he thought. After all, he was the expert in the field. He gave Amanda a boyish grin and reached up for the chart, but as he opened the door he made his face a mask of composure. Family members would be waiting, and for them, he needed to look appropriately somber.

To his surprise, there were no anxious visitors at the patient's bedside. Phipps shrugged and focused on the victim. He lay on a gurney, still strapped to a rigid board

12

which the paramedics had used to transport him. One side of his face was covered in a large purple bruise, the eye on that side swollen shut. His looks were the least of his problems, however. Glancing on the chart, Phipps saw that his pelvis and left femur were broken, along with a few ribs and his neck.

His neck. Phipps gazed at it, dispassionately, trying to gauge the extent of the trauma to the spinal cord. They'd need an MRI to see which vertebrae were damaged, and whether the injury could in some way be improved. Repaired, he knew, was out of the question, but if a piece of bone was pressing on a vertebra or a nerve, some pain might be relieved. He scrawled a note on the chart. *Methylprednisone.* This medication was a corticosteroid that reduced damage to nerve cells, decreasing inflammation near the site of injury. It seemed to cause some recovery in patients if given within eight hours of injury.

He looked at the man, little more than a stationary bundle of sheets and mangled bone, and judged him to be in his early twenties. A small diamond stud sparkled from one earlobe. His hair was dark and curly, and needed a washing. And yet Emerson Phipps knew that this patient would never again shampoo his own hair, or change his earring. Without even seeing an X-ray, Phipps sensed that the C-1 vertebrae was crushed, the one that controlled the arms, legs, and even breathing. It would be a miracle if the poor guy found the strength to go on living once he realized his fate.

Phipps sighed and prepared to leave the room when something — an instinct he couldn't define, an unnatural stillness in the room, a sweet thin odor that he only now was just beginning to notice — made him stop, and reach instead to the carotid artery for a pulse. Phipps' trained fingers felt nothing. Puzzled, he put on his stethoscope and listened for a heartbeat. Again, nothing. He sighed and put the stethoscope back in his pocket. This patient was dead, most likely by a heart attack — and, judging by the extent of his injuries, it was probably a good thing.

Idly he wondered why an alarm hadn't sounded when the patient had stopped breathing. The ventilator was there, and the patient was on it. Just then Phipps noticed the power cord to the ventilator. It lay on the floor, unplugged.

A stab of alarm pulsed through his body. Why wasn't the guy on a heart monitor? *Some clumsy EMT knocked the cord out,* he thought. It happened, more often than any hospital wanted to admit. His second thought was one of self-preservation. *They're not insinuating I had anything to do with this . . .*

Phipps knew the nurse Amanda would have noted the time she phoned, and luckily he had been prompt in answering her page. He'd checked in upon entering the hospital so he was covered there, as well. Timing was everything, and this morning, Phipps had done it all perfectly.

And yet he didn't want even a hint of a scandal. Twice he'd been called to appear before the hospital ethics committee on charges of negligent behavior, just because he'd started a few surgeries later than scheduled. Both instances had been dismissed, but of course the newspapers had carried the stories. *Did Surgeon's Tardiness Lead to Death?* He swore under his breath. He was not about to let this night create another hassle with the hospital administration.

Emerson Phipps knew how to disable the machine's built-in recorder system, and he did it quickly and with a calm that came from making life and death decisions every day. He checked that no one had entered the room without his hearing, and then, taking a quick breath, he plugged the respirator back in.

While the machine made its reassuring hum and pumped oxygen into non-functioning lungs, Emerson Phipps jotted down a time of death. Calmly, he paged Amanda in the nurses' station and told her the patient had coded. She gasped and hurried into the room, her pretty face puckered with worry.

He placed a reassuring hand on Amanda's shoulder and locked his eyes with hers. "Poor guy couldn't take the trauma," he said softly. "His body was just too battered."

Amanda bit her lip and Phipps could see tears in her eyes.

"He's just a few years younger than me," she whispered. "A college kid. Way too young to die."

Dr. Phipps nodded gravely. "Ask Dr. Chan to notify the family," he said, putting the chart back in its holder. "I've been called out on urgent business."

He saw the look of dismay cross the young nurse's face.

"I hate to leave you with all this," he said, his eyes dropping down to the pink ribbon she wore on her scrubs and lingering there a moment before once more meeting her gaze. "You organized the cancer walk back in the fall, right?"

She nodded, blushing again, and he smiled. "Make sure you see me for a check next time. I'm happy to help." He glanced at his watch, the pink gold glinting under the fluorescent lights. "Look, if I didn't know how competent you are . . ."

She exhaled quickly and shook her head. "You go, Dr. Phipps. Go and do what you need to do. I'll handle this and track down Dr. Chan."

He smiled. "You're an angel, Amanda."

Twenty minutes later he was seated in his BMW, speeding north to Maine.

The sun rose just as he crossed the bridge from New Hampshire, a rosy ball rising up out of the blue water and climbing effort-lessly into the sky. After stopping for coffee and a stale blueberry muffin, Phipps climbed back into his car and drove an hour or so more, up the coast to the working-class city of Manatuck. He waited with the fishermen in the line for the first boat of the day, noticing the admiration of the ferry workers as he purred past them and onto the ramp. "Get used to it," he said softly. "You're going to be seeing a lot more of this car." Twenty minutes later, he steered the sedan off the ferry and onto the island of Hurricane Harbor.

He drove slowly past the trim little cape that served as the ferry office. A few clumps of people stood waiting to board the ferry, but Phipps paid them no attention. Instead he headed up the hill, past the little café with its window boxes crammed with flowers, the dingy little bar, and the hotel, a stately Victorian structure upon whose wide porch a few tourists were already perched. Beyond the few buildings that served as the island's center was a crescent-shaped piece of land called Long Cove, a sheltered inlet of water dotted here and there with lobster buoys and one or two small sailboats. At the fork in the road, Phipps turned right, where a small wooden sign said simply, "Pemberton Point" and beneath that, in capital letters, "PRIVATE."

His heart quickened as he drove down the wooded road. He knew he shouldn't have come — Mark had advised him to lay low — but he couldn't help himself. His longing to see the estate again was so intense, he was willing to drive three hours for a ten- or fifteen-minute look. *The buyer won't be at the property,* he reasoned. *Not this early in the morning . . .*

The buyer. *Let her enjoy the feeling, because it wasn't going to last.* If all went ac-

18

cording to plan — and it would — he would be the one with the keys to Fairview sometime Monday afternoon. *She's about to be broadsided and she doesn't even know it.* The thought filled him with the same adrenalin that flooded his veins in the operating room.

Phipps knew that his purchase of Fairview was a gamble, but he was a man used to taking chances and having them go in his favor. As he turned down the curving, tree-lined driveway that led to the Trimble estate, he felt a surge of anticipation. Nevertheless, he drove slowly on the dirt road, careful to keep the rocks from spinning up and damaging his paint job. *I'll have it paved next week.*

He slowed to a stop and looked up at the main house, as impressive as any English manor or French chateau. *Fairview,* he whispered. The very sound filled him with a longing that was almost unbearable. He said it again, letting it roll off his tongue.

The property was as beautiful as it had been the previous Saturday when he'd raced up from Boston and submitted his offer, as breathtaking as the first time he'd laid eyes on it, all those years before. It was more than the house, or the staggering view, or the formal gardens landscaped to perfection. It was the whole idea of an island retreat and what it represented. A mini-kingdom, *his* mini-kingdom, with tennis courts, an airstrip, and an indoor pool. It was an estate that rivaled any along the Atlantic coast, a property that was the envy of everyone who knew tony Hurricane Harbor, of anyone back in Boston who knew exquisite taste. It represented everything he had ever worked for, the life he had carefully crafted. *Mine,* he thought. *It will soon be mine.*

He let his eyes linger for a moment more on the weathered shingles and listened to the crash of the surf beyond the house. Phipps had made arrangements to get inside, but the person with the key wasn't due until eight o'clock. Phipps looked at his watch with impatience. Twenty minutes before the hour. He thought fleetingly of the elderly real estate broker upon whose frail shoulders the whole deal rested, and wondered if she was the one meeting him. What the hell was her name? Jean? Joan? Jane. Jane Farr. She still had all her marbles, he had to give her credit for that. And those penetrating eyes . . . It was as if she'd seen right through him, and known, somehow, that Fairview was something he would acquire at any cost. She'd come up with the whole thing . . .

Phipps looked at the time again. *I wish to hell she'd get here.* Jane Farr hadn't wanted this meeting, but with nearly six million dollars on the table, she'd been easy to convince. The whole thing had been easy, which was just the way Phipps liked it.

He decided to walk to the back of the house, stretch his legs before he began driving once more.

He strode across the verdant grass, damp with the morning dew. A few gulls cried out as he rounded the corner, their shrieks like screams against the early morning stillness. A rabbit darted from behind a clump of beach roses, and Emerson Phipps jumped. *I'm not used to peace and quiet. I'm used to life or death.*

The cove was calm, save for the sound of a gentle swell buffeting the rocks below. Phipps peered over the craggy cliffs that jutted out like fingers and saw a path winding down to the small beach below. He'd hire a landscaper and put in stairs, so that his nephews could scamper down there and not break their necks in the process. His thoughts wandered back to the emergency room and the unfortunate patient he'd seen hours earlier. Poor Amanda had seemed rattled by the whole thing. *I'll call her later. She may want to talk.* The memory of the young nurse and her bouncy little ponytail made him smile. She was pretty, in a wholesome, earnest way, not like the angular models he usually dated. *Maybe I'm ready to give all that up. Be the kind of person my sister thinks I am . . .*

He glanced again at his watch and noted that it was nearly eight. With one last look at the cove, he turned and started back to the front of the house. There was a small orchard on the southern side of the estate, and Phipps wondered what fruit he would soon be harvesting. He wished he'd brought his PDA, but it was tucked in the glove compartment of the BMW. That, too, could wait for the journey back to Boston.

As he approached the orchard, he heard what sounded like a low moan. He turned in the sound's direction, expecting to see the elderly real estate agent, perhaps with a sprained ankle, hobbling toward him. He saw no one, but a shingled garden shed with its door ajar caught his attention. He listened intently. There it was again: a cry of pain, and it seemed to be coming from the shed.

Phipps shook his head. He was off duty, for Chrissakes, and the last thing he wanted to do was play hero doctor. Nevertheless, he strode across the lawn and entered the shed, stepping gingerly on the old wooden floor. The smell of compost, oil, and cut grass mingled into a pleasing mixture he associated with summer. Inside it was dark, and dusty, and he waited for an instant so his eyes would adjust, all the while listening keenly so he could locate the victim. "Hello?" he called out. "I'm a doctor. I can help you."

A crackling sound split the silence and Phipps felt a jolt run through his torso. Without warning his legs buckled beneath him, and an instant later he was collapsing onto the floor of the shed. He heard the soft thud of his bones against the worn wood, felt the floor rush up to meet his face like a slap. He tried to speak, to wonder aloud what had happened, but his tongue was fat and heavy and he couldn't move his lips. *I'm paralyzed,* he told himself with surprise. *I've had some kind of stroke or something . . .*

He heard a muffled movement, the sound of something heavy being dragged across the wooden floor. His brain was scrambling to figure out what was happening: the moan of pain, the sudden crackle, his quick collapse. *Not a stroke,* he realized, *some kind of attack!* Before he could follow this line of reasoning further, he heard a grunt of exertion and saw the blurred outline of a body just beyond his line of vision. Another grunt, and then a searing pain as the weight of something very heavy came crashing down on his skull.

Emerson Phipps felt the warm gush of his own blood coursing like a red river across his face, spilling down the gullies of his cheeks and making a waterfall off his jutting chin. He heard another grunt and instinct kicked in, warning him to move before he was bludgeoned again. His battered brain begged his legs to run, or crawl at least, but it was useless — he couldn't even feel his toes. He was incapacitated, like so many of the patients he'd treated over the years. Images flashed before him like flickering strobe lights — his car, little Celina with her gap-toothed baby smile, the rows of trees lined up like sentinels in the orchard — and then, just before the blow that would split open his skull, Emerson Phipps lost consciousness.

ONE

Darby Farr slowed her fast run to a stop and pulled her cell phone out of the liner of her Lycra running shorts. *Finally,* she thought. *The buyer for the Costa Brava mansion is stepping up to the plate.* The fact that it was a sunny Sunday morning didn't matter in real estate, at least not to Darby Farr. Her position as the top selling agent for San Diego's Pacific Coast Realty meant that she conducted business at any hour of any day, to virtually anyone willing to buy one of her listings, the most inexpensive of which was a mere million dollars.

Out of habit, she glanced quickly at the display before answering. What she saw made her heart, already pounding from her run, race even faster. Displayed on the screen was a number from a place she'd spent ten years forgetting, a place that still haunted her dreams. With a trembling hand she switched her phone to silence, stashed

25

it back in her shorts, and ran toward the beach.

The boardwalk was dotted with bikers, bladers, and skateboarders, but Darby barely noticed their presence. While her feet beat a steady drumbeat along the wooden walkway, she sifted through a confusing maze of long-forgotten images. She saw the red pickup she'd stolen and driven cross country to San Diego's Mission Beach. The cash that she'd found in her aunt's desk and stuffed in her denim jacket. She remembered her final trip on the ferry, the gulls wheeling and circling, the sky a brilliant blue like today . . .

She shook her head. Her long glossy black hair rippled and she forced the unwelcome memories out of her mind. She'd kept the past buried for ten years, and she wasn't about to let it resurface now. *Focus on your breathing,* she told herself. *Forget everything else but the coffee waiting for you back at the bungalow . . .*

Sirens wailing down the next street brought Darby's thoughts back to the present. She ran off the boardwalk and onto Pacific Street, slowing her pace to begin her cool down. The next street was Palm, a mix of homes built in the 1950s, most of which had been restored in the past decade. She admired the Arts and Crafts-style home of her neighbor, Doug Henderson, who was sweeping off his front porch as usual and humming show tunes. He gave Darby a little wave as always. She smiled and waved back, then walked up the neat little path that served as her walkway.

"Your phone's been ringing and ringing," he yelled from the porch. "I don't think your voice mail is picking up."

Darby groaned. Her answering machine was ready for retirement, but she'd been too busy to replace it this week. "Thank you," she called. She picked up her newspaper and tucked it under her arm.

"Hey!" yelled Doug. "Got a second to taste something for me?"

"This wouldn't be another one of your little tests, now would it, Doug?" Darby walked across the grass, a smile playing about her lips.

"Oh, come on," her neighbor cajoled, disappearing back into his home.

Darby waited, enjoying the rush of post-run endorphins. She stole a glance at the headlines, heard a thrush singing in one of Doug's flowering shrubs.

"Here you go," Doug said, emerging back on the porch and offering her a blue china cup full of steaming tea.

She frowned. "Now Doug, you know the rules: white cups only. Using a colored one is cheating." She took a moment to note the pale yellow color; inhaled the tea's rich aroma. "However, I think I'm going to get this one even with your flagrant disregard of the rules."

She took a sip and smiled.

"Doug, you've gone all out today. This is one expensive cup of tea." She took another sip. "It's delicious: sweet and lingering. I taste fresh grass, seaweed, and a hint of the woods."

Doug waited expectantly. "What do you think it is?"

She smiled. "I know what it is. Hongyokuro, a rare grade of Gyokuro, from the Yame region of Japan near Fukuoka. 'Precious Pearl Dew' is the translation. Harvested in the early spring, I believe."

"Unbelievable!" He shook his head. "Palate memory, huh? That's what you call it?"

She nodded. "That's right."

"Your mom was Japanese, right? Is this a tea she used to make?"

Darby laughed. "My mother couldn't have afforded this. She was a 'Constant Comment' drinker from the day she set foot in America." Darby thought back to the first time she'd tasted the exquisite green tea

28

now in her hands. "I tried Hongyokuro two years ago, over at the Beach House Tea Room." She took another sip and handed him back his cup. "Delicious. Thanks for letting me enjoy it again."

Back at her bungalow, Darby removed her sneakers and placed them on the stoop, then reached discreetly into her jog bra to find her house key. Opening the door she inhaled the rich smell of coffee, as welcome in the morning as an embrace. She loved teas of just about every variety, but coffee was what got Darby Farr fired up each morning.

I want nothing more than to sit in the sun and read the paper, she thought, but her intuition told her such leisure wasn't to be. As the most sought-after real estate professional in San Diego County, she had a duty to an ever-growing list of clients with properties to market and sell, and an even longer list of eager buyers craving her expertise as a broker. She loved every minute of it, despite the fact that her newspaper often went unread. Sighing, she poured herself a cup of Hawaiian Morning Blend and took a long sip. She savored its flavor for a minute more, then pulled out her cell phone and turned it on.

Ten missed calls. Ten, all from the same

number. Her heart sank. She knew where the calls had come from, and could guess who'd made them. She just didn't know why.

Darby Farr took another sip of coffee, fighting the feeling of nausea that threatened whenever she thought about her hometown and Jane Farr, the only living family member she had left in the world. Her aunt Jane had swooped into Darby's life just as she was entering her teens, becoming her guardian and destroying her previously blissful childhood. A predatory woman with shrewd eyes and jet black hair, Jane had devoured Darby and the town of Hurricane Harbor, Maine, like a fish hawk in a stocked pond.

Darby took a deep breath and another sip of coffee. It had been hard work, putting distance between herself and the craggy island. It had meant attempting to forget the people and things she had loved, too. Darby didn't know if it was coincidence, or the fact that her thirtieth birthday was in sight, but lately she had wondered whether it was time to face her demons, chief amongst whom was Aunt Jane Farr. And yet, there was so much at stake . . .

Darby looked at the last call from Maine. Fifteen minutes had elapsed; perhaps Jane Farr had given up on reaching her runaway

30

niece. *If she calls again, I'll answer,* Darby promised herself. *If not, I'll forget all about it.* A second later, the ring of the phone made her jump.

Darby braced herself for the voice of her aunt, a sound she recalled as quite similar to the rasp of a rattlesnake.

"Is this Darby Farr?"

"Who's calling please?" The speaker's voice was definitely not the one she remembered as belonging to her father's only sister.

"This is — this is Tina Ames. From Hurricane Harbor. I worked with your aunt . . ." She paused and Darby felt a strange sensation in the pit of her stomach. Apprehension, mixed with curiosity . . .

Darby heard the other woman sniffle and attempt to regain her composure. "I've been trying to reach you all morning. Jane's in the hospital in Manatuck. She's in a coma and the doctors don't think she'll pull through." The woman choked, and Darby could hear her soft sobs.

Jane Farr was on a bed, comatose. The news shocked Darby, and yet she felt oddly detached as well.

"What happened?"

"She has a brain tumor, and it was scheduled to be removed next week. But this morning, she was rushed to the hospital for

31

the operation, and she still hasn't come around." The sound of Tina's sniffles grew louder.

"I'm sorry about Jane. I appreciate your tracking me down and I hope you'll keep me in the loop . . ." Darby paused, not wanting to state the obvious "when she dies" and add to Tina's pain.

Tina blew her nose. "There's something . . . something she'd like you to do."

"Me?"

"Yes." Tina paused. "Your aunt needs you to finalize a deal she's been working on for months."

"What are you talking about? A real estate transaction?"

"The sale of the old Trimble property, Fairview. One of the prettiest places on the island. You must remember it . . ."

"Look, I —"

"Just listen. Last week your aunt sat me down and made me promise to call you if anything happened to her. She knew her surgery would be risky, and that there was a chance she'd be hospitalized before they got her on the table." She paused, took a breath. "I'm the one who types up all the documents for your aunt, and believe me, the sale of Fairview is a done deal. I've got all the files, and everything's in order. The parties pass papers on Tuesday."

"Tina, I'd like to help, but I'm really busy with my own work. And I'm on the other side of the country. I'm sure you've got brokers there who can handle this for her."

"I know where you are, Darby. I'm only asking for a few days of your time. And as for other brokers, your aunt didn't trust them to handle this. She wants you."

"I'm not even licensed to practice real estate in Maine."

Tina barked out a laugh. "You think your aunt hasn't got that figured out? You'll take the Maine law portion of the exam on the plane. You pass it, and you're licensed."

"That's impossible!"

"Not for Jane Farr it's not. That means you'll get the commission, too."

Darby shook her head. Her compassion for Tina was fast turning to irritation. Who was this woman and why did she think she could summon her to Maine on what certainly appeared to be a whim? Her aunt had always been a master manipulator, and apparently nothing had changed.

She struggled to keep her voice neutral, despite her annoyance.

"Look, it's not about the money . . ."

"Jane says it's always about the money," Tina interrupted, "which in this case is $5.5

million with a 6% commission. You get half and Jane keeps half. It's not exactly pocket change."

Darby closed her eyes. *No amount of money is worth the pain of going back,* she thought. *I'm just not ready . . .*

"I'm sorry, but I can't help you."

Tina was silent for a moment. When she spoke again, her tone was stony. "Are you getting what I'm trying to tell you? Your aunt is lying here unable to brush her own teeth, never mind conduct business. You've been given power of attorney to handle her decisions: medical, financial, you name it. And, in the event of her death —" Tina choked a little, "you've been appointed her personal representative. You've got responsibilities here. This isn't some whimsical jaunt back to Maine." She paused and continued. "No one can force you — least of all me — but I hope you see that it's the right thing to do. If it's money that's on your mind, the real estate company will pay all of your expenses, and, like I said, you'll earn commission as well."

The implications of Tina Ames' words struck Darby like a blow. Why, after ten years of silence, had her aunt chosen her to step in like this? Was there truly no one else to whom Jane Farr could turn? Darby knew she was not bound by law to go to Hurricane Harbor, and yet it seemed the old woman had made it impossible for her to refuse. *And,* she realized with some surprise, *I'll admit that I'm intrigued . . .*

"Your plane leaves today at 12:45 your time," Tina continued. "Your ticket and a packet of documents are waiting at the ticket counter. I'll meet you in Portland when you land, just before nine." She paused. "I think you'd better get packing."

The phone went dead and Darby looked at it incredulously. Ready or not, she was headed to Hurricane Harbor.

"Ms. Farr? Ms. Darby Farr?"

The voice was confident and strong. Darby Farr's eyes opened instantly and looked into the perfectly made up face of the flight attendant.

"I'm sorry to wake you," she continued smoothly. "A message just came in from the Portland Jetport. Your aunt's assistant, Tina Ames, will meet you at the baggage claim."

Darby Farr nodded. "Thank you. How long until we land?"

"About an hour. Coffee?"

"Thanks." Darby twisted her hair into a quick bun before accepting the steaming cup. The flight attendant gave her a smile

35

and offered cream and sugar.

"Congratulations," she murmured. "You passed the exam."

Darby shook her head and took a deep breath as the flight attendant continued down the companionway. The first hurdle was over: unbelievably, she was now licensed to sell houses in Maine. *Time to take a look at what the heck I'm doing here,* she thought.

Darby fingered the mysterious manila envelope she'd been given at the ticket counter back in California. She took a sip of her coffee, opened the packet, and began reviewing the typed pages.

On the top of the pile was the agreement for the sale of Fairview. Darby scanned it quickly, seeing nothing out of the ordinary. As Tina Ames had mentioned, the transaction was scheduled to close on Tuesday. Purchasing the property was a corporation called Pemberton Point Weddings, whose president was a Peyton Mayerson from Boston. The sellers were listed as Mark and Lucy Trimble. The deed to Fairview, also enclosed, confirmed that they owned the property.

Darby took another sip of coffee and sat back in the spacious first-class seat. She pictured Mark Trimble as he had been ten years earlier: tall, tanned, and handsome.

He had a square jaw and a wide, easy smile, straight brown hair that he parted on the side in a casual style. His teeth were straight and very white, thanks not only to good orthodontics but to the deep tan he acquired from his hours on the water as an avid sailor and sailing instructor.

In her early teen years, Darby — along with just about every girl in the sailing class — had had a huge crush on Mark, something his sister, Lucy Trimble, could never seem to fathom.

"Ugh," she'd exclaimed when her friend Darby had confessed she found Mark to be "sort of cute." "Are you kidding? I'm counting the days until he goes away to school! He leaves his dirty socks all over the front parlor and chews with his mouth open. You call that cute? I call that *disgusting!*"

Darby had shrugged and let the matter go — at fourteen, she preferred to admire boys from afar, anyway. By the time she was sixteen, she had put Mark Trimble out of her mind as a romantic prospect. He was off at college and never seemed to have time for his local friends.

Darby's thoughts turned to Lucy Trimble. A lithe, blonde charmer with the same good looks as her brother; she'd been Darby's closest friend until the third year of high school. Darby remembered the surprise she'd felt when Lucy did not show up for their first day as high school juniors.

"She's in Connecticut, at a boarding school," Mrs. Trimble had sniffed on the phone when a concerned Darby had called.

Connecticut? Darby's confusion had turned to anger over her friend's abrupt departure. *Why didn't she tell me? She didn't even say goodbye . . .*

After a month, she was over her anger, and phoned Mrs. Trimble for Lucy's address at her new school.

"It's best if you don't contact her at all," Lucy's mother answered crisply. "Her adjustment will be hard enough without hearing from her island friends."

Island friends. She'd said it like Darby carried a disease her precious Lucy could catch. Darby, dejected, told herself she'd lost her friend forever.

Unlike her brothers, Lucy didn't stay behind the ivy walls. Whatever the reason for her foray into the world of boarding school, it was a short tenure. By the following summer, Lucy Trimble was back on the island and enrolled in the senior class at Hurricane Harbor High. And yet she had changed . . .

Darby's initial delight at the return of her

38

friend turned quickly to despair. Lucy Trimble had transformed into someone Darby barely recognized. Frequently drunk or stoned, even in class, her friend exhibited all the classic symptoms of chemical addiction, but no one — not even her parents — seemed to care or comment on her bizarre behavior. *That was the summer she became an addict,* Darby realized with a pang.

I could have done something to help her. I could have told someone . . .

The flight attendant interrupted her thoughts with the offer of a refill. Darby accepted more coffee and went back to looking at the documents spread before her.

It was clear from the contract that Peyton Mayerson was buying Fairview to operate a wedding retreat, something the company name indicated as well. Pemberton Point Weddings was an apt choice. Even though the estate was named Fairview and locals referred to it as "the Trimble place," the beautiful promontory which jutted out from the property into the crashing surf was known as Pemberton Point. No doubt the promontory would be the spot where lucky brides and grooms would pose for their wedding photos, perhaps even take their vows.

A glossy four-color photograph caught

Darby's eye. It was an advertisement for Fairview, and penciled in the margin were the two publications in which it had run: the *New York Times* and *Boston Magazine*. Pretty pricey advertisements, Darby knew, but demographically perfect for a buyer of this ilk. Darby regarded the photograph with a critical eye. She saw a magnificent structure, with eight bedrooms, a giant wraparound porch filled with wicker rocking chairs, and several jutting eaves. Fairview's symmetry and design were truly unparalleled.

Darby recalled what she knew of the property's history. Built in the style of the sprawling, shingle-style mansions of the turn of the century, the house was the residence of a notoriously cantankerous steel baron from Pittsburgh, the great-grandfather of Lucy and Mark's mother. According to local legend, the gentleman was asked by a Pittsburgh newspaper reporter to describe the view from his dwelling's huge porch. Looking out upon the crashing surf and massive boulders, a sight that anyone would find divine, the man waved a dismissive hand and pronounced the view "fair." Or so the story claimed.

Darby remembered the home's high ceilings, ornate ballroom, and sweeping main staircase. Fairview was a gem, and Jane Farr had marketed it as such. *No one who sees Fairview forgets her,* read the advertisement on her lap. Darby had to admit that her aunt's sappy copy was probably dead on.

She glanced over the property description detailed in the listing packet. A multitude of outbuildings dotted the property's twenty acres, and all of them were conveyed with the sale. A guesthouse, gardening cottage, garage, and caretaker's house, along with a fanciful gazebo, were listed as part of the property inventory. Darby found a release from the buyer concerning the condition of the entire property. It seemed all of the buildings had been scrutinized by Pemberton Point Weddings' team of building inspectors and deemed satisfactory.

Darby gathered up the papers. She was still drowsy, but now that she'd done her homework, sleep was an appealing option. As she tried to slip the papers into the envelope, she met with resistance. Something was stuck at the bottom.

Reaching in, her fingers touched a piece of paper. It was an index card, three by five inches, without lines. In handwriting Darby recognized as belonging to her aunt was scrawled a single line: *Subject to planning board approval for zoning change and liquor license by 6/21.* The sentence was initialed by "PM," "MT," and "LT."

Darby frowned. The index card appeared to be an amendment to the contract, although it was a highly unusual and sloppy one. What could her aunt have been thinking, using such vague language? An index card? And yet Darby knew of multimillion dollar deals that had been scribbled on paper napkins . . .

She looked back at the purchase and sale agreement, but saw no reference to a planning board meeting. Apparently this little scrap of paper represented an unmet condition to the contract. A planning board meeting on the twenty-first of June. *That's tomorrow,* she realized with a shock.

The transaction was not quite a "done deal" as Tina had said. The zoning change was no doubt to modify the current residential status of Pemberton Point to commercial, since Pemberton Point Weddings was to be more than just a home business. Certainly a liquor license was a key component in Peyton Mayerson's plans to host elaborate and expensive weddings. Darby knew that, although a few towns in Maine were still "dry" — meaning alcoholic beverages could not be sold within the city limits — Hurricane Harbor was not one of them.

Generations of cocktail parties, dances, and wild nights at the town's bar had seen to that.

Nevertheless, the successful sale of Fairview was now contingent upon the common sense of a group of volunteers, serving on a town committee that met once a month to decide issues of licensure and zoning. These islanders would listen to the proposal to modify the zoning code, as well as for a permit to serve and sell alcohol, and then they would vote. It was a process as old as democracy itself, and one, Darby realized with a sinking heart, over which she had no control.

She leaned back in the airplane seat and closed her eyes. Worry was settling like a wet blanket on her shoulders, weighing her down with a damp feeling of doom. She exhaled slowly and tried to relax, but one question kept pounding at her brain. *What in the world am I doing?*

TWO

Tina Ames was tall and thin, with a long, straight nose and large dark sunglasses, which she sported inside the terminal although it was nearly ten P.M. She carried a large turquoise pocketbook over one shoulder and a can of Diet Coke in her hand. Her hair was a mass of red curls in a shade that nearly matched her long finger-nails.

"Knew it was you," she said, extending her free hand and shaking Darby's vigorously.

"How? Because I'm the only Asian woman in the airport?"

Tina gave her a sharp look. "Nah, I've seen your picture. You look pretty much the same as the one Jane's got in her office. Still got the long hair, the pretty almond eyes . . ." She contemplated Darby for a moment and then cocked her head to the side, like an egret on the lookout for a school of minnows. "You look a little older. Wiser, maybe. Where's your other bag?"

She lifted her duffel. "I've got everything with me. I'm only here for a few days."

Tina Ames pursed her lips and said nothing. She turned and began to walk toward the exit doors, her heels clicking on the hard floor of the terminal.

Darby watched her walk away. After a few seconds, Tina stopped and turned around.

"Let's get a move on. You're on the clock, you know."

"When is my flight back?"

"You really want to discuss this now?"

"I do. You've dragged me all the way across the country. I'm not going a step farther until I know when my flight back is booked."

Tina shook her head slowly and looked off to the side. "Well, that depends."

"On what?"

"On whether you plan to stay for your aunt's funeral."

"She's not —"

"Not yet. But the doctor says it could be any time." She dabbed at her eyes with a tissue and Darby could see that beneath the sunglasses they were red from crying.

The two women stood for a moment. Darby absorbed the news of her aunt's condition and tried to think about her options. She was a master negotiator, and part of her talent was knowing when to back down — at least for the moment. "Look, I'm sorry that my aunt's health is failing. I'm sorry that she didn't have anyone else to call. But I do have a life and career back in California, and I hope you understand that I want to be on that plane back to the West Coast as soon as possible." She approached the distraught woman, placing a hand on her shoulder and giving a gentle squeeze. "I'm sorry if we got off to a bad start. Let's go."

Tina sniffled and led Darby out of the airport to the parking garage, where a large GMC truck gleamed in the overhead lights. "Meet Thelma," she said, with a flourish and a brave attempt at lightening the mood. "She's loaded with every option from heated seats to a GPS system, and she's your aunt's pride and joy."

Darby regarded the massive vehicle. Her aunt had a penchant for driving enormous trucks with female names. "Jane's taste in transportation hasn't changed much in ten years," she noted. "I left Maine in Reba, and the truck before her was Scarlet."

Tina forced a chuckle. She unlocked the doors and the two women climbed in. She dabbed at her eyes again and gave a sad little hiccup.

"Are you okay to drive?" Darby asked.

She nodded and started the truck.

The two women were quiet for a while and Darby suspected that Tina was making every effort to compose herself. Finally she took a deep breath. "I'll say this to you just once, Darby, since you've spent seven hours flying clear across the country. Your aunt can be a giant pain in the ass."

She glanced at Darby's surprised face and nodded.

"I mean, have you ever met someone more unbelievably opinionated, stubborn as the day is long, and vain as Jane Farr?" She shook her head. "I've seen her call a broker a lazy son-of-a-bitch to his face, in front of his own clients! Man, I thought that guy was gonna sue her skinny ass." She paused. "But I'm not telling you anything new, am I?"

"Nothing I haven't thought myself a hundred times."

"I know."

Tina pointed out the window at the grass bordering the highway. In the sweep of Thelma's headlights, Darby could just make out the shoulders of Route I-95, dotted with tall, spiky flowers in shades of blue, purple, and pink.

"Loads of lupines this year."

Darby nodded. "I forgot how pretty they are."

In June, the blooms of the wildflower were everywhere, elegant splashes of color that stretched on for miles. Darby remembered picking lupines as she walked home from school, the way the stems were so sturdy it was easier to yank the whole plant out of the ground then tear them. She saw her mother's gentle smile as she trimmed the stalks, and the careful way she arranged them in a vase on the kitchen table, as if they were a work of art. She swallowed at the memory and her throat felt rubbed raw.

"What I'm trying to say is, I understand how you and your aunt could have your . . . differences, and I appreciate that you came anyway." She gunned the truck and passed the first vehicle they'd seen since the airport. "The thing with your aunt, is that despite her shortcomings, she is a hell of a woman. Her strengths outweigh her weaknesses by far, and you can't say that about everybody. I guess I hope you'll remember that side of her, too."

Darby looked out the window. The last person she wanted to talk about was Jane Farr, dead or alive, but she didn't want to upset Tina again. "Tell me about this deal," she said. "Especially tomorrow's meeting."

"You don't mean the planning board?" Tina snorted. "That's a formality."

"It's a condition of the property sale, is what it is."

Tina sniffed. "Well, in my opinion, it's no big deal. Peyton's got to get approval to do her resort the way she wants. The land is zoned residential single family, and she wants to put little cottages up, plus use it in a more commercial way. And she needs to serve booze, naturally. Who ever heard of a wedding without champagne?"

"Jane did her homework before she got sick, though. She spoke to all of the committee members and they all support the project. No one anticipates anything but the board's good wishes and the permit."

Darby smiled grimly. She'd heard that kind of talk before. "So you've met the buyer?"

Tina nodded. "Peyton Mayerson's in her late thirties, from Boston, working with a small group of investors to create this wedding destination resort. You know, people from New York and Boston book the whole damn place, have their wedding, take their sails on the bay, yuck it up at their posh lobster bakes — it's really catching on in

Maine. Seems everybody and his brother want to get married on the rocky coast and have what they think's a real authentic experience. The ministers can't even keep up with it." She snorted. "Most people I know get a bun in the oven, then go to the JP. None of this croquet on the lawn and tents set up on the grass." She swerved to avoid a dead animal in the road. "You know the Trimbles, right?"

"Mark helped my father run the sailing program at the yacht club. He's older than me, but we know one another. Lucy and I were friends for several years. I never really got to know Mr. and Mrs. Trimble."

Tina waved a manicured hand. "No matter. They're long gone, and so's the big brother — Wes, I think he was called? Anyway, it's just Mark and Lucy and they've been very easy clients. Jane would tell them to do something — bam! — they got it done. Fix this, paint that, whatever, they'd get somebody to take care of it. Neither one seems to have too much attachment to the old place, and it's been years since they lived there. Mark, especially, seemed relieved that the place is selling so soon. Who wants to keep taking care of a big empty house?" she sniffed. "If you ask me, I don't think Fairview was a very happy home."

Tina's cell rang and Darby watched her keep one hand on the truck's steering wheel while she fished around in the turquoise pocketbook for her phone. "We're on our way," she said. "We'll be there before eleven." When she snapped her phone shut, Darby saw that her pointy face was puckered with worry.

"That was the minister of the church your aunt goes to, you know, the one on the corner?"

Darby nodded. Jane had moved to Hurricane Harbor and become immersed in the little village church with a fervor Darby always suspected had more to do with listings than religion. Tina cleared her throat.

"She wants us to stop at the hospital in Manatuck. She thinks your aunt won't make it through the night." She looked at Darby with concern. "You think you can handle it?"

Darby shrugged. "What about you?"

"I don't know. I guess we'll find out."

Darby dozed for ten minutes or so, her mind darting into worrisome corners like a wild animal trapped in an abandoned cabin. She saw Mark and Lucy Trimble, Jane Farr, and the house she'd grown up in. Her parents were there too, smiling and reaching out their hands to hug her . . .

51

She woke with a start. Tina was parking the car at a large brick building that Darby recognized as Manatuck Community Hospital.

"We're going across in half an hour, so we don't have much time."

Darby stretched and followed Tina Ames across the parking lot and into the hospital. The lobby was well lit, with a large screen television and plenty of chairs, some of which, even at this late hour, were filled with waiting patients and family members.

A slim, petite woman with short frosted hair was waiting by the front desk. She gave Tina a smile of recognition.

"That's her," said Tina. "The minister of the church."

"Actually I'm the associate minister," the woman corrected, coming toward them. She proffered her hand. "I'm Laura Gefferelli. Your aunt has told me about you. I'm sorry you have to come back to Hurricane Harbor under such difficult conditions."

Darby shook the woman's hand. "Thanks."

Laura glanced at Tina and continued. "They've moved Jane over to a hospice room. They've got her on drip morphine so she's in no pain."

The three walked down a corridor and

into another wing of the hospital. Laura waved to several of the nurses; she was obviously a frequent visitor to the hospice wing. Minutes later she was opening the door of a quiet, dimly lit room with carpeting, an upholstered couch, and several paintings. In the middle of the room was a hospital bed upon which a frail woman lay sleeping.

Darby moved nearer and gazed down at the face that had once been so terrifying.

Age had softened her aunt's features, the way water wears down the jagged rocks in a stream. Her hair, formerly jet black and severely styled, was now dove gray and cut in a soft bob. Her eyes were closed and she appeared to be breathing easily.

Darby reached out and touched her aunt's shoulder. She felt the hard knob of bone beneath the thin sheets. *Somewhere in that mind are all the times we spent in opposition, all the battles we waged and the insults we flung.*

"Tell me what happened."

Laura Gefferelli nodded. "Jane was having transient ischemic attacks — they call them TIAs, or mini-strokes — and realized something was wrong. Dr. Carver, the neurosurgeon at Manatuck, did a CT scan and found the tumor. He recommended surgery, pretty much immediately. Jane got a second opinion down in Portland, and that physician concurred. This was last week, right Tina?"

Tina nodded.

"Yesterday, I stopped in to check on Jane," Laura continued. "She was prostrate on the floor with an excruciating headache. I brought her here and had them page Dr. Carver. An hour later, she was in the operating room. Dr. Carver believes the surgery relieved most of the pressure, but Jane hasn't regained consciousness. We're just hoping that she's strong enough to recover." She paused. "Personally, I believe she is heading toward a very peaceful death. She's in no pain. She's just slipping slowly away."

Tina made a small strangled sound. Tears ran down her face, streaking her mascara so that she looked like a sad clown.

"You have been such a good friend to her," Laura Gefferelli said softly, touching Tina on the arm. "Your friendship meant so much to Jane. She told me before the operation that she could always count on you, no matter what. You were like family."

Darby felt a coldness wash over her. Is that what Jane Farr had said? That you could count on family? She felt a rolling sensation in her gut. *Where was her support when I needed my family the most?*

Oblivious to the two grieving women,

54

Darby backed away from her aunt and her painful past. Across the sleeping patient, Tina sniffed and sighed, taking Darby's movement as a signal that it was time to leave. "You're right, Darby," she nodded. "We'd better go get our boat."

The gray-shingled building that served as the state's ferry terminal was a trim structure surrounded by a white picket fence and neatly mowed lawn. As she steered the truck into line for the ferry, Tina explained that the old terminal had burned five summers earlier during a severe thunderstorm. "Your aunt gave some money to the new building fund. Her name's on a granite marker over on the water side."

"It's almost 11:30," Darby noted. "Surely there isn't a ferry at this time of night?"

Tina nodded. "Yep. That was part of the deal Jane made when she gave the money. Weekend ferries at one A.M., so that islanders can party on the mainland, go to the movies, whatever, and still get home. Sunday through Thursday, the last one's at 11:30," Tina grinned. "Kinda made her a hero, making negotiations like that."

Darby glanced at the building her aunt had helped create. The little parking lot was well lit, and Darby thought she saw two

55

people holding signs.

"That couple over there — they can't be protestors?"

Tina parked the truck and yanked her keys out of the ignition. "They're picketing, all right. The state wants to put a bridge here, some huge thing like they did over in Canada, you know, to Prince Edward Island? The vote's not for a couple of months, but people are pretty upset already. They've got petitions and whatnot, a citizen's group, you name it." She reached for the turquoise pocketbook and slung it over her shoulder.

"I'm goin' to grab our tickets and a Diet Coke. You want anything?"

"Just the bathroom."

"Back of the building," Tina slammed the truck door. "Unisex, but a sorry sight better than one of those port-o-pottys, which is, if you remember, what used to be here." She began strutting toward the picket fence, her heels clicking against the parking lot like the hooves of a deer. Darby saw the protesters try to hand her something but she waved them away and kept walking.

The night air held the tang of the Atlantic, a musky, sharp scent that seemed more intense than it did on the West Coast. Overhead a gull cried, his body glowing white against the stars. Darby walked across the parking lot, feeling the salty air on her face. In the faint glow of the parking lot's lights, she noticed more lupines blooming against the back of the building, their pastel shades luminescent in the moonlight.

Darby opened the bathroom door and stepped inside. It was dark, without the benefit of the overhead lamps outside, and Darby's eyes strained to adjust to the dimness. The heavy door shut with a bang. She ran a hand down the cool surface of the wall, hunting for the light switch, and heard a small sound like an animal exhaling . . .

Her pulse quickened. There was something trapped in the bathroom. As Darby reached for the door handle to escape, she felt the force of someone grabbing her from behind in a bear hug, pinning her arms back in a painful squeeze. She screamed and twisted toward her attacker. Getting a good look at a face before escaping meant identification. Of course, that would be the last thing her assailant would want . . .

A huge man loomed over her.

Bushy black hair in the form of a beard and thick black eyebrows covered most of his face. A tangle of black curls sprung from his head and his plaid flannel shirt. The smell of unwashed skin assailed her senses, but that was the least of Darby's problems.

"Where ya headed, little girl?" His voice was thick, slurred, dangerous.

Quickly she reacted with the defensive fighting skills she'd honed at San Diego's Akido Academy. Keeping her breathing controlled and forcing herself to focus, she brought her knee up hard, hoping to connect with his groin. Instead, she encountered hard muscle — his thigh. She refused to give into the panic that was rising like bile in her throat.

"Who the hell do you think you are? Let go of me!" Her screams were accompanied by the hardest stomp on his foot she could muster.

His eyes widened in surprise. Darby could see the edge of a large tattoo on his forearm.

"You always were a wildcat. A little Oriental spitfire." He lunged closer, his face now only inches from hers.

"I saw you in the truck with Tina," he whispered, his lips brushing the edge of her ear. "What're you doing back on the island, Darby Farr?"

Cold dread washed over her body. *He knows my name . . .*

She took a quick breath and forced herself to focus. His arms were on her neck, squeezing against her throat. With all the strength she could muster, she raised her arms above

58

his shoulders, and brought them down hard on his forearms. He pulled his hands back in surprise, the hold broken. Darby tried to flee the small space, but her attacker's instincts were too quick. Before she could wriggle out of the bathroom, he lunged at her torso, pinning her against the grimy wall.

A second passed with no sound. Darby's attacker let out a low chuckle, crystallizing her dread into pure fear.

"Where'd you learn those moves, huh kitten?" He gave her arm a wrench that made her wince in pain, and then, to her surprise, shoved her away.

"Stay away from the island," he snarled. His eyes, cold and black, seemed to bore right through her. "Unless you want to end up like your parents."

Darby felt for the doorknob behind her back and yanked it hard. Pain shot through her wrist as she swung open the heavy metal door.

"Don't threaten me, you sack of shit," she spat, backing away and beginning to run.

The door clanged shut as Darby dashed toward the truck, his throaty laugh ringing in her ears.

Tina was sipping a Diet Coke when Darby,

panting, reached the truck.

"What the hell?" Tina asked, seeing the younger woman's ripped shirt and bloodied hand.

Darby looked back toward the bathroom. "Call the police. That guy — there —" She pointed at the flannel-clad figure now slouched by the outside of the bathroom door. "He jumped me in the bathroom."

Tina's mouth set in a grim line. "Soames Pemberton," she said. "You okay? What'd he do?"

"Pinned me from behind, told me to stay off the island." She tried to catch her breath. Soames Pemberton — the name was definitely registering. For some reason, she didn't want to mention his threat about her parents. Without meaning to, she shuddered. "Is he as dangerous as he seems?"

"Oh yeah. He's as bad as they come, now. Used to be a boat captain and drive this ferry, but the state yanked his license when he came back from the Gulf. Drug use — heroin to be exact." Her eyes lingered on the man before flitting to Darby. "Was he high? Could you tell?"

"Possibly. I couldn't exactly administer a drug test." She rubbed her wrist. "Why isn't he locked up?"

"Has been, here and there. But you barely

turn around and he's out again, you know?"

Darby did know, all too well. In California there were similar creeps who never seemed to get what they deserved.

Tina gave her another of her sideways glances. "Soames' grandfather or great-grandfather owned the whole of Pemberton Point at one time, from where the Trimble estate is right clear around to the cove. I think the family got it way back from the King of England or something. Little by little they sold chunks of it off, and I think the only piece of land any Pembertons own now is Soames' sorry little doublewide on the property line."

She started up the truck and followed the line of cars onto the ferry, then parked behind a small economy car and turned to face Darby. "I'm surprised you don't remember him. Left before you did and joined the Navy. Became a SEAL — you know, the ones who never get taken prisoner? It was a big deal for the island. Only a small percent of guys make it, and Soames was one of them."

"I think I do remember. There was a parade and a ceremony at the dock." She had the sudden image of her father, tanned and smiling, holding tightly to her hand. He had spoken to Soames Pemberton, told the

61

powerful-looking young man something in a low voice. After that he'd clapped him on the back, wished him good luck.

Darby remembered the look in the Navy SEAL's eyes. Cold and hard, like metal. It had matched what she'd seen in the restroom just minutes before. "What happened to him?"

"Nobody really knows. He finished his training and got sent to the Gulf War, the first one, in the early 90s, some top-secret guerilla warfare missions that he could never talk about. He came back with that post-traumatic stress disease, plus the heroin habit. And he was never what you'd call a nice person to begin with."

Her voice softened. "An island's not an easy place to live, you know? It pushes some people right around the bend. They start talking to themselves, running around in their pajamas in broad daylight, that kind of thing. But Soames?" She shuddered. "He's become a monster, pure and simple."

"Then let's call the cops. Get him locked up, at least for tonight."

Tina put the truck keys in the turquoise purse. Her brilliant blue eyes were suddenly brittle and Darby could see she was furious. "Believe me, it will only make it worse. Listen, just stay away from Soames Pemberton. One of these days he's gonna kill someone and get locked up for good, but until then, he's like a great white in a plastic kiddie swimming pool."

She reached across Darby and yanked open the glove compartment, rummaged around and pulled out a small cylinder which she tossed on Darby's lap. "Pepper spray. I got a bunch of 'em. Stick it in your pocket and don't be afraid to use it. Way more effective than calling the cops any day."

Darby fingered the spray and jammed it in her denim jacket as instructed. She'd used the stuff back in California on a guy who'd grabbed her when she was out running, and he'd hit the pavement like a sack of bricks, giving Darby enough time to sprint to safety and call the police. "I wouldn't have the least problem giving Soames Pemberton a blast or two," she said.

"Good." Tina looked at her carefully. "You want some night air? Let's go on top."

The two women left the truck and climbed up a set of stairs to an observation deck. The ferry began moving, heading purposefully across the bay with engines sounding as if they were at full capacity. In the wake of the vessel, two porpoises followed along, their bodies jet black and shiny in the foamy water. Tina pointed through the darkness at a small island, no bigger than a parking space, where Darby could see nothing but boulders and a few spruce trees. "Your aunt sold that a couple of months ago. Two million dollars. Amazing what these flatlanders will buy."

The sky overhead was studded with stars. Darby and Tina picked out the few constellations they recognized: the Big Dipper, the Pleiades, and the Little Dipper. Outwardly, Darby Farr looked content, her episode with Soames Pemberton nearly a memory. Inside, however, her thoughts churned like the water behind the boat. Any minute now and she'd see the island emerging out of the inky black night. Was she prepared?

She let her thoughts wander back to California and the various deals she'd left in her assistant's capable hands. Enrique Tomaso Gomez, or "ET" as Darby called him, was an aging Ricky Martin, debonair and suave, his back always ramrod straight and his sense of propriety even straighter. Because she depended so much on her solo employee, Darby compensated him well, paying a hefty salary plus commission, most of which, she suspected, he spent on designer-label clothes. He favored silk shirts, open at the neck to reveal a thick

64

forest of slightly graying chest hair, and pressed pants.

Just then the ferry's engines slowed as the vessel entered the slow harbor zone. Darby took a deep breath and looked toward the bow of the boat. There it was: Hurricane Harbor. In the darkness she could just make out the tiny ramshackle ticket office, just as she remembered, with a curving road leading up the hill and past the Café.

Darby reached out to grab the handrail with shaking hands. Her heart was beating so quickly she could barely catch her breath. She felt like an engine that was constantly revving and would seize up at any moment. *Get a grip. This isn't life or death.*

Tina motioned to return to the truck and Darby followed her down to the parked lines of vehicles. Tina started the engine and drove off the ferry and onto the road.

I'm back, Darby thought. *I never thought this day would come, but I'm back on Hurricane Harbor.*

She stole a glance in the passenger side mirror. *I look exactly the same.* Straight black hair parted in the middle and hanging to the middle of her back; arched black eyebrows; and dark, almond-shaped eyes. Anyone looking would see a slim half-Asian, half-Caucasian woman in her late twenties.

Your typical Islander, Darby thought wryly. *Just another kid from Maine.*

If Darby Farr's outward appearance hadn't changed in ten years, neither had the look of her hometown. Even in the dark, Darby could see that the Café and neighboring bar were exactly the same: tall, wooden structures with weathered paint and tattered awnings. So, too, was the Hurricane Harbor Inn, where Darby had waited tables one summer. Inexplicably, Darby felt strangely comforted by the familiar buildings. *These landmarks feel like a life raft,* she thought, as she watched Tina maneuver the truck on the narrow island roads.

The bar was called The Eye of the Storm, or, in local parlance, "the Eye." It was the only real nightspot on the island, unless one counted the gas station on the other end of town, where islanders often hung around the dumpster and downed a six-pack or two. Darby remembered at least one occasion when she and Lucy Trimble had managed to sneak into the Eye and order rounds of Cape Codders. While picking at their chicken wings and fried clams they'd gotten pretty drunk. One night the two girls were so inebriated they had passed out on the floor of Fairview's potting shed, only to have the gardener scream bloody murder when he discovered them in the morning.

The road curved uphill from the Hurricane Harbor Café and around a bend Darby had once known very well. She held her breath and there it was: Long Cove, stretching before them in moonlit beauty, a smile-shaped piece of beach with gently ebbing water. It had been Darby's playground as a child and her sanctuary as a teen. Now, as an adult, she saw it for what it truly was: a beautiful piece of nature, unspoiled and tranquil. Her heart ached for what she knew lay around the next bend.

As if anticipating Darby's tenseness, Tina slowed the truck and lowered the volume on the radio. They rounded the bend, and there was the low white farmhouse with its wide front porch, framed by magnificent maples that Darby knew turned a vivid bright orange in October. In the darkness she could make out a tricycle parked on the patch of green lawn in front, and a swing hanging from one of the maples. Darby's eyes welled with tears. Once again she told herself to get control of her emotions.

"That's one sale I can never forget," Darby said, keeping her voice deceptively light. She thought about what the house had meant to her and made a vow. *I'll never forgive Jane for letting it go,* she thought. Tina glanced her way but said nothing. Instead, she honked at a battered red jeep as it passed.

"What's Donny doing out so late?" she wondered.

"Who's Donny?"

"One of the Pease boys. He's the caretaker for Fairview, plus he fixes things at the Hurricane Harbor Inn." Her voiced sounded a little pinched and she cleared her throat. "You must be exhausted. I'm taking you right to Jane's so you can get a good night's sleep. We'll tackle all this Fairview stuff in the morning."

Darby nodded. As Tina steered the truck around a curving road past the old Ice Pond, the ringing of her cell phone startled them both. She answered it and listened for a minute, her posture stiffening. "Shit," she muttered. And then, "Thanks."

Tina said nothing as she slowed the truck before a tall Victorian that Darby recognized. It was Jane Farr's home, the house from which Darby had fled ten years earlier. Tina turned into the driveway, parked and turned to Darby, her full red lips pursed.

"I'm going to give you this truck," she announced. "Your aunt can't use it now and anyway, I figure you're sort of used to driving her vehicles?"

"Very funny." Darby smiled in the darkness. "How will you get home?"

"Donny. I'll give him a call and he'll pick me up." She sighed and placed the truck's keys on the dashboard.

"Tina, is there something you're not telling me? Something to do with that phone call?"

Tina turned to face Darby and nodded. Outside a lone cricket chirped mournfully. "That was Laura Gefferelli, calling from the hospital. I'm sorry, Darby. Your aunt is dead."

THREE

For a woman who'd made a small fortune selling houses, Jane Farr's own property was downright modest. A neat little Queen Anne Victorian with a turret and a trim, picket-fenced yard, it gave every impression of propriety and poise. Darby remembered the polished wood floors, crisp white moldings around the doors, and furniture covered in lots of flowery chintz. She recalled an impression of warmth: fires crackling in the fireplaces; the walls painted in soothing tones — an environment that lulled a visitor into thinking they were in a safe haven, when in fact the cozy home was a lioness' den.

Darby Farr was in for a surprise.

While Tina flicked on lamps and overhead lights in each of the rooms, Darby saw that, although the "bones" of the house hadn't been altered, gone were the furnishings that had given it a welcoming atmosphere. The oversized sofas, chairs, and occasional tables were missing, and the walls, once dotted with tastefully done oil paintings of the craggy Maine coast, were bare.

"This is a bit of a shock," said Tina, as she pointed to the gleaming exercise machines that now lined the walls of the living room and front hall. A treadmill took up most of the dining room. A rowing machine blocked one of the fireplaces. Even the kitchen was not immune: in place of the old farm table Darby remembered was a large computer monitor and printer. Jane's comfortable home had morphed into a YMCA with office space.

Tina looked at Darby and shrugged. "She got into exercise in a big, big, way," she explained. "Might have been some sort of late-life thing, I don't know. It started with one of those tummy crunching machines, the kind they sell on television? Then it kind of went off from there." She waved a hand in the general direction of the exercise machines. "Anyway, your aunt was in very, very, good physical shape. I've seen her doing that machine over there —" she pointed to a bench press, "with so many of those big weights on it, I thought for sure it would collapse and crush her to death. And you should have seen her on that treadmill! She

71

walked so fast the thing couldn't hardly keep up with her. No sooner would she finish with that, she'd take a couple swigs of water and start rowin', or jumpin' rope." Tina paused and shook her head. "Hard to believe she wasn't strong enough."

"What do you mean?"

"It just seems strange that a woman as physically active as your aunt couldn't survive that operation, you know? I mean, she was in here all the time, and when she wasn't in here, she was down at that office, making deals left and right. Does that sound like the feeble old lady you saw lying in that bed?" She shook her head, and then pointed out a window to the backyard, shrouded in darkness. "Can you see the little guest cottage? Stay there, and I think you'll be pretty cozy. You can come in here to cook or use her computer. Or jog a few miles."

Darby followed Tina's clicking heels out the back kitchen door, past the giant computer monitor and across a little expanse of lawn. The moonlight was even brighter, and by its glow Darby spotted a neat little garden, then caught a whiff of what smelled like lavender. She barely remembered the cottage. It had always been full of yard equipment — rakes, shovels, the lawn mower, and mulch, and had seemed more like a shed than a living structure. Tina stooped to adjust a little mat outside the door. She straightened up, yanked open the door, and turned on a light. Darby stepped inside.

The cottage was bigger and brighter than it appeared. Wide plank floors painted light blue and whitewashed walls gave it a light, summery feel. A full-sized iron bed, with a yellow and blue patterned quilt, anchored the room, with a little white writing desk nearby. A comfortable armchair on a braided rug took up another corner. Tucked back through a small door was a tiny bathroom and kitchenette.

"It's adorable," she said.

Tina smiled. "Lucky she didn't get the chance to turn this into a gymnasium. Got enough room? It's not exactly what you'd call spacious."

Darby's bungalow in Mission Beach was larger — but not by much. "Small spaces suit me. I spent a lot of time on boats when I was a kid." An image of her mother laughing as she tried to hoist sails while her father smiled from his vantage point at the tiller filled her with a sudden sadness, but Tina interrupted the memory.

"I'll get your bag. You must be tuckered out."

Darby nodded. "I am. Tomorrow —"

"Don't think about it now. Get a good night's sleep."

Darby watched as Tina disappeared into the darkness to retrieve her suitcase from Thelma. Sleep was fogging her brain like mist over the harbor, and yet one fact kept pounding relentlessly. Jane Farr was dead. Tomorrow, plans would be underway for her service — whatever form it would take — and before the week's end, she would be laid to rest. Whatever remained unsaid between the aunt and niece would stay unsaid. Their relationship, best described as stormy, was over.

I could go back to California tomorrow, Darby thought. *There's nothing binding me here.* She was now her aunt's personal representative, but any duties associated with her aunt's estate could be handled long distance. *And the Fairview closing . . . I could find another broker to take care of it. Jane's dead. I can do what I want.*

And yet, as Darby drifted off to sleep a half hour later, she knew she would remain on Hurricane Harbor until Jane's memorial service. Her aunt had summoned her to Maine, almost from the grave, as if challenging her to one final power struggle, and Darby Farr wasn't about to back down.

■ ■ ■ ■

Donny Pease woke just after dawn on Monday morning. He headed down the steep back stairs to his kitchen in time to see a young fawn step tentatively through his vegetable garden and back into the woods. He smiled at this glimpse of nature. The little fella was probably nibbling on the buttercup lettuce shoots that were just starting to poke out of the ground. Donny shrugged. He didn't mind sharing, especially with a creature as magical as a spotted young whitetail, and he never had been that fond of lettuce to begin with.

As was his regular routine, he ate a bowl of oatmeal and drank a cup of strong coffee, relishing the jump start he always got from the bitter beans. He was more tired than usual, having picked Tina up at midnight from Jane Farr's house. He pictured Tina's face, her eyes puffy from crying. She'd loved that old battle-axe Jane Farr, although Donny couldn't for the life of him see why.

Once his dishes were washed and put back in the cupboard, he took special care shaving his lined face and combing what little hair remained on his head. Today he would meet the new owner of Fairview — his new boss if all went well — and he wanted his first impression to be especially good.

Donny didn't need to be at Fairview until eleven o'clock, but there was no sense waiting until the last minute to get ready. He was always prompt, and he prided himself on his preparedness. Being ready for any situation imaginable was a trait that made him an exemplary property manager and a reliable boat captain as well. You just never knew what would happen with a house or a boat, and it made darn good sense to be ready for just about any calamity: an ice storm, a burst pipe, an oil leak, you name it.

Donny paused and thought about the last time he'd checked on the old Trimble property. Must have been a week, yes, a week ago. Donny didn't imagine anything much had happened to the place since that time, but what if something had? In his years as a caretaker, he'd seen just about everything from squirrels running rampant in a house (then chewing every piece of window sill in an effort to get out) to pot-smoking teenagers partying their brains out in a yacht parked right in the owner's yard. What if something had happened at Fairview since his last visit?

Talk about a good impression! What kind of caretaker would this new owner think he was if a nest of rodents were living the high life in the master bedroom? Donny Pease fought his mounting panic as visions of Fairview fiascoes danced in his brain. *There's plenty of time,* he thought. *Plenty of time to take my key and go over there and fix what needs to be done.* He took a deep breath to steady himself, and remembered what Tina always told him. *One thing at a time.* Tina! He'd nearly forgotten. Today was the day he picked her up mid-morning for their weekly visit with Donny's aging father. Donny thought a moment. The island was small and he was getting an early start. *I can go check on Fairview and still scoot out in time to meet Tina.*

When he felt calmer, he put on a light jacket, grabbed the keys to his truck, and headed out the door.

The ride to Fairview took only a few minutes and Donny was pleased to see that the day would be beautiful. His tires crunched on the long winding driveway, and he anticipated the rush of pride he always felt when he saw the house appear around the bend. This time, though, he felt a sense of puzzlement instead of joy. A sleek black car was parked directly in front of the house's main entrance.

Donny Pease parked and walked past the gleaming automobile. It was a BMW, and he knew enough about cars to know it was mighty damn expensive. No doubt it belonged to the new owner, as nobody he knew on the island would buy such a thing. He struggled to remember the new owner's name and came up with it at last. Peyton. The woman was named after a damned movie.

Donny took the key out of his khaki pants pocket and let himself in. "Hello?" he called, relieved to see nothing furry running across the glossy wood floors. With a thoroughness bordering on reverence, Donny walked through the many rooms of the grand old house, inhaling the lemony smell of the polish he'd used on the banisters, checking to see all was in order as he had so many times before. Fairview was as silent and still as a mill pond at dusk.

Once satisfied that the house was shipshape, Donny headed onto the vast back deck to inspect the rest of the property. He paused for a moment to listen to the waves breaking against the jagged cliffs, a sound he never tired of hearing. It seemed odd that the BMW's owner was not inside the house, but the weather was fine and the grounds lovely. No doubt she was strolling through the orchard or admiring the dramatic view.

Donny walked across the deck, noticing that the finish was looking a little dull. Normally he re-varnished the entire thing at the end of June, and it was looking like it needed it. *That's something I can offer to do right away,* he thought. *Show her I know this place inside and out.*

He took the steps down to the lawn and glanced toward the ocean. Nothing. He looked at the orchard, noticing the grass was getting ready for a trim, when he spotted an unusual sight: both doors to the garden cottage were wide open. That was strange. The building looked like a charming little home, but it was used as a shed for lawn and garden equipment. No one but the landscapers ever opened the building.

Donny walked slowly across the green expanse and toward the outbuilding. In the air over the cottage were two black ravens, flying in slow arcs around the cottage doors. That, too, was unusual. He felt a growing sense of uneasiness. Something was wrong.

The garden cottage was flanked by several old trees that marked the end of the manicured lawn and the beginning of a thickly wooded section of the property. The sun was still very low in the sky so the trees cast dark shadows. Donny heard a rustling in the bushes and jumped. *Probably just a squirrel,* he thought. Then the shape of a man seemed to dart through the gloom.

"Hey," he called out as he approached the building. Had he really seen a person, or was his mind playing tricks on him? "Who's there?" he cried hoarsely.

A blue jay shrieked from a tall pine, just as a thudding blow felled Donny Pease from behind and he crumpled, like a dead leaf, onto the dew-soaked ground.

Peyton Mayerson could no longer ignore the sun streaming through the Hurricane Harbor Inn's thin curtains. She frowned and opened her eyes, willing the slight headache just beginning behind her eyes to go away. She glanced at the sleeping man beside her and felt a curious mixture of lust and revulsion. Emilio Landi was gorgeous: there was no denying that. His soft curly brown hair framed a face that was classically Roman: long aquiline nose, strong chin, and full, sensuous lips. His body was flawlessly muscled and proportioned and he knew how to show it off. *Too bad he can't speak a damn word of English,* Peyton thought. *Then he'd be just about perfect.*

She stretched languidly and climbed out of the rumpled king-sized bed, being careful not to wake him. Peyton had some business with her partners to attend to on this sunny Monday morning, then the silly town meeting at ten A.M., and then the little howdy-do with the caretaker at eleven. Given everything she needed to accomplish, it was certainly easier to let sleeping Italians lay than to pantomime every single thing on her agenda. She shook her head with mild frustration. Despite her best efforts to teach Emilio even rudimentary English phrases, he remained unable to communicate except through gestures or his native tongue. In the month since they met, she'd picked up more Italian than he had English, despite the fact that they were in America! She arched an eyebrow as he rolled over, revealing tight abs of which Michelangelo's *David* would have been envious. Maybe this Roman God of a man — however well endowed — was truly *stupido.*

Quietly she entered the bathroom and turned on the water for a shower, thinking that whatever Emilio Landi was lacking in terms of brains, he more than made up for as a lover. Peyton couldn't recall a time when she'd been so physically spent by someone with a seemingly inexhaustible capacity for lovemaking. She regarded herself in the mirror and saw an attractive yet determined woman, thirty-five years old, gazing back at her. *I've got a sexy Italian lover in my bed, and yet I haven't let this relationship dull my business sense one bit,* she thought proudly. *I'm still making things happen . . .*

She tested the water temperature, shrugged off her silk robe and shivered. Even though it was late June, the mornings still held a chill in Maine. *I'm sick of this place,* she thought. *Sick of this substandard hotel with its local-yokel clientele.* She sighed and then smiled. One more day! Tomorrow at this time, the deal would be done. *Finito.* Not only would she be off this dismal island, but she'd satisfy her partners, the men she thought more and more of as greedy Boston sleazebags. What had happened to turn Tony Cardillo — and even Reggie, who was always Mr. Mild Mannered — into such bullies? *Something else must have gone south for them,* she reasoned. One of those mysterious South American schemes they only hinted at. Why else would they be breathing down her neck and threatening to tell the New Jersey guys? She couldn't believe that the money she owed them — a mere drop in the proverbial bucket — was worth the attention they'd given her deal.

None of it mattered, anyway, because the purchase of Fairview was nearly complete. They'd have their precious acreage and she'd be back to civilization. As she entered the shower and felt the steaming water caress her skin, she pushed away any doubts that threatened to destroy her confidence. *It will all work out,* she told herself. It simply had to.

A stone's throw from the Hurricane Harbor Inn, Darby Farr sat at her aunt's mahogany partner's desk in the compact office of Near & Farr Realty, sorting through a stack of files with growing impatience. She'd located one folder, neatly labeled FAIRVIEW 1, which contained the same contracts she'd reviewed on her flight the day before. Her annoyance stemmed from her inability to find the rest of the Fairview files in any of Jane's cabinets, drawers, or on her desk. She made an exasperated sound. "That's it! I give up."

Tina poked her head around the corner of the door.

"Hell of a lot of rummaging going on for 8:15 in the morning," she commented.

83

"Why you didn't just sleep in a bit more, I don't know. It's just a little town meeting, nothing to sit here poring over papers about." She paused, saw that Darby was still deep in thought, and sighed. "Anything I can do?"

Darby looked up at the redhead's concerned face, her eyes dark from lack of sleep, and sighed. "Maybe. My aunt's got a file here for Fairview numbered 'one', but I'll be darned if I can find any others. It doesn't make sense to number a file unless there are others, right? Somewhere there must at least be a 'two' kicking around."

Tina shrugged. "You would think so. But your aunt was doing some odd things lately, so I wouldn't put too much store in what you find."

"What kinds of odd things?"

"Oh, this and that . . ." She shrugged. "Trips to the hardware store in Manatuck at all hours of the day, for one. In the past week, she probably went over there two or three times."

"What was she buying?"

"I don't know. I never saw anything. When I'd ask her, she was vague and said she needed supplies for 'projects'." Tina snorted. "Your aunt was not the type to sit home and build a bookcase or learn basket weaving. If she wanted something, she hired somebody to take care of it for her. Her idea of a night at home was running on one of those crazy machines. I'll bet she didn't even know how to swing a hammer."

"Even if Aunt Jane wasn't a fixer-upper, going to the hardware store a few times isn't exactly strange behavior."

Tina sniffed. "There were other things, too. She was distracted, you know? Forgetful. And that was never, never, your aunt. Not for as long as I knew her."

"Forgetfulness could have been caused by the tumor, Tina. Maybe even the trips to the hardware store had something to do with the pressure on her brain."

Tina looked doubtful. "Maybe." She rifled through a stack of documents on an adjoining occasional table. "I don't think there are any other Fairview files. Hopefully the one you've got has all the relevant docs . . ." She stopped. "Speaking of forgetfulness, I nearly forgot to tell you that Mark Trimble called. He said he's looking forward to seeing you at the meeting."

"Thanks." Darby stood and glanced at Tina's worried face. "Forget about that other file. I'm sure you're right — it's no big deal."

Tina nodded and hurried to answer the

ringing phone. A moment later, she was back.

"Laura Gefferelli is on the phone."

Darby looked puzzled and Tina whispered, "The minister."

Darby picked up her line and said hello. The voice on the other end was gentle.

"I know you have a lot on your mind today, Darby, but I was hoping we could meet and discuss Jane's service."

Inwardly, Darby groaned. She wasn't looking forward to dealing with the details of her aunt's death, but as personal representative, those details were now her responsibility, however uncomfortable she felt. "How about this afternoon? I have a meeting this morning, and I'm not sure how long it will take."

"Planning board, right?" Laura Gefferelli chuckled. "No telling how long those guys can talk. I have to be there, too. We can touch base then."

"Is it part of your ministry to attend town committee meetings?"

Again Laura laughed, a light, musical sound that Darby welcomed. "It should be! God knows I go to enough of them." She paused. "I'm attending today on behalf of a woman's shelter we're setting up on the other side of the island. The church bought

86

a small raised ranch over there, and we just found out that the septic system is partly on the neighbor's yard. Luckily the neighbor is being very understanding, but we need to get permission from the board to continue renovating the structure." She sighed. "You know how it goes, I'm sure."

"I do. I'll keep my fingers crossed. If I can help you while I'm here . . ."

"You have enough on your plate," Laura said quietly. "We're the ones who are here to help you."

Darby felt a knot in her throat at the other woman's kind tone. "Thanks," she said quickly, fighting to regain her composure. "I'll see you shortly."

Tina Ames was standing in the doorway, touching up her manicure with practiced dexterity. She blew on her nails, sending the scent of polish wafting toward Darby, and gave her a knowing look. "Awful lot of folks are gonna miss that Jane Farr." She shook her head sadly, then glanced at her watch. In a flash, her mood changed from melancholy to anger. "Where the hell is that Donny Pease?" she fumed, striding to the window. "I'll have his hide if he forgot to pick me up."

Forty minutes later, Darby scooped up the

only file on Fairview and walked two blocks from Jane Farr's office to the town hall. A brick building constructed in the late 1800s, the hall held the island's few administrative offices, including those of the police department, as well as a tiny library and the town meeting room.

Darby pulled open the heavy door. Inside, the meeting room was set up theatre style with a few long tables across the front where the planning board members sat. Although the meeting wouldn't start for another fifteen minutes, already several people were milling about, claiming their seats, and greeting fellow islanders.

Darby glanced at the others and spotted a tall man dressed in a polo shirt and khakis. He turned around and she locked eyes with Mark Trimble.

She would have recognized him anywhere. He had a strong, square jaw, and eyes that were very blue against his tanned skin. His face was rugged-looking, but friendly, although perhaps a little more lined than Darby remembered. *He's still a heck of a handsome guy.*

He strode across the room to hug her and she caught a whiff of suntan lotion.

"Darby Farr! I can't believe it's you." He flashed his grin again and gave her an appraising glance. "You look fantastic. Still the same beautiful girl you always were. Man, your dad would be so proud of you. What was it he used to call you when we were racing? Wasn't it Little Bird?"

"Little Loon. He always said my mother was as graceful as a swan, but that I darted through the water like a loon." She cleared her throat. It felt raw again. "You look pretty good yourself."

Mark laughed. "Why, thanks. Have you seen my sister yet?"

"No. Will she be here?"

"Not a chance. Lucy likes these things about as much as a hangover." He glanced around the room. "I, on the other hand, find these exercises in democracy highly entertaining. So did your aunt." He paused. "I'll miss her, Darby. Lots of us on this island will miss Jane Farr. I want you to know how sorry I am that she's gone."

"Thanks." She forced herself to focus on the steady stream of people filing in, hoping Mark didn't see the way she was fighting to stay in control of her emotions. "How did you know she died?"

"Oh, you know life on an island. There are no secrets." He pointed in the direction of the door. "Look, there's Peyton and Emilio."

A tall woman with upswept brown hair and a handsome, curly-haired man entered and surveyed the room. The woman's eyes settled on Mark and she gave a nod and a small smile. She indicated where her partner should sit and then glided up to Darby and Mark.

"Mark, darling, it's all so exciting." She gave him an air kiss and turned to Darby with an eyebrow raised. "And you are . . . ?"

"Peyton, this is Darby Farr, Jane's hotshot niece." Mark paused a moment. "Jane passed away yesterday and Darby is taking over for her."

Peyton seemed to make an effort to appear as if she cared. "I'm sorry to hear that. Well, welcome Darby." She directed her glance back at Mark. "Lot of people, aren't there? Considering it's just a city council thing? Of course, there's hardly anything to do on this island. Quaint and charming, but rather boring when you compare it to the city. The resort should bring a little life to the place now won't it? We'll have some shows, and a martini bar, and a first-rate restaurant, not like that blah little Hurricane Harbor Inn. So pedestrian. As if all anyone wanted to eat was broiled haddock night and day."

Darby listened, taking in the woman's expensive clothes and careful makeup job. Peyton Mayerson was close to forty, she guessed, and was already taking advantage of plastic surgery to keep time at bay. Darby caught the scent of her fragrance, and smiled in surprise.

"You're wearing *Fleurettes*," she noted. "It's lovely."

Peyton Mayerson raised her eyebrows in surprise. "That's correct. How in the world did you recognize it?"

"I love vintage perfume. My aunt used to wear Molinard's *Verveine*." She paused, remembering the scent of Jane Farr as she'd brushed by her niece so many times, off to list an island property or meet with a buyer. "If I'm not mistaken, Molinard introduced the two perfumes the same year, 1948."

Peyton pursed her lips. "*Fleurettes* was *reintroduced* in 1948," she corrected. "The fragrance first debuted in 1908." She gave Darby a patronizing smile. "In case you're wondering, I'm wearing the original."

"We'd expect nothing less," grinned Mark. He waved in the direction of Emilio Landi. "Why didn't you bring your fiancé over?"

Peyton Mayerson tittered. "Hold your horses, Trimble . . . we're not engaged yet." She tilted her head in his direction. "Mark's

91

talking about Emilio Landi, my Roman boyfriend. Gorgeous, isn't he?" She blew a kiss in his direction. "I have no doubt we'll get married one of these days, right at Pemberton Point perhaps. Emilio's an absolute doll. No head for business, but he's very good at *other* things." She laughed again. "Hey, how about a drink tonight? See if we can shake up this sleepy old town?"

"Good idea," said Mark, as the sound of a gavel rang through the room. "I'll have my people talk to your people."

Peyton laughed again and strutted back toward Emilio, her heels clicking on the polished wooden floor.

"So," whispered Mark as he leaned toward Darby. "That's Peyton Mayerson. Do you think my ancestors are rolling over in their graves when they contemplate her at the helm of their precious Fairview?"

"Pemberton Point will never be the same."

"Let's hope not."

His words had an unexpectedly bitter ring. Darby looked up, but he had turned away and she could not read his expression.

The gavel sounded and the room grew quiet. The man wielding it called for order, and then ran his committee through several agenda items in quick succession. "Now we come to Pemberton Point Weddings, Inc., looking for a change of zoning for the property known as Fairview, over there on the Point, and along with that a liquor license." He cleared his throat. "I think we've gone over this request enough and I feel comfortable voting to grant what the buyer, Ms. Mayerson, needs."

"All those in favor —"

The door to the committee room burst open and Darby, along with the rest of the crowd, spun toward the commotion. A powerfully built man filled the door frame. He wore a white T-shirt that showed off his bulging biceps, jeans, and black combat boots. His face was clean-shaven, with a jagged scar over one cheek, and he sported a short, military-style buzz cut. He surveyed the room as if looking for possible threats, his cold eyes taking in each person. Darby recognized those eyes — they belonged to the man who'd assaulted her at the ferry terminal. *Soames Pemberton.* Her anger turned to fear as he reached into the pocket of his jeans and began pulling out an object . . .

There was a horrified gasp from the audience, and then a low chuckle from the intruder. "What are you scared of? Think I got a weapon, or something?" He pulled a piece of paper from his pocket and brandished it before the room. "I thought you'd like to see this little item I found in my great-granddaddy's things."

Soames Pemberton moved deliberately toward the planning board members and held the paper up as if taunting them. Slowly he unfolded it and pretended to read it for the first time. "Why look at this. It's a deed from Thaddeus Pemberton to his son, Josiah, written about a hundred years ago."

He paused for effect and scanned the room. "My great-grandfather was a Methodist, deeply devoted to the Lord. He believed in the devil and all the ways he could lead us astray." A slow smile crept across his face. Darby felt her palms grow clammy.

"That's why he decided, all those years ago, that any Pemberton lands had to be free of alcohol, dancing, and wild women. Old Thaddeus put that right here, in writing." He waved the paper and said softly, "There isn't going to be any fancy resort on Pemberton property."

The room erupted in conversation, punctuated with a shriek that Darby suspected came from Peyton Mayerson. The man with the gavel banged it repeatedly, to no avail.

The gavel banged again and Soames Pemberton chuckled, raising the hair on the back of Darby's neck. "I've got copies for all of you," he said, making his way toward a table in the back of the room. He picked up a stack of paper, approached the planning board, and began passing sheets out.

Darby's throat felt dry and she avoided making eye contact with Soames. She heard the rustle of paper and saw Mark accept a copy. After a cursory glance, he handed it to Darby.

Quickly she scanned the photocopied document. It had the look of an original deed, plus the archaic language, but this version contained a much shorter description of the property than the documents she'd painstakingly reviewed.

Darby stood and felt the eyes of the room upon her. "This deed refers to an abutting piece of property up on the road," she said. "Not the parcel in question."

The members of the planning board breathed a sigh of relief and turned toward Soames Pemberton for his response.

"The little lady is right," he said, his eyes staring straight at Darby with icy hatred. "This is all that's left of the property once owned totally by the Pemberton family. Great-granddaddy's widow sold it all — every last little piece — except for this worthless ten acres of cow pasture." He gave a sly look around the room. "You see, she couldn't sell this piece, because it had already been deeded to my grandfather before she got her hands on the estate. But old Thaddeus Pemberton made it clear in this deed: No drinking, dancing, or whoring, on this *or any other piece* of Pemberton property."

Everyone in the room was silent, listening to the deep, flat, voice of Soames Pemberton. Finally the silence was broken by one of the planning board members.

"Somebody put this in plain English," she said.

The man with the gavel looked imploringly toward Darby. She rose from her chair, feeling her legs shaking beneath her.

"If this piece of Pemberton property was conveyed first, and there was a covenant on this, as well as all the rest of the land, it would seem that these restrictions do apply to all former holdings of Thaddeus Pemberton." She paused, trying to swallow. "Even Fairview."

The room exploded in arguing and the planning board chairman turned to the rest of the members. Darby heard him mutter, "This board can't approve anything without a legal opinion." The other members nodded. "I'll entertain a motion to postpone this decision until our next meeting, twenty days from now." Darby heard someone make the suggested motion, and then the chairman asked for a vote. A moment later he banged the gavel and the din dropped to a dull murmur, with the only audible sound Peyton Mayerson's voice screaming obscenities at her lawyer. Darby turned to Mark Trimble.

"I'm sorry, Mark. This restriction — it's totally from left field."

Mark nodded. "You remember my parents and their blow-out cocktail parties. No one ever mentioned an anti-drinking law to them, that's for sure." He fixed his eyes on Darby and said carefully, "This means the deal is off."

Darby's heart sank. "I'm afraid you're right. That amendment to the contract — the one written on the index card — stipulated that Peyton needed this approval to proceed. She didn't get it, so the contract is null and void." She thought a moment, her natural optimism giving her an idea. "I wouldn't say it is dead in the water, though. We can certainly grant her an extension, give her some time to figure out, with her lawyer, how to approach this . . ."

"No." Mark's tone was sharp. He looked around the room and lowered his voice.

"Let's get out of here, go somewhere we can talk." Around him, the noise of the crowd had barely abated, and Darby thought she could hear an angry Peyton Mayerson above the din.

Mark rose from the folding chair and offered an arm to Darby. "There's more to this than what's happened today," he confided. "I know just the place where we can talk privately."

Darby stood and scanned the room for Soames Pemberton.

"He's gone," Mark said, steering her toward the exit with a firm hand. "Chances are, you won't be seeing Soames for a while."

Darby recalled the look of pure menace in the man's face and suppressed a shiver. *Let's hope not,* she thought.

It was a short walk from the town office to the harbor and the dock where Mark's boat, *Lucy T,* was moored. She was a large, beautiful sloop, and the pride Mark felt in her fine lines and handsome rigging was evident.

"Isn't she sweet? Almost as nice as the real thing, my adorable sister." He pointed at a smaller boat tied up beside the *Lucy T.* "That cute little Seafarer belongs to the minister. I've been giving her private lessons and she's turning out to be a heck of a sailor."

Darby glanced at the twenty-four-foot vessel and then back at Mark. "Is that how you've been spending your time, teaching and taking care of Fairview?"

Mark jumped aboard and glanced quickly at his cell phone, before jamming it into a pocket. "Pretty much. I still teach at the yacht club, too." He flashed the grin she remembered so well. "Guess I'm still trying to figure out what to do with my life. Having a significant trust fund makes it that much harder to find motivation, not that I'm whining about it or anything."

Mark grinned again and wiped off the canvas seat of a director's chair with his hand. "Come aboard, Darby. We'll sit out here in the fresh air." He darted quickly below deck, emerging with a folder of papers which he placed on a small side table. "You do any sailing in California?"

Darby hesitated, still on the dock, her heart beginning to thud in her chest. With the exception of the ferry ride, she hadn't set foot on a boat for more than ten years. She'd convinced herself that it wasn't fear that kept her off the sea, but a lack of interest. When invitations came her way to sail in the bay of San Diego, she politely declined, thinking to herself that she had better things to do. Now she knew the truth. She was petrified.

Mark misinterpreted her delay. "Hey, don't worry about your shoes. I'm not one of these boat owners who care about that. Come on, climb aboard."

He reached out a hand and Darby grabbed it.

"Thanks," she managed. She wondered if Mark could see how her legs were shaking. She sank into a deck chair and waited for her body to return to some degree of normalcy.

"Thirsty? I've got some drinks below."

"Sure." She took a deep breath and felt her pulse slowing.

Mark disappeared below deck, and Darby heard the clink of glasses. She took out her cell phone and called the office of Willis Foster, the Trimble family lawyer. "Have him call me as soon as possible," she told the secretary who answered.

She glanced idly at the papers on the table. On top was a file folder, the same kind Jane Farr used. She looked at the tab. File 2 was written in neat letters.

Mark reappeared with two glasses of an amber liquid, one of which he handed to

Darby. "Ginger ale." He raised his glass in a toast. "To old friends," he said.

"To old friends," echoed Darby. She took a sip, feeling the crisp carbonation on her tongue. *What was Mark doing with Jane Farr's folder?*

"Your boat's a real beauty," she said, admiring the pristine condition of the *Lucy T.* Every inch was scrubbed and shining, from the aft decks to the polished stairway banister.

Mark grinned. "Thanks." He snapped his fingers. "I almost forgot. I've got some nibbles for us." He hopped up and went below deck. Darby heard him rummaging in the boat's little galley. Carefully, she lifted the cover of the file folder.

Inside was a contract for the sale of Fairview. Darby scanned the page and stopped, confused. The name of the buyer was not Peyton Mayerson, but an Emerson Phipps, III. She let the folder close.

Mark Trimble emerged from below deck a minute later carrying a tray with a few cheeses, crackers, and some sliced fruit. He eased himself into a deck chair next to Darby and offered her the plate. "You never answered my question. You do any sailing in California?"

"No," she admitted. "I admire the boats

from the shore, but I haven't been on the water in a long, long, time." There was an awkward silence. Darby spread some aged blue cheese onto a rice cracker and popped it into her mouth. "So who is Emerson Phipps?"

Mark managed a shaky laugh. "How did —"

"This folder is twin to one in Jane's office and I've been looking for it. I recognized it immediately, and yes, I looked inside. I don't mean to snoop, but I'm now the listing agent for Fairview, and I have a right to know what's going on. So why don't you stop with the snack service and tell me exactly what is happening."

Mark took a deep breath. "I was about to do just that." He took a sip of his drink and continued. "Phipps is an old college friend. We were in a few classes together our second year at Dartmouth, and he came up here to see me the following summer. We were twenty or so at the time. He visited twice, and then he never came again. But he never forgot Fairview, or so he says.

"About three weeks ago, I had a call from Phipps. It was quite a surprise, as we hadn't been in touch since graduation. He went to medical school after Dartmouth and became a surgeon in Boston. Spinal injuries, I think. He's done quite well from what I hear. Anyway, he saw an ad for Fairview in some Boston magazine. He recognized the place and tracked me down. I told him to get in touch with Jane and left it at that. Last week he called again and I said he was too late. He chuckled and said it was never too late to buy something if you had the right price. I told him about Peyton and the contract and figured that was the end of it."

He took a long drink, draining his ginger ale.

"Jane called me a day later. She'd spoken with Phipps and she seemed excited. We met in her office and drew up another contract, one that only went into effect if Peyton's fell through."

"A backup," Darby said softly.

"That's what she called it. A backup. She said it was a long shot but that you never knew how things would turn out." He paused. "Wouldn't she love to know what happened today! Soames Pemberton shows up with that old deed, totally taking Peyton out of the picture . . ."

"And now Emerson Phipps is our new buyer." Darby reached for the folder and opened it. Her brow knotted with concern. "The price on Peyton's contract was $5.5 million."

"I was waiting for you to notice," said Mark. "When Phipps came on the scene, Jane told him the price had gone up to $5.8 million. She wasn't going to budge, and Darby, he didn't even care. 'The price really doesn't matter,' he said. Jane was in heaven."

"I bet," Darby said dryly.

"I think she had a premonition that something would go wrong with Peyton's plans, you know? She'd been at this so long; it was like she could predict the future."

Darby thought back to the planning board meeting. Not even Jane Farr could have imagined a scene like that. A nagging suspicion entered Darby's thoughts. Could her aunt have known about the old deed? She told herself no, that Jane would have been just as surprised by the revelations of Soames Pemberton.

She looked back over the pages and noticed only one signature in the seller's area.

"Lucy hasn't signed this."

"She will," Mark stated confidently. "She doesn't care who buys Fairview, she just wants out."

"I see that Phipps had no contingencies — no building inspections, no water tests, and no financing. He's paying cash?'

Mark nodded. "Yup." He took out his cell phone and glanced at his calls. "He's due to call me any time now," he said. "He wants to know as soon as possible what happened at the Planning Board meeting, and whether or not he's the lucky winner."

"I wouldn't make that call just yet," said Darby. "I want to speak to your attorney to verify the legitimacy of Soames' claims. I was hoping he'd call me back this morning."

"Does it matter? Whether the restrictions are enforceable or not, Peyton didn't get her approval for a liquor license or a zone change. The contract says if she doesn't get that approval by the end of today, the deal is off. I think that puts Phipps on top."

"I'd still like to check with Willis Foster." She paused. "And if Emerson Phipps is, as you said, the lucky winner? What happens then?"

"He's going to drive up from Boston and buy the house this afternoon."

"Today?" Darby forced herself to focus. In the space of an hour, one deal had crashed and burned while another, even more lucrative one arose, like a phoenix, from the ashes. *This is why I love real estate,* she thought. *And why my aunt had loved it, too.*

FOUR

Darby listened while Mark relayed the events of the planning board meeting to his sister. When he mentioned the backup offer from Emerson Phipps, his tone changed from enthusiastic to incredulous.

"What do you mean you won't sell to Phipps?" Darby heard him say. "It doesn't matter who the buyer is, don't you see that, Lu? Who cares if it is Peyton and her silly Italian sidekick, or Phipps? What matters is that we are done with it; that we can travel, or buy new homes, or just sit around and paint. I know, I know, you don't just sit around and paint. The point is, what do we care who purchases the place?"

There was a pause while Mark listened to his sister. Finally he said in a subdued tone, "Okay. Thanks."

He clicked off his cell phone and turned to Darby with a frown. "She'll do it, but she's not happy." He rose and stretched his legs. "I don't get it. Yeah, Phipps is an arrogant son of a bitch, but why should she care if he takes a major headache off our hands?" He ruffled his hair in frustration. "Plus he's paying more money!"

"Lucy says she remembers Emerson Phipps. You were around that summer, Darby. Do you remember the guy?"

Darby thought a moment, and then shook her head. "No, I don't. Maybe when I see him, I'll have some recollection." Possessed of a photographic palate memory, Darby was unusually good at remembering faces, too. And yet the name Emerson Phipps did not spark any associations.

"Is this why Lucy hasn't signed the back-up offer yet? If she doesn't feel comfortable with this sale . . ."

"Who knows why she's going off on this tangent? She's got a big gallery opening in July and the annual art show this weekend. Maybe it's tension from trying to get ready. She's got a copy of the offer, and she says she hasn't even opened the envelope!" he sighed. "She's doing well, you know, as an artist. Her career is poised to really take off."

He ran a hand through his hair and continued. "I don't know what her story is, but she'll get over it. She'll definitely get over it

107

and sign anything we need her to sign. After all the work I've done to get this place sold . . ."

Darby debated her next comment and her instincts as a realtor won out. "Mark, have you thought about keeping the property for a while, at least until the vote on the bridge is over? There's a good chance that you and Lucy could make even more money if that bridge from Manatuck is constructed."

Mark Trimble wheeled toward Darby, taking her by surprise. A dark look contorted his face. "Wait? Wait? I've been waiting my whole life to get rid of that place. It's a prison, Darby, a fucking prison. I won't own Fairview one day longer than I have to. And you know what? I don't care if the man in the moon buys it." He rammed his hand on the side table and papers from the file scattered on the deck. The blast of a horn signaling the arrival of a passenger tour boat broke the silence.

"Shit, I'm sorry, Darby." He ran a hand through his thick hair. "I shouldn't take it out on you. It's just that — well, I didn't expect Lucy to react in this way. I thought she'd be happy." He sighed. "She's been through so much, I thought she'd be able to let the old place go as easily as I can." He knelt and collected the papers and placed them back in the file. "She's headed over to Fairview shortly. Let's go over there together. I know she'd love to see you, and I sure as hell hope she'll sign this backup offer."

Darby consulted her watch. "Okay. I'll do my best to point out the advantages of this sale, but I represent both you and your sister. If she refuses to sign, the deal is off."

He looked up quickly. "I'll just have to hope she comes around," he said.

"Stop at the office," Darby requested, as she and Mark climbed into his vintage blue convertible. "I need a copy of this contract."

"Fine. I'll run over to the Café for a sandwich. Want anything?"

Darby declined. They pulled into the parking lot and he strode across the street.

Tina met Darby at the door. "Mark Trimble's attorney returned your call. It's on your voice mail."

"Thanks." Darby listened to the message, wondering whether the restrictions on the Pemberton property could possibly be for real.

"That old covenant against drinking and dancing could certainly be legitimate," the voice on the machine equivocated, "but then I can't be sure until I have a chance to look at the old deeds in the registry on Manatuck. Prohibitions like that were common at the time. Why, we even have some dry towns remaining here in Maine."

Darby groaned as she saved the message from Willis Foster. *A typical lawyerly response,* she thought. *It tells me absolutely nothing.*

Her gut told her that the crazy story was somehow the truth, and yet she had a hard time imagining that Soames Pemberton had merely happened upon the old deed. *I'll go to the registry myself and search the records,* she thought. *Chances are, I can find what I need in an afternoon.* She rose and made copies of the agreement with Emerson Phipps. Whoever he was, a twist of fate was putting him in the position to buy his dream house. *Some people are born lucky,* Darby thought.

Copies in hand, Darby was about to leave when the door flew open and Peyton Mayerson, boyfriend in tow, burst into the office.

"Darby Farr," she spat. "Where do I stand on my purchase of Fairview?"

The handsome Italian man beside her was silent, his hands jammed into the pockets of a rich, chocolate-brown leather jacket.

"Ms. Mayerson, Signor Landi — won't you both have a seat." Darby indicated two wooden chairs in her aunt's small conference room.

"I'm not in the mood for tête-à-têtes. Just tell me, do we still have a deal?"

"I'm afraid not, Ms. Mayerson. An amendment to the contract stipulated that you would have planning board approval today, or the deal was null and void."

"I don't remember any amendment," Peyton sputtered. "What are you talking about?"

Darby withdrew the contract from her file and showed her the index card. "Aren't these your initials?"

"On this scrap of paper? Who cares? That can't be legal, and besides, I've changed my mind. I don't care if I have approval from that board."

"You can't throw a wedding without dancing and booze," piped Tina from across the office.

Peyton glared at her. "That fool of a man and his ridiculous claims! If it hadn't been for him . . ." her voice trailed off and one glance at her face revealed the fury she felt.

Her companion cleared his throat. "*Scusi,* the house — it is still possible we buy him?"

Darby nodded. "Yes. It is still a possibility.

My clients want to sell Fairview, and as quickly as they can."

"Then we have some time to figure this out," Peyton said, making an effort to calm herself down. Darby caught the faint scent of the rare French perfume once more. "Right? It isn't as if anyone else is lined up to buy Fairview."

Darby remained silent.

"Oh my God," screeched Peyton Mayerson. "Are you telling me someone else wants to buy it?"

"I can't answer that."

Peyton pulled a cigarette out of an expensive leather purse. Her hand was shaking as she lit it and took a long drag. "Wonderful, just wonderful." She inhaled once more and seemed to get control of her emotions. "I'll take it without the board's approval then. How's that? I'll call the other investors and come back with an offer that will satisfy that greedy bastard Mark Trimble." She gave Darby a shrewd look. "I see his car in the parking lot. Just what the hell are you two cooking up? Do we have a deal or not, Miss Farr?"

Darby answered carefully. "No, Ms. Mayerson, we do not have a deal at this point. But my clients certainly welcome your offer."

"Welcome my offer? How dare you . . ." she snatched up her purse and gave Darby a murderous look. "We'll see who ends up with Fairview," she hissed, sweeping out the door. Emilio shrugged and followed her, his leather jacket swaying as he walked.

"Whew," Tina said once they were headed down the street. "That woman is so obnoxious I can hardly stand it. Do you think she will come back with more money for Fairview?"

"It's possible." *She certainly didn't like hearing there was other interest on the property,* thought Darby. *In fact, she had seemed almost desperate.*

"I doubt she can outbid the new guy. From what I hear, he's got deep pockets."

Darby glanced at Tina. "How did you hear about a 'new guy'?

Tina paused and looked down at her bright red fingernails. "Your aunt mentioned something about it last week. She was pretty excited about his interest in Fairview. She called it an 'obsession'."

"Why didn't you tell me there was a backup? Why wasn't there a copy of it in my file?"

"I didn't know there was one," Tina said earnestly. "Jane mentioned that this doctor was a great prospect if the deal with Peyton flopped, but she never told me he signed anything. To tell you the truth, I wasn't sure if this mystery man was for real or not. He never came into the office, and your aunt wasn't making tons of sense. I kind of listened and then chalked it up to the tumor."

Darby pulled out the index card and looked at the scribbled date. Was this why her aunt had seemed distracted in the week before her death? Because she was trying to figure out a way to make the sale of Fairview an even bigger moneymaker? Darby shook her head and wondered if Jane Farr had let greed cloud her once-razor sharp judgment. She put the index card back in the file and faced Tina. "I hope you remember that contracts and offers are confidential."

"I know, I know. I'd never spill the beans, but you know as well as I do that things get out on an island." She gave Darby a meaningful look.

Darby opened the door and scanned the street for Mark Trimble. Tina was right — Hurricane Harbor had always been a place where everyone knew his or her neighbors' business. Most of the islanders' gossiping was harmless, but with a multimillion-dollar deal at stake, Darby feared loose lips could turn out to be deadly.

Donny Pease came around slowly, wincing as the pain in the back of his head registered. What the hell had happened? He dimly remembered driving his truck to Fairview to meet with the new owner. And then? It was a blur. He tried to get to his feet. His head throbbed and his sixty-five-year-old limbs were stiff from lying on the ground. He wasn't sure how long he'd been unconscious, but it must have been an hour at least.

"Some bastard clocked me," he muttered to himself. "Clocked me one good, but he didn't kill me." He chuckled to himself. The Pease men were notorious for being hard headed; at least that's what his mother had claimed on more than one occasion. "Comes in handy," he muttered again, with another painful chuckle.

Slowly he pushed up with his hands and rose to his feet, feeling the back of his head gingerly for blood. There was none, but a nice lump the size of a golf ball had formed just over the rise of his shirt collar. It was tender to the touch and he nearly yelped in pain. Still, he felt lucky to be alive.

The garden shed was fifteen feet in front of him, and Donny remembered he'd been on his way to see why the doors were ajar. Cautiously he made his way to the building and peered in. What if his attacker was hiding in the shed? Shouldn't he grab a rake or a shovel, to be on the safe side? Inside it was as dark as a cave. Donny could barely make out its contents, although he knew, practically by heart, where everything was located.

As his eyes adjusted to the darkness, he frowned in amazement. What had been an orderly storage room now bore the marks of a rampage. All the tools were strewn on the floor in a haphazard mess, like that game children used to play called "Pick up Sticks." Stacks of clay pots once destined to be filled with red geraniums and placed on the back deck had crashed to the ground from their shelves, and most were smashed into jagged pieces. A bag of compost was ripped open, gutted like a dead animal. The riding mower looked untouched, but oozing around the front tire was a thick substance Donny took to be gasoline. Funny that the air didn't smell much like gas . . .

He plowed through the debris, his anger mounting at the destruction, until he saw that the puddle came not from the machine, but from a man lying face up on the wooden floor. Without knowing how or why he knew, Donny realized he was dead.

Instantly Donny looked at his face: was this poor guy someone he knew? But the head was crushed so completely it was impossible to find any features among the pulverized flesh. Donny stared, stupefied, a feeling of nausea building within him like a wave. Who was this guy, and why was he here? Who had attacked him so brutally? Was it the same person who'd knocked him out, and if so, was he waiting to kill Donny at this very minute?

A feeling akin to curiosity kept Donny Pease from fleeing the scene. He willed his eyes to travel down the body and saw something lodged in the victim's chest: a pair of gardening shears, sticking out of the torso like a meat thermometer.

Donny Pease took it all in for another full minute: the prostrate figure, the tools littering the floor, the gasoline that wasn't really gasoline but blood . . . and then, overcome with fear and disgust, he bolted faster than he thought capable out of the garden shed and into the noon sunshine. As he lost his breakfast on the boxwood hedge, he saw a curious sight: an angel, wandering out of the woods behind the shed, the front of her white dress all streaked with blood.

■ ■ ■ ■

Peyton Mayerson gave a half-hearted wave at the ferry as it receded into the distance. *Finally!* she thought. *Emilio will be off souvenir shopping for a few hours, and I can do what I need to and get this damn deal back on track.* God, he got on her nerves. If he wasn't so wonderful between the sheets, she'd have ditched him a long time ago, or sent one of the New Jersey guys to take him on a very long ride. She smiled, but then her grin slowly faded. They'd be after her if she couldn't come up with the money she owed them. If she couldn't make this deal happen . . .

Peyton got behind the wheel of her Mercedes and felt the calming quiet of the leather interior embrace her like a cashmere wrap. It was good to be alone, to have a chance to think. She went over her conversation with Darby Farr and felt her anger rising. The nerve of Mark Trimble, that smug greedy bastard! Darby Farr hadn't said as much, but he was going to sell Fairview right out from under her, after she'd worked so hard to convince her investors that she could make them money. Big money.

She took a deep breath. She couldn't afford to get emotional now. She had to come up with a plan, and fast. Who was this new buyer? How quickly was he or she prepared to move? She knew Mark Trimble was too smart to tip his hand, but that sister of his . . .

Lucy Trimble is the weak link in that partnership, Peyton thought. *Perhaps she can be influenced.* Peyton thought about what she knew about Lucy Trimble. She was an artist, and apparently quite good. She had some sort of substance abuse problem, although the island scuttlebutt was that she'd kicked it. She still looked like a junkie — scrawny and pale . . .

Peyton started her car and heard the rich rumbling of the engine. Lucy Trimble's studio was in her house, a mile or so from the ferry dock. As the Mercedes hummed down the island road, Peyton worked out a plan of attack. She'd appeal to Lucy Trimble as an artist. Flatter her and offer to put her work in a Manhattan gallery. That would work, she was sure of it. What hick Mainer would turn down the chance to be famous in New York?

She parked in front of a small house with an attached garage and walked up a muddy path to the door, hugging her Armani jacket more tightly around her torso. The wind had picked up and it whipped her long hair in her eyes. It would be a rough ride to Manatuck. Maybe Emilio wouldn't have such a pleasant journey after all.

"Knock, knock, anybody home?" she called out in a high voice. A cat meowed from the side of the house and Peyton jumped and swore under her breath. She waited, listening intently. There was no other sound, so she tried the door. To her surprise, it opened.

Peyton's first thought was that a security system might sound, but after a minute or two, she realized the property was unprotected. Trusting islanders! Leaving their doors practically wide open . . .

The entrance led directly into a sitting room, and Peyton tiptoed in. A worn couch and a comfortable chair were arranged in front of a fireplace with a simple wooden mantel. A painting hung above it, and Peyton guessed it was one of Lucy's. She stopped to scrutinize it. *She really is quite good,* she thought. Now that she thought about it, perhaps her offer of the Manhattan gallery wouldn't be smoke and mirrors. Lucy Trimble had the talent to actually make some sales off this dinky little island.

She walked farther into the house, into

the barn that served as Lucy's studio. Canvasses were stacked against one wall and finished works were everywhere, waiting, she supposed, for frames. A door was ajar leading into another room and Peyton walked gingerly toward it. Inside it was gloomy and dark, the shades drawn against the June sun.

Peyton began retracing her steps to the studio when she noticed an envelope propped against a small occasional table. She picked it up and saw it was unopened. The envelope was from Near & Farr Realty, and written on the outside were the words, "Back Up — Please Read." With shaking hands, Peyton opened the envelope and pulled a set of folded papers out.

It was another offer on Fairview, and for more money, too. Peyton stared at it, her thoughts swirling. *Mark Trimble, that son of a bitch,* she thought. Beside her, the cat rubbed against her legs and brought her back to reality.

Angrily she shoved the envelope into her jacket pocket and hurried back to the studio. Despite her mental state she noticed a particularly vibrant painting and stopped. It was a cove full of boats, their hulls bright shapes against the blue water. It really was quite good, and she picked it up for a closer look. A price tag was on the back and she squinted to read the numbers. $20,000. Lucy Trimble, the junkie artist, was getting twenty grand? She grabbed another painting and flipped it over. $25,000. *Holy shit.*

Still clutching the second painting, she reached back for the first one, and though they were unwieldy, she made her way to the door. She'd get them off this island, to the city where she knew people who would buy them without asking questions. While it wouldn't settle her debt with the New Jersey guys, it would be a small down payment.

She emerged from the house holding the two canvasses and looked around. The yard and road were deserted. She hurried to her car, struggling against a particularly strong gust of wind. She pushed a button on her keys and the trunk to the Mercedes popped open. Quickly Peyton stashed the paintings, using a large beach towel to conceal them. Emilio didn't have a set of keys to her car, so she wouldn't have to worry about him.

Peyton drove as fast as she dared back to the Hurricane Harbor Inn and parked her car. After locking it securely, she went back up to her suite. The bedside clock said the time was noon, leaving her an hour and a half until Emilio came back on the ferry.

She opened her travel jewelry box and

pulled a folded piece of paper out from under some diamond earrings. It was time for Plan B. Her hands shook and she sat down on the bed for support. After a moment, she pulled the envelope with the contract out from her jacket, and searched for the buyer's name. Finding it, she grabbed her Blackberry from the bedside table. Using the hotel's wireless internet connection, she accessed a free IP Relay site used by the hearing impaired to send telephone messages. She typed in the number from the piece of paper. When the space came up for her message, she took a deep breath and typed:

Emerson Phipps, Hurricane Harbor, Maine, Immediate.

Peyton knew that when the call was placed and someone (she imagined a man) answered, her message would be read by the well-meaning IP Relay telephone operator. By federal law, every call was put through. To protect the privacy of users, phone companies were not allowed to keep records, making IP Relay the perfect vehicle for thieves, scammers, extortionists, and anyone else involved in illicit activities.

Including someone ordering a hit.

Her task completed, Peyton Mayerson turned off her PDA, replaced the number in her jewelry box, and pulled a bottle of scotch from her suitcase. The room's mini fridge had a small freezer with a few ice cubes, and Peyton clinked them into a glass. Then she poured herself a tall one and quickly drank it down.

Darby held on to the dash as Mark Trimble drove the classic convertible expertly down the winding roads to Fairview. Only minutes before, Tina Ames had called Darby on her cell phone with the unbelievable news of Donny Pease's grim discovery.

"Donny doesn't know who the poor bastard is," Tina had confided. "He's not good at things like this. Can't even shoot a duck he's so squeamish. Says he can't stop running to the bushes and puking." She'd taken a deep breath and continued. "Hurry up and get over there before the cops do. I'm staying put here at the office, but I'm worried about Donny. And I sure as hell want to know who the dead guy is."

Now, as the road turned to dirt, Mark slowed the car to a crawl. "It's got to be Phipps," he muttered. "I hope not, but it would explain why he hasn't returned my calls."

Two massive stone pillars, both stamped "Fairview" in imposing block letters, loomed on the left. Mark took the turn down the long driveway.

Darby caught the clean scent of pine in the air and inhaled deeply. Both sides of the roadway were lined with enormous evergreens, a type that was once called "mast pine" because of its usefulness to wooden sailing ships. *It still feels timeless,* she thought. *Like a medieval hunting lodge in France . . .*

They rounded a bend and there was the sprawling mansion Darby remembered. She exhaled at its beauty and Mark nodded, but said nothing.

Three vehicles were parked in the circular driveway: a truck Darby guessed belonged to Donny Pease; a police cruiser; and a black BMW sedan. Darby glanced at Mark. His face was grim.

"That's Phipps' Beamer," he muttered, opening the door of his car and climbing out.

They crossed a wide expanse of lawn together. Darby recalled games of croquet on this very spot in which the object had been less about getting a ball through a wicket than not spilling a Rum and Coke. She pushed the past out of her mind and matched Mark's pace, her pulse quickening.

A man was seated on the lawn about fifty feet from the side of a little building Darby remembered as a gardening shed. Someone had dragged an Adirondack chair onto the grass, and the weary soul was slumped in it, looking pale and haggard.

"That's Donny Pease," explained Mark. "We'll talk to the poor guy later."

A strange smell assailed their nostrils as they stepped into the garden shed.

"Now just hold on a minute there," a voice boomed from the darkness.

"Chief Dupont," Mark said. "I'm glad to see you."

Hurricane Harbor's chief of police plodded out, his boot smashing a piece of something as he walked. " 'Course you're glad to see me," he said. " 'Cause it looks like we've got ourselves some real excitement here on your estate."

Darby remembered the chief as a trim, athletic man, with hair just starting to gray at the temples. Now, however, his muscular physique had turned to fat, and his once-friendly demeanor seemed tired and suspicious.

He ran a pudgy hand through his crew cut.

126

"Well, if it isn't little Darby Farr," he said, whistling under his breath. "I heard you were on the island, but I wasn't sure I'd get to see you before you flew the coop again. Where is it you're living now? Texas?"

"California," she said.

"That's right, California." He thought a moment. "California. You must like it there. Little easier to blend in, I imagine."

Darby felt her cheeks burning. "Now why would you say that, Chief?"

Mark interrupted the exchange. "Can we see the body? I believe I know the victim and can make a positive identification."

The chief touched his chin thoughtfully. "Is that so?"

"Yes," answered Darby. "Mark and my aunt were working with a doctor from Boston for the purchase of Fairview, and Mark recognizes the vehicle in the driveway."

Chief Dupont nodded, his tiny eyes shrewd. "Go ahead then, take a look. Seeing as how we haven't found any identification, and old Donny out there isn't gonna be much help, let's see what you come up with. But I warn you: it's not a pretty sight. Not only was he stabbed, but the man's face was pounded thin as a veal cutlet. Maybe you want to stay out here, Darby."

"I'll be all right," she said, struggling to keep her anger in check. "Thanks for your concern."

"Watch your step, then. There's liable to be some evidence on the ground and we don't want to destroy anything."

Darby followed Mark into the shed, picking carefully around the debris Chief Dupont had crushed minutes earlier. Garden implements appeared to have been pulled off the walls, and pieces of terra cotta pots lay broken on the floor. Seeping past the tire of the riding mower was a dark puddle of blood, and in front of the mower was a body.

Darby noticed the garden shears first. A wet circle of red ringed the steel of the shears, like a bull's eye on a dartboard. They had been thrust into the victim's chest in the area of the heart, and Darby suspected that the damage done by the puncture was substantial. Her eyes traveled up to the victim's head. Whatever represented a face — nose, cheeks, lips — was now obliterated. The killer had smashed the facial features to such an extent they were pulverized. No doubt the victim's eyeballs remained, but the orbital sockets around the eyes were so swollen they formed a solid, bloodied mass.

She noted sandy hair and a dimpled chin, and suddenly she flashed back a dozen years. *Emerson Phipps.*

Mark echoed her thoughts. "It's Phipps. My God, who could have done this?"

Darby scanned the shed floor, and noticed blood and pieces of human flesh on a stone angel. "He must have been struck with that garden statue. That's what did such a number on his face."

"Wasn't just struck with it," said Chief Dupont, coming alongside the tractor and standing by Darby and Mark. "He was mashed with it, sort of like a mortar and pestle kind of thing. Whoever did this hated the guy. Wanted to teach him a lesson." He looked down at his fingers for a moment, fiddling with a ragged cuticle. "You got a positive identification for me?"

"It's Emerson Phipps, M.D.," said Mark. "He lived in Chestnut Hill, outside of Boston."

"I've got his full address back at my office," added Darby.

"Well that's a start. I've got the medical examiner coming in from Augusta, and she should be here —" he consulted his watch, "in ten minutes or so. She'll determine the time and cause of death, although from the looks of it, I'd say we can blame that pretty little garden angel. Those shears were more for decoration, looks like. The icing on the proverbial cake."

Mark Trimble and Darby exchanged a glance and began heading out of the shed.

"Hey," Chief Dupont called out after them. "I may have more questions for you two. Don't leave the premises. Got it?"

The warm sunshine and clean air was a welcome contrast from the dank darkness of the garden shed. Neither Mark nor Darby said anything for a minute or two. They had walked the distance from the shed to where Donny Pease was seated when Darby sighed and said, "We need to tell Lucy."

"I know. I thought she would be here . . ."

"She was here," said Donny, surprising them both with his thin voice. "She showed me her bloody hands . . ."

"Her what? Christ, Donny. You're going off the deep end." Mark gave the older man a menacing glare.

Darby kneeled before the Adirondack chair and looked into the man's pale face. "He's in shock," she said to Mark. To the older man, she pleaded, "Tell me, Donny. Tell me what you saw."

He seemed to focus in on Darby's eyes. "I remember your parents," he whispered. "They lived at the cove . . ."

"That's right, Donny. Now tell me what you said about Lucy Trimble. You thought you saw her . . ."

"I saw her behind the shed, dressed all in white, like an angel. She was there, and then she ran." He pointed across the wide lawn, "That way, to the cliffs."

Mark jerked his head up and met Darby's eyes. "The cliffs . . . ?" he asked, and then, he was off, sprinting across the lawn with Darby close on his heels. She barely felt the grass against her ankles or the stiffening sea breeze. Panting, they reached the edge of the grass where the land dropped off in a dangerously dramatic fashion, its sides studded with huge slabs of ancient granite and a few tufts of grass.

"Lucy," Mark yelled into the wind. "Lucy!"

Darby scanned the small beach below, and saw clumps of seaweed, a discarded lobster buoy, and more rocks. She glanced to the right, toward a rocky outcropping frequented by small bands of gulls, and saw a mooring ball that had washed up on shore and somehow become wedged between two boulders. Oddly enough, legs were sticking out from the ball . . .

"She's down there!" cried Darby, pointing at the huddled form.

"Sweet lord," said Mark, "Not Lucy! Tell me she isn't . . ."

Darby was already scrambling down the sheer precipice. "Get the chief and have him call for an ambulance. Find some rope and a blanket. We don't have a minute to lose."

FIVE

The emergency medical technician slammed the back door of the ambulance with a curt nod to Darby and Chief Dupont. Mark Trimble was already inside the vehicle, crouched beside his sister with another EMT.

"She's going to make it," the EMT said, as he opened the driver-side door and climbed in. "Her fall caused a few broken bones, but we don't see any signs of internal trauma."

"What's all that blood from?" Chief Dupont asked. "Can you tell?"

"Not from any wound that I could see." The technician pulled his door closed and started the ambulance. The chief turned to Darby with a frown.

"My guys took a sample, but it doesn't take a genius to figure out she's wearing Phipps' blood. It's all over her white blouse, for Chrissake. Backs up the old guy's story,

133

too. Apparently she didn't want to sell the old place, probably had sentimental reasons — and so she killed this guy Phipps."

"That doesn't make sense," Darby said. "For one thing, Donny Pease saw Lucy running *before* he discovered the body. Why wouldn't she have taken off before he came to?"

"He surprised her in the act," the chief said confidently. "Happens all the time. Then Miss Trimble had a fit of remorse and threw herself over the cliff."

Darby shook her head. "Lucy wasn't attached to that house. She and her brother both wanted to sell it." *Although Lucy hadn't wanted to sell it to Emerson Phipps.*

"I'm not arresting her — not yet, anyway. I need the medical examiner to get here and give me a time of death. Then you can bet I'll be bringing Miss Lucy in for questioning."

He leaned back on the heels of his scuffed shoes and regarded Darby.

"So, where are you staying while you're here? Your aunt's place?"

Darby nodded.

"You here until her memorial service?"

"I'm not sure."

She saw the chief raise his eyebrows at her indecision. Her feelings about the old

134

woman were complicated, to say the least. *Am I staying for her service? My schedule has opened up. I could take a more active role in putting Jane Farr — and my past — to rest.* She made a mental note to call the minister about arrangements.

"There's a new restaurant in Manatuck with family-style dinners and such," continued Chief Dupont. "If you're not busy, we could talk about old times . . ."

This is exactly why I'm single, Darby thought. She shot him a grimace that she knew he'd interpret as a smile.

"Thanks, but I'm not up to a dinner date. Will you call me when you know the time of death?"

Charles Dupont nodded. "What will you do in the meantime? There's no place to hide on this island."

Darby kept her anger in check. "I won't be hiding," she said briskly. "I've got a funeral to plan."

Real estate deals do not always work out. As skilled as she was, Darby Farr knew that there were forces beyond her control that could scuttle a transaction, and she did her best to prepare her clients for that possibility ahead of time. Still, there were times even Darby was caught off guard.

Mark Trimble's reaction to the abrupt end of his second Fairview deal astonished her.

"Easy come, easy go," he said lightly, as he perched on the edge of his sister's hospital bed. "I mean, it was a good deal, don't get me wrong, but maybe it was too good to be true?" He gazed down at Lucy Trimble's bandaged arm and pale complexion. "Besides, Lucy didn't like the guy anyway."

Darby pulled up a chair and sat down by the hospital bed.

"You've got your priorities straight, and I like that," she said, watching Lucy's chest rise ever so slightly with her breathing. "But I get the sense you feel responsible for what happened today. Selling your estate doesn't mean you're a neglectful brother. I'll call Peyton as soon as I leave the hospital. She still wants Fairview. We can make a deal happen."

"But I didn't listen to my sister, Darby," he said, his voice a whisper. "Lucy told me how she felt and I didn't even care. And now . . ."

"She had an accident, Mark, and she's going to be okay. Seeing Phipps upset her, and she had an accident."

"But the blood . . ."

"She was trying to help the guy! Isn't that

what she said to you in the ambulance? You can't think for a minute that she had anything to do with his death."

"No." Mark stood up, walked across the room and looked out the window. With its proximity to Manatuck Harbor, the hospital's rooms boasted a few five-star views of the ferry landing and a seaweed processing plant. "I saw her lying there, and all I could think of was Wes."

He turned and Darby saw the pained expression on his face. "I've already lost one sibling. I can't bear to think that Lucy . . ."

There was a soft knock on the door. Laura Gefferelli, holding a bouquet of lupines, peered into the room. "May I come in?"

Mark nodded and the minister closed the door softly behind her. "How is Lucy?"

"Stable. No internal injuries, thank God." He gave a guilty glance at Laura. "I mean . . ."

Laura smiled. "I couldn't agree with you more. Thank God." She walked to the bed and put a hand on Lucy's shoulder. "Has she regained consciousness at all?"

"No."

"She will. Her body is just recovering from the shock." She turned to Darby. "And how are you holding up? You couldn't have imagined such an eventful trip east."

"I'm fine, thanks." Darby glanced at her watch. The courthouse in Manatuck was a short walk away; if she left now, she would be there before they closed. "I think I may do a quick deed search for Fairview," she said. "I'd like to see if I can find any proof of that anti-drinking language in the original deed."

Mark sighed. "I don't even care anymore, Darby. Lucy and I can keep Fairview, rent it out or something. Maybe I'll even move back in there."

"No way." The voice was feeble, but all three heard the words clearly. Lucy Trimble's eyelids flickered and she said again, "No way are we keeping that house."

"Lucy!" Mark rushed to the bed and bent over his sister. "You scared me, Lu. I couldn't take it if something happened to you."

Lucy Trimble swallowed painfully and Laura offered her a sip of water through a straw. She accepted, wincing as the liquid touched her parched lips.

"Thanks, Laura." She winced again. "Darby, I thought I heard your voice. It's good to see you. Sorry I'm such a mess."

"I'm glad you're okay, Lucy. That was quite a fall."

Lucy tried to lift her head up, but sank

back on the pillow in pain. "It wasn't a fall," she said firmly. "Somebody gave me a good, hard shove."

Her brother gasped. "What?"

Lucy nodded. "I walked over to Fairview for one last look. I saw the BMW, Donny's truck, and the shed with the doors open. When I saw the body . . ." she paused and looked at Laura Gefferelli. "I've got to tell them the whole thing."

"You're not up to it," Laura said quietly. "Tell them later."

Lucy shook her head. "No. This is the time."

She motioned for another sip of water and Laura once again complied. When Lucy spoke, her voice was stronger than before.

"You know how much I hate Fairview," she said, her eyes searching Mark's face. He nodded and she continued. "I want nothing more than to sell that place and be done with it once and for all. I don't care if it becomes a wedding resort, or a dog kennel, or if it burns to the ground. But I didn't want it sold to Emerson Phipps."

She took a ragged breath, her eyes focused on Mark. "I was sixteen the summer Phipps came to visit you." She turned her head slowly toward Darby. "You must remember that summer? We were having such a

139

blast . . ."

Darby nodded. She had only a hazy memory of Emerson Phipps, and the image of him mangled on the shed floor at Fairview wasn't helping.

"He visited for a few days in late June, and then he came again in July. And it was on his second trip that he raped me."

"What!" Mark exploded out of his chair, his eyes blazing. "That bastard! How . . ."

"The details don't matter," Lucy said wearily. "I played tennis with him, I saw him that night in the library, he gave me some whiskey . . ."

Suddenly Darby saw it all: Lucy, laughing in her tennis skirt and sleeveless blouse, swinging her racket and talking to her brother's charming friend from Dartmouth; Mrs. Phipps' vacant glance at the dinner table, as she pushed away her chair and retired to her private wing; the easy friendliness of Mark Trimble, offering a sunset sail, but his friend turning it down, looking instead at the lithe teenager in her tennis whites, his eyes a cold blue . . .

Darby shuddered. She knew now why Lucy had not returned to school that summer, why she had changed from a carefree girl to a careless addict. She understood it all, except for one thing.

"Why didn't you tell me?" she whispered. "We were best friends. I could have helped you."

"I wanted to," Lucy said softly. "I wanted to with all my heart. But I was ashamed, Darby. I thought that if I didn't say anything, it would go away." She exhaled and closed her eyes for a brief moment. "But of course, it didn't." She bit her lip. "Six weeks or so later, I knew I was pregnant. I had to tell someone, so I went to see Dr. Hotchkiss. He promised that he wouldn't tell my mother, but of course he did. He wasn't going to keep something like that from the most powerful family in town."

"You went away to school," Darby said. "You went to boarding school in New York."

"I went to a home for unwed mothers in New York," said Lucy. "My mother told everyone I was at a private academy, but I was tucked away in Albany until the baby was born. Not even my father knew what was going on."

Mark looked dumbfounded. "I can't believe it. Phipps . . . he did that to you. Why didn't you ever tell me, Lucy? All these years . . ." His voice took on a hard edge. "I'm sorry I wasn't the one to kill him."

"Somebody beat you to it," said Laura Gefferelli, placing a calming hand on his trembling arm.

Darby stood up, her mind racing. "Lucy, what happened after you found Phipps?"

"I think I went into some sort of trance," she said. "I looked down, and the next thing I knew, I was covered in blood. I got up and ran across the lawn and toward the ocean. I stopped at the edge of the cliff, screaming. I felt a hard shove, and all of a sudden I was falling . . ."

"Did you see who pushed you?"

Lucy's eyes were brimming with tears. "I know it's impossible, but I keep thinking it was Emerson Phipps."

Given Lucy's painful news, Darby decided to postpone her trip to the Manatuck courthouse, and instead made a coffee run to the hospital cafeteria. Although she hadn't eaten since eight A.M. that morning, the sight of the doughnuts and stale muffins repulsed her. As she made her way back to Lucy's room with the steaming Styrofoam cups, she saw the bulky form of Charles Dupont passing the nurse's station. Her heart sank. His presence could mean only one thing: Lucy Trimble was about to be questioned for murder.

Chief Dupont looked up as she approached. "Why thank you, darling, don't mind if I do." He grabbed a coffee and gave her a hard look. "Shouldn't you be planning a funeral?"

"It just so happens that I have been meeting with Reverend Gefferelli in Lucy's room," she said. The chief didn't need to know what they'd been meeting about, she reasoned.

"That so? I'm here to ask Lucy Trimble a few questions, now that we know what time of day Dr. Phipps was killed."

Darby kept herself from asking and opened the door. "Coffees," she announced. "Coffees, and Chief Dupont."

The others were silent as he made his way inside the room. He regarded Lucy's open eyes with satisfaction. "Why you're awake, Miss Lucy. That will make the job of questioning you that much easier."

He pulled up a plastic chair and eased onto it. "Normally I would ask you all to clear out of here and leave us alone. But if you can keep your mouths shut, I'll allow you to stay, seeing as how Miss Lucy is pretty banged up." He glanced at Mark Trimble. "Do you understand what I'm saying?"

Mark nodded. The chief grunted and turned back to the hospital bed. After a sip of coffee, he gave Lucy a hard look that made Darby shiver. "Let me get right to the point. Where were you on Sunday morning, Miss Trimble?"

"Sunday?" Mark questioned.

Dupont put up a hand. "Yes, Mr. Trimble. That's what the medical examiner tells me. Dr. Phipps was killed with a blunt instrument yesterday morning between seven A.M. and eleven. The gardening shears stuck in his gut were a nice touch, but they didn't kill him."

Mark Trimble rose to his feet. "You can't think Lucy had anything to do with Emerson Phipp's death," he cried. "That's ridiculous!"

"Mark, please," said Lucy. "He's just doing his job." The effort of talking seemed to exhaust her and she took a long breath. "Sunday I was at the church, in the kitchen. I went in around seven A.M. and was there until the service started at nine A.M. I attended worship, and then came back and cleaned up. I was home around eleven A.M. or so."

"What were you doing in the kitchen before church started?"

"I was preparing for communion, cutting cubes of bread and pouring the juice into the communion glasses."

"That takes two hours?"

144

"It takes longer than you think," she said.

Laura Gefferelli interrupted. "It has to be cut up into small cubes and arranged on the platters. Plus Lucy made coffee and helped set up for the hospitality hour."

The chief turned back to Lucy. "So there were other church members present?"

"Rhonda Davis and her sister — Lillian's her name, I think — showed up at 8:15."

"You were alone until that time?"

"Yes."

The chief shook his head and was about to comment further when Laura Gefferelli spoke up once more.

"Chief, I don't know if it's helpful, but I saw Lucy in the kitchen on my way to the sanctuary. That was at 7:30, maybe even earlier. I could tell she'd been working for some time, as the glasses were already full."

"Did you speak to Miss Trimble?"

"No, I didn't."

"Why not?"

"I was praying." She turned her calm blue eyes toward the chief and continued. "Every Sunday I wake at sunrise, get ready for the service, and spend as much time as possible in quiet contemplation until the service starts. I've always done it. I find it helps center and prepare me for my duties as a minister."

145

"I see." Chief Dupont turned to Lucy. "Lucky for you Reverend Gefferelli has a set routine." He scratched his head and frowned. "That's all for now, I guess, but I may be back with more questions. You'll stick around, right, Miss Trimble?"

Lucy nodded.

Darby rose and walked Chief Dupont out of the hospital room. "Do you have any other leads?" she asked.

He looked at her warily. "Maybe. Why would you want to know?" His cell phone rang and he answered it with a curt yes. She watched him narrow his eyes and nod.

"My deputy just found Emerson Phipps' wallet in the woods not far from Fairview," he said. "There was no money, but his driver's license was still intact."

"I don't mean to tell you how to do your job, Chief Dupont," said Darby quietly. "But I don't think Lucy Trimble was anything but an innocent victim today. In fact, she says she was pushed from that cliff. Whoever murdered Emerson Phipps may have been the one who hit Donny Pease and shoved Lucy. She could have been killed as well."

The chief appeared to consider Darby's statements. "I suppose you have a suspect in mind?"

"Soames Pemberton's trailer is in the woods, not far from Fairview. He could easily have seen Phipps' arrival Sunday morning in the BMW. Perhaps Soames lured Phipps into the shed, killed him, and returned the next day looking for money."

"Soames? He's got one or two screws loose, but he's not a murderer." The chief turned and started down the hospital corridor. "Look, I'm not discussing my case with you, Darby Farr, and I'd like it if you kept your suppositions, however plausible they may seem, under your hat." He paused and glanced back at Darby. "Tell Lucy Trimble I said get well soon."

Darby watched the bulky form of the chief as he rounded the corner. She thought back to the morning's planning board meeting and Soames Pemberton's appearance with the old deed. Could he have come before the town knowing he'd killed a man in cold blood only twenty-four hours earlier? *Soames is a madman,* thought Darby. *I know that firsthand . . .*

She entered Lucy's hospital room to find Mark Trimble pacing the floor, eyes blazing with anger. He whipped toward Darby, his hands gesticulating wildly.

"Can you believe Chief Dupont thinks Lucy had something to do with this? That man is an idiot."

Laura Gefferelli sat quietly by Lucy's bedside, observing Mark Trimble's anguish without comment.

Lucy tried once more to calm her brother down. "Mark, please, he's just doing . . ."

"I know, I know, his job," Mark scoffed. "Lucy, if you're a suspect now, imagine if he knew about what Phipps did to you. If he were to find out . . ."

"I think we need to let you sleep, Lucy," said Laura softly. "I see they've given you Vicoprophen, which should help with the pain." She leaned over the hospital bed and gave Lucy a hug. "Don't worry about the art show," she said. "I'm organizing a few volunteers to help me and we've got it covered."

"Thanks," Lucy said with a weak smile. "You'll probably sell more paintings without me."

"I doubt that, but we'll certainly give it our best." Laura turned her gray eyes toward Darby. "Care to sit down with me in the cafeteria? I'd like to go over a few details about your aunt's funeral."

Darby felt a pang of guilt. With all that had happened at Fairview and the hospital, she'd nearly forgotten about Jane Farr's memorial service.

"Sure," she said. She turned to Lucy. "You and I need some time to catch up. I'll be back to talk after you've rested."

When Lucy nodded, Darby gave her shoulder a small squeeze and left the room.

The fluorescent lights of the cafeteria buzzed overhead. The two women chose a table and pulled out plastic chairs.

"Want anything?" Laura Gefferelli asked, gesturing toward the coffee machines and food.

"No, I'm all set." The air reeked of macaroni and cheese, but Darby was beyond hunger. She gave a sigh and regarded the older woman. "I'm still in shock over Lucy's news that Emerson Phipps raped her. I remember that summer, although I barely remember him, but I certainly have memories of the way Lucy changed. She kind of withdrew into herself, you know, and then her problems with addiction started."

Laura nodded. "That's often the way it progresses. The shame, the inability to process the rape, and the effort of acting like all is normal — it's more than anyone can bear, especially a vulnerable girl of sixteen." Her normally relaxed face hardened with anger. "When I think of the way Lucy's mother reacted . . ." she paused, and with only minimal effort, seemed to calm herself down. "In Lucy's case, the fact that she was sent away probably saved her from going completely over the edge. She's told me before that there were some caring individuals at the home for unwed mothers, and they tried to make a very painful experience less traumatic."

Darby pictured Lucy giving birth in New York, away from her family and friends, and then handing the baby off to strangers . . . coming back to Hurricane Harbor, pretending that she'd spent the academic year at a prestigious boarding school.

"When did she tell you?"

Laura thought a moment. "A month or so ago. We were working together at the Coveside Clinic, and she chose to open up."

"I wish I had known she was in such pain," Darby said quietly.

Laura shook her head. "From what little I know of your story, Darby, you were in pain yourself. You'd suffered your own trauma." She took a small notebook out of her pocketbook. "Forgive me for getting down to business, but I have a meeting after this and I want to get some details together for Jane's service."

"You go from one meeting to another. Do you ever sleep?"

Laura Gefferelli laughed. "Not much, hence the bags under my eyes. This meeting is about that Women's Center that I told you about, on the west side of the island. We did get our approval for the septic system, by the way, so the project is on track." She paused, and looked down at her notepad. "The whole thing was actually Jane's idea. She was like that, you know, she thought big. Instead of adding a wing onto something, Jane suggested a new building, found it for us, and helped fund it. She really was a remarkable woman."

Darby was silent as Laura ticked off items from her list: Scripture passages, pallbearers, music, flowers . . . She tried to listen but her mind wandered from images of Jane Farr to Lucy Trimble as a teen. The past — her Hurricane Harbor past — was intruding upon her present. She heard herself agreeing with things Laura was saying, without knowing, or caring, what they were.

Her confused mental state was abruptly interrupted by a deep cough.

"Excuse me," said a voice tinged with a British accent. "I'm looking for Darby Farr."

Darby looked up. She was ten inches away from a rugged face with a thick shock of dark hair, unquestionably the sexiest face she had ever seen.

She said nothing for a moment or two, drinking in the feeling of lust that was overwhelming her whole body. Then she willed herself to take control of her hormones and answered.

"I'm Darby," she managed. "What can I do for you?"

He smiled and held out a hand. "Miles Porter, journalist from the *Financial Times* of London. I wonder if I might have a word?"

They shook hands and Darby glanced toward the amused face of Laura Gefferelli. Quickly she introduced the other woman and invited Miles to take a seat.

Laura rose from her chair. "Actually, Darby, I really need to get back to the island. I have to work on this service and get ready for my meeting. Nice to meet you, Miles." She gave Darby a little smile and left.

Miles Porter pulled up a chair and sank gratefully into it. "I'm bushed. I flew in yesterday and drove up from Boston this morning. I'm afraid I'm not my usual chipper self yet."

You look pretty darn good anyway, thought Darby, noticing the way his khaki pants fit in all the right places. "What are you doing in Maine?"

"I'm here to write a story for the FT about real estate," he said. "Specifically, high-end waterfront property." He paused and pulled a business card out of the pocket of a tweedy jacket. "Actually, I was supposed to meet up with your aunt. Tina at the office just told me of her passing. Please accept my condolences."

"Thanks. You didn't know until you arrived in the United States?"

"I didn't know until I rang the office an hour ago to say I'd be a little late for our appointment." He touched his fingertips together and said lightly, "Turns out I was quite late."

"I'm sorry that you weren't notified, Mr. Porter. I checked her appointment book but I didn't see your name."

"It's Miles. Please don't worry on that account. It's a business trip for me, and besides, Tina said I could get an even better story from you."

"She did?"

He laughed. "She suggested the bicoastal angle — you contrasting the Maine market with the California coast. I think it's a very good idea. What do you say? There's a free dinner at the restaurant of your choice in it for you. I'm afraid it does need to be tonight, however, as I have to be back in

Boston tomorrow."

Darby considered. Although she wasn't in the mood for socializing, the *Financial Times'* affluent, international readership represented just the kind of buyers she coveted as clients. "I'll do it, but it's going to cost you," she warned. "I have pretty expensive tastes."

"Seeing you in person, I wouldn't doubt it."

He gave her a frank look and she felt the color rising in her cheeks. *Since when am I someone who blushes?*

"The restaurant I'm choosing is called Firefall," Darby said. "It's —"

"Fabulous."

"You know it?"

"I love it. I was hoping you'd pick Firefall. They have room for us at seven. Will that be too late?"

Darby glanced at her watch. "The ferry back to Hurricane Harbor leaves in fifteen minutes. I need to shower, and change, and it takes about an hour to get there . . ."

"That's if you're going by car," Miles said, smiling at her surprised look. "I'll pick you up at the Hurricane Harbor dock at 6:30." He rose and gave her another grin. "Bring a warm jacket."

Six

Firefall was an intimate restaurant tucked into the exclusive coastal town of Westerly, up the coast from Manatuck some seventy miles by car. Traveling in a fast boat across the bay cut the journey in half, and before Darby would have imagined it possible, she and Miles Porter were seated at a corner table, a full-bodied bottle of Barolo before them. Darby felt a little shaky from the boat ride, but she was surprised to note that being on the water was becoming less traumatic with each outing.

"To Jane Farr," said Miles, clinking glasses with Darby, an impish smile on his face. "I never actually met your aunt, but we shared a few wonderful conversations on the phone. She was not afraid to express her opinion, so much so that I wonder if the FT would have printed half of her comments!" He chuckled. "For instance, she told me that any buyer she'd ever worked for was a total

155

fraud. 'You can't trust a word they tell you,' she said. 'And the bigger their wallets, the bigger their lies'."

Darby rolled her eyes. "The old 'buyers are liars' routine," she said. "You hear it all the time in real estate, and it was one of my aunt's favorite sayings. Unlike most agents who laugh it off, I think Jane actually believed it." She took a sip of the ruby-colored liquid. "This wine is delicious."

"Glad you like it. This particular vintage is one of my favorites."

"Corino 99?"

"That's right. I'm impressed."

"I've tasted it before."

The waiter appeared and took their orders for dinner. Miles pulled a small tape recorder from his pocket and placed it on the table. "Can we get the questions out of the way before dinner?" he asked.

Darby nodded. "I don't like being taped, but I suppose that's the easiest way for you," she said.

"It is, but I have a pad of paper with me as well. Whichever you prefer, I'll do."

She took another sip of the wine, feeling it warming her throat. "Well . . ."

"Paper it is," Miles announced, shoving the tape recorder back in his pocket and withdrawing a small spiral notebook and pen. "The last thing I want to do is make you uncomfortable."

For the next ten minutes or so, Miles asked Darby questions about waterfront real estate, coaxing from her a few tips that he could share with his readers in the United Kingdom. When the waiter arrived with their appetizers, he closed the notebook and said, "Great. Your insightful comments, combined with a few breathtaking photos, will please my editors back in London." He grinned and met her eyes across the table. "Thank you."

"Thank you," Darby said, gazing down at the artfully arranged trio of pates before her. "This looks absolutely fabulous."

"Let's hope it tastes as good as it looks." Miles tried a bite of his appetizer. "This little place has quite the reputation. I read about it in a travel magazine back in London. I can see now the glowing review was well deserved."

"Do you write for magazines as well?"

"No, I'm strictly a newspaper man, myself, although I enjoy reading just about anything."

"Were you always a financial features writer?"

He shook his head. "I've only been writing for the FT for two years now. Before

157

that, I was an investigative reporter for the *New York Times*, based in London."

"Interesting. How did a Brit get that job?"

He grinned again. "By going to school in the States. I attended Columbia University and did an internship at the *Times* while I was a senior. That led to employment following graduation, and, eventually, to them sending me back to London. I did that for many years, and I must say, I miss it."

"Why did you stop?"

For the first time, Miles Porter's warm eyes lost their merry look. He looked down at the table and then back up at Darby.

"Someone close to me — one of my most trusted sources — was shot in the back in Piccadilly Square. I spent months digging for information, clues — any scrap of evidence I could find. I was an investigative reporter, after all, so I figured I could unearth something . . . but the murder was never solved. All the wind went out of my sails, so to speak, and I found I no longer had the drive I needed to ferret out the truth."

Darby put down her fork and nodded slowly. "I know what you mean," she said. She thought back to her parents' deaths and how her life had seemed to abruptly halt. It was like a sailboat suddenly losing wind, she realized. Funny that she had never thought of that analogy . . .

Miles poured more Barolo into Darby's empty glass. "Not to stay on such a gruesome subject, but I must ask: what's happened on the little island of Hurricane Harbor to get everyone in such a tizzy? I heard a small item on the radio, something about a doctor from Boston found killed in a garden shed."

Darby thought for a moment. If the police had released the name of the victim, they'd obviously located his next of kin and informed him or her of the murder. She knew that she wouldn't be revealing any confidential details if she told Miles Porter what little she knew of the crime.

When she had finished recounting the facts of the case, he let out a low whistle.

"That's a big story for a small island," he said. "I suppose an AP reporter is on his way up here as we speak." He paused as the waiter removed their plates and poured them each more wine.

"You sound almost wistful," she said. "As if you'd like to be covering this story yourself. Do you miss it that much?"

"I'll admit it: I do. When Sarah was killed . . ." Darby saw him wince slightly as he said her name — "I threw every ounce of strength I had into solving her case. I failed, and began to question my whole reason for being. I have come to realize as the years have passed that some mysteries can't be solved. Her death may be one of them."

The waiter returned with their entrees, which he placed before them with a small bow. "Enjoy your meal," he said, leaving them to gaze at the masterful presentations alone.

"I almost hate to eat it, it's so beautiful," breathed Darby.

"That's the duck?"

"Quail."

"Mmm, well if you can't manage to tuck into it, just let me know," Miles said cheerfully.

"I said I 'almost' hate to eat it," Darby reminded him. "Fortunately or unfortunately, I have a healthy appetite. There's rarely a time when I can't eat."

"I daresay you wear it wonderfully."

Darby looked up and Miles was gazing at her with an intensity that felt like heat. She felt the color rising in her cheeks and gave a small laugh.

"Why, thank you sir. *Bon appetit.*"

The two enjoyed several bites in silence. Darby's quail was delicately flavored, with a very light glaze that enhanced, rather than overpowered, the tender meat. She offered Miles a bite and he accepted.

"I've never had anything like that," he marveled. "So fresh! Here, try my beef. You do eat beef, I hope?"

"Definitely." Darby tasted a morsel and smiled. "That reminds me of something my mother used to make," she said. "A French dish — *Boeuf à la Lyonnaise.*"

"Your mother was French?"

"No," Darby laughed. "She was Japanese. But she was also a talented cook who decided to tackle the art of French cuisine."

"How intriguing! Tell me more."

"I think I was nine or so when she found a copy of Julia Child's book, and that was the start of her love affair with *la cuisine Francaise.*" She smiled at the memory. "Not all of her efforts were successes. There were the soufflés that didn't rise, the gateau that was more like soup — but she persevered. I guess that was true of her personality in many ways. She taught herself English, she grew to love sailing, and she made herself fall in love with the coast of Maine. She was quite a determined woman."

"And your dad? Tell me about him."

"He was an adventurer. A world-class sailor who raced around the world. He

161

wasn't afraid of anyone or anything, and he rose to any challenge."

"Did they meet on the island?"

"No. They met in Boston, at a world cup sailing event. My dad was there representing the American team, and my mother was part of a Japanese delegation on a tall ship. They saw each other at a cocktail party and fell in love."

"The classic 'love at first sight'," commented Miles. "What brought them to the island?"

"They didn't come up here right away. They lived in Boston, where Mom worked as a translator, and Dad continued to race the world cup circuit. When my mother became pregnant with me, he decided it was time to embrace the landlubber life. Somebody told him about the job as the sailing director at the Hurricane Harbor Yacht Club. They moved up here and I was born a few months later, at the hospital in Manatuck."

"So you are a Maine native."

"No, being a native is a generational thing. I was always an anomaly on the island. Not a native, not a summer person, not your white-bread American. Hard to categorize."

"That's not necessarily a bad thing," he teased.

"True, but it isn't always easy on an island." Darby placed her fork on her plate and sighed. "That was delicious."

"I agree." He glanced at his watch. "We have time for coffee, or an after dinner drink before the boat meets us. What would you like?"

"Coffee, thanks." Miles ordered coffees and asked for the check. The waiter returned a few moments later with two steaming mugs.

Miles added some sugar to his and took a sip. "Did I hear there is a suspect in the Fairview case?"

"For an ex-investigative reporter, you're awfully curious." She grinned. "Maybe you should be writing about this murder after all."

He thought a moment. "I can't say it hasn't crossed my mind. There is something so compelling about a mystery, isn't there? Come on, tell me what you know."

"My instincts tell me a local guy named Soames Pemberton could be guilty. He's a former Navy SEAL with some big-time anger management issues, a substance abuse problem, and a history of criminal behavior. Hopefully, he's the one Chief Dupont is focusing on."

"This Soames character sounds like a

163

total beast."

Darby nodded. "Murder seems like something he'd relish, and yet . . ."

"What?"

"I don't know. Something about it doesn't feel exactly right, that's all." Darby finished her coffee and shrugged. *Was it his appearance at the planning board meeting the day after the killing took place? Was that why she felt he was the wrong man?*

"I can't explain it. When I can, I'll give you a call."

"It's a deal."

They rose and left the restaurant, walking the short way to the private wharf where the sleek speedboat waited. Darby felt her palms grow clammy, but she climbed into the boat without her legs wobbling too much. Thirty minutes later, Darby was thanking Miles Porter for dinner and walking through the damp grass to Jane's guest cottage. She undressed and got into bed, wondering, as she drifted off to sleep, why in the world she doubted Soames Pemberton's guilt.

Darby awoke the next morning with the sun. Her first thought was to contact Peyton Mayerson and discuss a new offer, but it was barely past dawn and too early for calls.

Instead, she tied on her sneakers and went running toward Fairview. She had barely looked at the old estate the day before, and she wanted a chance to see the grounds without Chief Dupont and his deputies breathing down her neck.

The morning air was clean and crisp. Darby ran past the cove and through the village, along the harbor and then up the woodsy hill and out toward Pemberton Point. The road soon turned to dirt and Darby kicked up small dust clouds as she ran. She came to the massive stone pillars, ducked under a "crime scene" tape, and ran down the road.

The house loomed up before her. She avoided looking toward the garden shed, and instead, crossed the wide green lawn to the house.

She peered in a window. A vast, empty room with deep paneling, parquet floors and two enormous fireplaces surrounded by marble loomed before her — the formal living room. Darby moved to another window. A second room, equally as large, adjoined the first room, and had been used as the casual, family space. In this room the look was rustic — rough-hewn paneling and two fireplaces built with local stone. The room had been large enough to accommodate not only two seating areas, but a game area, complete with a huge slate pool table.

The two living rooms were separated by a hallway wide enough to accommodate a car. This was the formal entryway, at its end was one of Fairview's most stunning features: a wide, arching staircase that separated midway into two mirror images. Darby knew the flying staircase was one of the finest examples in the Northeast. The effect was magical and grand, and Darby imagined brides floating down in a cascade of rose petals.

Darby left her vantage point and walked around the side of the house to peer in at the dining room. She remembered that an enormous table had presided over the room, with seating for ten or maybe even fifteen guests at a side. It was gone, as were the chairs and sideboards she remembered. Along with the elaborately carved mantel and fireplace, the only detail she could see was the giant crystal chandelier, now ghostly thanks to a few spiders who'd taken up residence.

The kitchen at Fairview had always been a bit of an eyesore, constructed as it was in the days before cooking was elevated from a servant's chore to an owner's pastime. Darby was curious as to whether Mark and

Lucy had updated the gloomy space, so she headed to the back of the house to take a peek. The sight of the ocean, however, made her stop dead in my tracks. *I didn't notice this incredible view when I was scrambling to save Lucy,* she thought. Fairview possessed an almost 300-degree vantage point, thanks to the jutting promontory of Pemberton Point. Here was the open ocean in all of its glory, crashing against the boulders and sending up a spray that misted the wild roses along the cliff. At one point there had been a low fence along the jagged edge, but it was now gone. What was the point? It had been generations since small children had played on the pristine lawns of Fairview.

Darby pulled her eyes away from the view and gazed back at the house. The wrap-around porch took full advantage of the scenic setting, and she recalled the solid line of wicker rockers that had once been positioned like sentries along the side of the house. There had been a ping-pong table at one end of the porch, where Lucy and Darby tested their lightning fast serves in endless world championships. Darby sighed. The past was all around her, and she felt it pulling her down, toward depths of sadness that would swallow her like quicksand.

She jogged to the far side of the house,

where a stand of blooming lilacs tried valiantly to prevent the erosion that was wearing away at the hill. Here the cliff was very sheer, and she marveled once more that Lucy had not been critically injured. Whoever bought Fairview would need to put in a retaining wall as soon as possible, Darby thought.

She was backing away from the cliff when she heard a low chuckle. Her scalp prickling, she turned slowly toward the noise. Planted squarely between where Darby stood at the rocky edge and the corner of Fairview was Soames Pemberton.

"Well, well," he said softly, moving toward her like a predator stalking prey.

Darby tried not to show her panic.

"Stay away from me, Soames," she yelled. She estimated the space between the big man and the edge of the cliff and tried to see the best way to safety.

He paused momentarily and seemed to weave back and forth. His pupils were glossy black circles and he licked his lips several times as if parched. *He's high,* thought Darby, knowing that made him even more dangerous. She felt her mouth go dry, waiting for him to make the first move.

Soames Pemberton lunged quickly for a large man, and he dove at Darby, forcing her to dodge him, her heel teetering on the edge of the grass and sheer cliff. Quickly she regained her balance and darted to his left, as fast as she was able, away from his grasp. His huge paw of a hand grabbed her T-shirt, and she twisted, the material stretching and then finally coming free from his hand. As tempted as she was to deliver a resounding kick that would break his jaw, she knew her smartest course of action was to run, and run quickly.

Without another thought she began sprinting.

He gave a grunt and she felt him behind her, in hot pursuit, but she forced herself not to waste precious time by looking back. *Make it to the woods,* she told herself. *Just make it to the woods . . .*

It was a sprint of pure adrenalin, a quarter of a mile covered in a blur. The woods rose up before her and she dodged the trees, barely slowing her speed. Somewhere there was a path she and Lucy had taken through these same pines, a path that led back to the main road. She was tiring, but she didn't dare slow her pace. She leapt over a huge maple that had fallen in a storm and grazed the back of her calf, barely feeling the injury. She was in flight mode, with every cell in her body telling her to escape.

A huge mass of granite appeared before her and Darby racked her brain to figure out where she was. The outcropping was dimly familiar. As tall as a two-story building, there were small caves between the boulders that she and Lucy had imagined held pirate treasure. Suddenly she knew she had missed the start of the path, and had run past Fairview's boundaries, into the abutting property, an undeveloped swath of forest belonging to the heirs of Thaddeus Pemberton. She had blundered into Soames Pemberton's lair.

All she saw of his leap from the boulder was a flash of something silver in the edge of her peripheral vision. He landed on her calves, sending her thudding to the ground with a force that could have knocked her out. His thick arms encircled her legs and he whipped her over onto her back, grunting with satisfaction at her terror. She felt the full weight of him on her pelvis as he pinned her arms out to their sides. Never before had Darby felt so trapped.

"Get off me," she spat, twisting to free herself from his body.

He grunted. "You shut up before I slit your throat. You're the enemy, you hear me? And you're dead . . ."

"I am not the enemy," Darby yelled. "I'm

here to bury my aunt. Tina called me and asked me to come. I didn't do anything to you.' She struggled against his considerable weight, not daring to look at his expression.

"You are the enemy," he insisted. "You've been hiding in these caves . . ."

He let go of Darby's right arm and grabbed his knife. Before he could use it, Darby rammed her knuckle into his glassy eyes with all the force she could muster. He cried out in pain and released her arms, but still she could not wriggle free . . .

The crack of gunfire echoed through the trees, and faster than Darby could have imagined, Soames Pemberton sprang up and fled. Slowly Darby rose to a sitting position, her head thudding, and looked for the source of the sound. She knew whomever had fired the gun was close by and that she was in great danger. Painfully, she rose to her knees.

A branch cracked to her left and Darby froze.

"You okay?" It was Charles Dupont, wearing jeans and his uniform shirt. He stopped beside her and squatted.

"I asked if you were okay."

Darby nodded. "What are you doing here?"

"Me? Why I'm a police officer, the chief

to be exact, out doing my job. What are you doing here? Didn't I tell you to stay out of the way?"

"I was out for a run. I know a path that goes through these woods . . ."

"This land belongs to Soames Pemberton, and surely a smarty-pants real estate agent like yourself knows that. You are meddling in my investigation, and you almost got yourself killed."

"You took a shot at Soames. Were you trying to hit him?"

The chief snorted. "If I'd been trying to hit him, he'd be lying here dead. I fired my weapon to get him off you."

Darby rose to her feet gingerly. Her ankle was twisted, but she wasn't about to tell the chief of her injuries.

His eyes narrowed. "You're hurt."

"No," she said, trying not to wince. "Not really."

"You could have fooled me. That leg needs to be looked at." He scanned the woods briefly then seemed to make up his mind about something. "Soames isn't going anywhere we can't find him, not on this island anyway." He paused a moment. "Come on, I'll take you over to the Coveside Clinic. They open at seven, and you need some attention."

Because she was in no shape to argue, Darby grudgingly acquiesced.

The Coveside Clinic was a trim, modest building with a wooden sign and a handicapped accessible ramp. "Look," Chief Dupont commanded, indicating a bronze marker by the front door. Darby exited from the police cruiser and walked closer to the marker. The inscription thanked a "longtime islander" for her "dedication and generosity."

"Your aunt," the chief said quietly. "She built this place."

Inside, the clinic was cheerful and clean. A nurse was on duty at the front desk, and Chief Dupont approached her, motioning for Darby to sit down. Darby complied and was surprised to see the familiar face of Laura Gefferelli enter the waiting room.

"What are you doing here?" Laura asked, a concerned expression on her face. "Everything okay?"

"I had a fall while I was running," Darby lied. "What about you?"

"Oh, I see a few counseling patients, and one or two prefer the early morning hours," she said. "It's pastoral counseling, incorporating the spiritual aspect into your more typical sessions. Lucy volunteers here too.

Are you waiting to see Yvette?"

"If she's the Physician's Assistant, then yes."

"She'll be with you in a moment." Laura gave Darby a searching look. "Mind if I sit down?"

Darby nodded. "Be my guest."

Laura sighed. "I've been thinking about you, Darby. About what's happened since you left California. There's quite a lot on your shoulders, and I want you to know that I'm here if you need to talk about anything."

Darby smiled. "Do I look that bad?"

Laura gave a kind smile. "It's not your outward appearance I'm concerned with. It's what's inside, the things you may be dealing with on top of your aunt's death, and now this." She hesitated. "May I give you a piece of advice? Allow yourself to grieve for Jane Farr, and help me with the funeral preparations. It's part of the healing process, and it isn't time you'll get back, Darby. I know you want to help Mark and Lucy, but please, think about what I'm saying."

"I will."

A fresh-faced young woman wearing white scrubs and carrying a clipboard entered the room. "Darby Farr?" she inquired.

Darby rose to follow the PA into the

patient room. Her ankle throbbed and she found it difficult to walk.

"That looks like a sprain," said Laura. "You may need crutches."

Darby groaned and accepted the help of the PA, feeling the eyes of Laura Gefferelli and Charles Dupont follow her as she left the waiting room.

Half an hour later, painkillers in hand, Darby was back at Jane's house to shower and change. After a quick cup of coffee, she wrapped up her throbbing ankle and drove to the office of Near & Farr, where a distraught Tina Ames met her at the door.

"What did that asshole Soames do now?" Tina ran a well-manicured hand through the tangle of red curls on her head. Darby could see she was fuming. "What's this I hear, he cornered you again?"

"Calm down. I went over to Fairview and he surprised me. I'm fine."

Tina yanked off an orange jacket and sat down at her desk. "You're hurt. Did he break something?"

"I twisted my ankle. I'll ice it, and it will be fine."

"I suppose I should tell you the whole story with him and me, because I can't help but feel some of his anger is misdirected at you."

"If you'd like."

She sighed and shook her head. "I was foolish to ever get mixed up with him, and now that I'm dating a nice guy like Donny, I really wonder about my sanity. What did I ever see in Soames, God only knows. Anyway, I was going through a bad patch and found myself at the Eye one too many nights, half in the bag and feeling sorry for myself. Soames was always there and he bought me a couple of drinks. I started to tell him things and believe it or not, he listened. One thing led to another and before I knew it, I was in his trailer on a stinky old mattress, and not just once, either." She gave Darby an embarrassed grimace.

"We've all done things we regret, Tina."

"I can hardly stand to think about it, but there it is. Finally I woke up one day and came to my senses. I told him we were through and he didn't much like that."

"What did he do?"

"He followed me around, hid out behind the bushes, you know, creepy stuff like that."

"He stalked you." Darby felt her anger toward Soames Pemberton rising again.

"Yeah, I guess you could say that. I reported him to the police. Not that it did much good. Just made him angrier. He surprised me one night at my mother's house and beat me up pretty good. I went back to the police and this time they listened."

"So then what happened?"

"He got some sort of suspended sentence, no jail time, but he has to go to counseling. I doubt it is making one dent in his perverted brain."

"How long ago was this, Tina?"

"Last year." She glanced down at her long fingernails then back at Darby. Her face was grim. "I told you, he's a dangerous man. I wish to God he'd take one too many pills and stumble off a cliff somewhere." She paused and gave Darby a dark look. "And don't think I wouldn't like to be there to give him a shove."

"Do you think he killed Emerson Phipps? Does it make sense to you?"

"Soames isn't about making sense," Tina said. "That's what I'm trying to tell you." She sighed and picked up a yellow pad. "Not to change the subject, but . . . this is your aunt's obit. We need to get it to the paper by noon and they'll print it in Wednesday's paper, plus the time of her service." She paused. "I hope you don't mind that I started working on it."

"Not at all." Darby sat down on a chair. "What have you got so far?"

Tina consulted the pad. *"Jane Jenson Farr, Real Estate Broker and Island Benefactress, came to Hurricane Harbor from Sarasota, Florida. Soon after her arrival on the island she established the New England office of Near & Farr Realty.*

Jane Farr was born in Connecticut, and attended local schools and the University of Connecticut, where she majored in business. She was a Vice President of a Florida import-export business before discovering real estate, a profession which quickly became a passion. She served on the Florida Board of REALTORS® and was a past president of the Maine Association of REALTORS®. Her many generous gifts to her community of Hurricane Harbor include major donations to the new ferry terminal on Manatuck, Coveside Clinic, and the Community Center."

Tina paused a moment. There were tears in her eyes.

"Jane Farr was predeceased by her parents, as well as her brother John, and sister-in-law, Jada. She leaves behind many friends in Maine and in Florida, as well as her niece, Darby Farr of Mission Beach, California."

Darby swallowed. "Very nice," she said.

"Should I have left you to do it? I'm sorry
—"

"No. It's perfect. Thank you."

Tina's eyes were moist as she nodded. "I'll send it in."

Darby rose from the chair, wiping her eyes with the back of her hand. "I'm going to hobble over to the Café for a muffin. Can I bring you back something?"

"Diet Coke."

The day was getting warmer, and a soft breeze was blowing off the bay. Boats were appearing in the harbor with more frequency and Darby knew that within a week, the little harbor would be full of vessels. Across the stretch of water she could see the tall mast of the *Lucy T,* and bobbing beside it, Laura Gefferelli's little boat.

She's right, Darby thought suddenly. *I need to focus on Jane's service, and details like the obituary.* She took one more look at the harbor before opening the Café's curtained doors. *I'll bury my aunt,* she vowed, *and then I'll see if I can't make peace with the rest of my past.*

SEVEN

Darby ordered a muffin and breakfast burrito at the Café and was waiting to pick them up when a friendly tap on the shoulder made her turn around.

"Miles!" she felt the physical reaction to his presence once more and hoped it didn't show. "I was going to call you. Thanks again for that fantastic dinner last night."

"The pleasure was all mine, I assure you." Miles was wearing jeans and a polo shirt with a light jacket. He raised his eyebrows at Darby's order. "Local fare? Any good?"

"Very good, if memory serves me right."

"Then I suppose I'll have to try one." He glanced around the Café and lowered his voice slightly. "Any news on the murder? Have the police apprehended the suspect?"

Darby shook her head. "No. They don't seem to be in too much of a hurry. I'm not sure what is going on."

Miles frowned. "Your leg — is it injured?"

"I had a little run-in with Soames Pemberton at Fairview this morning." She saw his look of concern and hastened to add, "I'm all right — fortunately for me, Chief Dupont showed up and scared him off. He basically fired a shot in the air, and let Pemberton escape." She thought a moment. "Why didn't the chief actually hit him? And why, once Soames ran away, didn't he pursue him? Instead he took the time to lecture me about staying away from the crime scene."

"Maybe this will muddy the waters a little." Miles Porter handed Darby a large gray envelope and she looked at him questioningly.

"Newspaper articles, about our friend Dr. Phipps," he said. "I did a little research online at the hotel this morning. It seems the good surgeon had a slightly checkered past."

"Interesting. I'll take a look at them this afternoon and call you."

"Not to add another duty to your 'to do' list, but I was hoping you might have dinner with me this evening?" Miles' smile was almost shy; Darby liked the contrast with his normally confident, capable, demeanor.

"I don't know if I'm up to it, Miles," she said truthfully. "I think I need to ice my

181

ankle and spend a quiet night. Besides, weren't you heading back to Boston today?"

"Quite right, that had been my plan. But this island, the murder, and the possibility for a really in-depth story . . . it's got me feeling energized again. I've decided to stay on a bit and have rented a little beach house for a few days. Maybe you know the property . . . I believe locals refer to it as the old Kendall place?"

"That's a great spot! I used to visit Mrs. Kendall when I was a girl. What a wonderful sandy beach, and the house has such character."

"I've checked it out, and although there is a modest kitchen, I think I'll be able to make you one of my specialties. I do hope you'll come. I promise it can be, as you say, a quiet night."

"I'll come on one condition: we spend some time trying to make sense of this murder."

"I'd love to. As I told you, I do love a mystery."

"Great. What can I bring?"

"Just your lovely self," he said lightly. "Shall we say around six P.M.?" Darby picked up her order and paid the tab, hoping that the flush she felt in her cheeks didn't show. "I'll look forward to it. Thanks for the reading material and I'll see you this evening."

Back at the office, Darby handed Tina her Diet Coke and half of the burrito with a flourish. "There you go, Tina. A little sustenance from the Café."

"Thanks. Let's get that ankle elevated while you have breakfast. I've got a bag of ice and a pillow."

Darby allowed Tina to help her get settled. The cold comfort of the ice plus the two ibuprofen she'd popped earlier were finally keeping the throbs at bay.

"Speaking of sustenance," said Tina. "I'd like to see some cash coming in here. Are you going to give our friend Peyton Mayerson a jingle and tell her Fairview's back on the market? If she wants to do her wedding thing, now's her chance to pony up and buy."

"Don't forget those old deed restrictions haven't disappeared," Darby said. "If they are legitimate, Peyton is going to have a hard time hosting weddings."

"They won't be any fun, that's for sure," sniffed Tina. "Didn't she say she wanted Fairview even if she couldn't do weddings?"

"She did, but she was pretty angry at the time. I'm sure she's already heard the news about the murder of Phipps. The time it takes to clear up this investigation will give Peyton just enough headway to line up her backers again. I've already called her, and when we speak, I'll do my best to convince her that she still wants the estate."

"What happens to a property when a guy gets bashed to death in the garden shed? That would affect its value, right?" Tina bit into the burrito and looked at Darby patiently.

"That depends," Darby answered. "When a property has a stigma attached to it, such as a violent death, the value is usually affected in an adverse way. But some stigmas — such as a ghost — can actually boost a property's value." She paused. "I've already considered how this murder affects a future sale, and I'm thankful Phipps' death occurred in the shed and not the main house."

"Would that have made a difference?"

"I think so. The garden shed is a utilitarian outbuilding — no one actually lives in it. Nevertheless, if the fact that a murder took place there proves troubling to a new owner, the shed can always be torn down and rebuilt, at a fraction of what it would cost to replace the main house."

Tina took a quick swallow of her Diet Coke. "I can't see that Peyton Mayerson being bothered one tiny bit about some guy who was about to ruin her plans getting murdered. Why, she'll probably make it some kind of tourist destination. The House and Haunted Garden Shed Tour. You'll see. She won't give a hoot about it."

Darby smiled. "Let's hope you're right. Mark Trimble tries to be philosophical about it, but he really is ready to move on with the sale of Fairview. And so is Lucy." She frowned. "Speaking of Lucy, I wonder if Mark has an update on her."

Darby went over to her desk and called Mark Trimble's cell phone. He picked up on the first ring.

"Thank God it's you, Darby. I was just about to call. I'm with Lucy. We're in intensive care."

"What?"

"It's drugs again. Heroin. The nurses found her in a stupor."

Darby sank into a chair, unwilling to believe what Mark was saying.

"What is her condition?"

"Alive. They think she might have done it on purpose. Like Wes." His voice broke.

"Oh, Mark." Darby's head was reeling. What more did this poor family have to suffer? "I'll get the next ferry. Do you need anything?"

"No." His voice was hollow, defeated.

"Just call me if you do." Darby hung up, her breakfast clutched in one hand, too stunned to move. The idea of Lucy Trimble taking her own life did not make sense. She turned toward Tina, feeling numb.

"That was Mark. Lucy's in intensive care with a heroin overdose."

"Good God," Tina breathed.

Darby grabbed her jacket from the back of her desk chair. "I'm going to the mainland," she said. "I need to be with my friends."

After waiting ten or so minutes for the next boat, Darby boarded the ferry, sinking into one of the plastic seats by a window. She sat in silence, and before long she was disembarking at the terminal and limping the few blocks to Manatuck Community Hospital. The morning sun was warm, the sky clear and blue, but visions of Lucy flashed before her eyes — Lucy as a happy young girl; Lucy as a wasted junkie; and Lucy as a successful artist, older and wiser. The image of Lucy as a relapsed drug addict did not fit Darby's visions, and she resisted even forming that mental picture.

Mark met her in the ICU waiting room. His face was pale and his voice, normally so resonant, shook. "She's going to be okay," he said. "They — we — found her just in time."

Darby gave him a hug and felt tears welling in her eyes. "Can I see her?"

He shook his head. "No. They're running some tests and didn't want me in there." He struggled to get a hold of his emotions. "I can't believe it. She's been clean for so long." He swore softly under his breath. "I really thought she'd kicked it this time. She's been so — happy, so focused on her art. Her work in the clinic, all the people she was helping . . . But addiction has too tight a grip on her, I guess."

Mark's voice was little more than a whisper. "How did she get that stuff into the hospital? She'll be awake soon, I suppose, but I don't think I can face seeing her again today. I'm too afraid of what I would say." He looked at Darby with a look of such vulnerability that her heart ached for him. "I don't know what to do. I'm angry."

Darby nodded. "Of course you are. That's natural."

He ran his hands through his thick hair. "What do I do now?" he asked. "My sister's a junkie, our house is a crime scene . . ."

Darby's voice was calm. "You're doing just what you should be doing, Mark. Don't worry about Fairview — leave that to me. I'll make sure that the estate is back in order as soon as possible. I've already contacted Peyton Mayerson and I think she'll want another shot at making this work. Please, leave it to me." She looked at her watch. "What you need is some food. Can I bring you something from the cafeteria?"

Mark shook his head. "Thanks, but I'll head down there myself in a little bit." He gave Darby a meaningful look. "I want you to know that I appreciate everything you've done. Your aunt would be so proud of you."

Darby gave him a tight smile. "Let me sell that house of yours," she said. "Then you can thank me."

Peyton Mayerson gave Emilio Landi a play-ful slap on his well-muscled derriere and rolled out of bed. She grabbed her silk robe and pulled it on, enjoying the feel of the fabric against her skin. Life was good again. First, the news yesterday on the hotel's cable channel that Emerson Phipps had been found murdered in the Fairview gar-den shed. Peyton was sipping coffee, wait-ing for Emilio's ferry, when she'd seen the report and nearly choked. Could she have ordered that hit, and had it happened that soon? When she heard the details of the killing, she knew it wasn't a professional job but some bloodthirsty hack. No matter. The murder had the exact same effect. She really didn't care how the competition was eliminated, as long as it was eliminated.

She smiled. It had been a pleasure to use the IP Relay service and type in "Hurricane Harbor Job Canceled." She pictured the hit man, some muscled bald guy named Vito or Mitch, answering his phone and hearing that message. *Like a kid hearing he had a snow day,* she thought.

Next had come the call from Darby Farr, inviting her and her partners to submit another offer for Fairview. No doubt that was a pride swallower for the prissy little agent! Peyton chuckled to herself. Any gloating she did would be in private. The important thing now was to salvage the deal and get the guys in New Jersey off her back.

"Off her back" made her think of the third pleasant thing that had happened on this beautiful Tuesday, and that was a leisurely encounter with Emilio, her personal Italian Stallion. God, that man was what the Italians called *splendido.*

She checked her watch. Nearly ten. She thought briefly about hopping in the shower, but just then Emilio rolled over and gave her his lazy Roman smile. Before Peyton

Mayerson knew it, she had slipped off her silk robe and slid back into his arms.

Darby and Laura were making an effort to talk about Jane's service while they waited for the noon ferry back to Hurricane Harbor. Laura had appeared only a half hour earlier, and together they had tried to see Lucy Trimble, only to be rebuffed by a police guard outside her room.

"You might as well go," he'd said, shaking his head. "She's going to be tied up for a while." Discouraged, the women left the hospital and made their way to the Manatuck dock.

"I have some scripture picked out to show you," Laura said. "It's about charity, which was certainly one of your aunt's best virtues."

Darby nodded. Her cell phone rang and startled them both.

"Hello?"

She listened for a moment and gave a quick intake of breath. "No," she said, in a tone of disbelief. Then she added, "I'll come to the boat as soon as I can." She snapped her phone shut and looked at Laura, her eyes flashing. "That was Mark Trimble. Lucy has just left Manatuck General Hospital in handcuffs. She's been arrested for the murder of Emerson Phipps."

"What?" Laura Gefferelli was aghast. "Lucy?"

Darby nodded. "They found a package of her cigarettes at the scene, as well as a painting smock covered in Phipps' blood."

"Surely they need more evidence than that? And what about her alibi? I saw her at the church that morning."

"They say they'll find all the evidence they need."

"My God, poor Lucy. This could push her right over the edge."

Darby gritted her teeth. "If it hasn't done that already."

The two rode the ferry back to Hurricane Harbor in silence. Back on dry land, Darby left Laura and headed directly to the berth of the *Lucy T.* She knocked purposefully on its gleaming sides.

A moment later, Mark Trimble emerged from below deck, his hair disheveled and a haggard look on his face.

"I can't believe this, can you? First the call that she is near death, and now this?" He lowered his voice as a tugboat chugged into the harbor. "Murder? My sister? She would no more kill someone than you or I! I'm absolutely in shock." He put his hands over his face and continued shaking his head.

"What happens now?" asked Darby.

"They will process her — you know, take the photographs, do all the paperwork, and then there's a hearing to see if they will set bail. I called our family attorney, Willis Foster. He thinks they probably will, as Lucy is a low flight risk. Assuming that goes as planned, I'll pay her bail as soon as I can."

"Does she have any idea how the cigarettes got there?"

"She probably dropped them." He ran a hand through his hair. "Darby, do you think the chief knows about the rape?"

Darby thought for a moment. "I don't know. Could Dr. Hotchkiss have contacted the police?"

"From what I hear, he's in a nursing home in Manatuck with dementia. It seems unlikely he would have contacted Chief Dupont, but who knows." He ran a hand through his hair again. "Darby, she's in a juried art show this weekend. What should I do?"

"Keep her in the show. She'll be free by then and hopefully cleared of these ridiculous charges. Do you want me to drive over to her studio? I'd like to take a look and maybe I could start transporting some of her work for the show?"

Mark grimaced. "You better not. Dupont told me not to take anything out of there. But if you don't mind, you could take a look and see how many she's got finished. I think she had a price list started."

Darby agreed to check the inventory and see what else she might find. "I may pay a visit to Dr. Hotchkiss as well. Who might know where he's located?"

"Laura, perhaps, or someone else at the church. I think a group of ladies visits people who used to live on the island." Mark rose and gave Darby a quick hug. "Thanks," he muttered. "It's good to know I'm not alone with all this."

Darby stopped in at the office to grab her keys for Jane's truck. Tina was on the phone when she entered, an incredulous look on her face.

"You've heard the news?" she asked, slamming down the receiver. "About Lucy?"

Darby nodded. "Unfortunately."

"Of all the stupid ass things. I swear, that Chief Dupont is just as lame brained as his father was. To even imagine that little Lucy Trimble would smash a guy's head and shove scissors in his gut — why it's ludicrous." She caught her breath. "How's your ankle?"

"Better. I'm going over to Lucy's, to take a quick inventory of her paintings for Mark. He's hoping she'll make bail so she can still sell at the Art Show."

"Good. That's just what that girl needs, something to take her mind off all this." She crossed her arms and regarded Darby. "Your aunt's obituary will be in tomorrow's newspaper. Somebody needs to call Helen Near and let her know when the service is. Do you want me to do that?"

Darby gave a quick sigh. "No, I will, Tina. Thanks for the reminder. Any chance you have her number?"

Tina handed her a piece of paper, and eyed Darby's limp. "Be careful," she warned. "We don't need you damaging any more body parts."

Donny Pease was touching up the paint on the porch at the Hurricane Harbor Inn when the tall lady from Boston with the funny name — Peyton, was it? — brushed by him with an impatient air. She seemed in a hurry to get somewhere, and as far as Donny was concerned, she could just keep on hurrying right off the island. *Now, don't go getting huffy,* he reminded himself. *It's*

194

flatlanders like her who put meat on the table.
Still, Donny knew there was a difference between people like Peyton and some of the other folks from away, people who didn't come over looking to change everything. Peyton and her kind were always trying to turn his pretty little island into some kind of hoity-toity suburb. They didn't care enough to talk to locals, or gather the wisdom of the old-timers who gathered for breakfast at the Café every morning. Naw, they didn't care about the way things had always worked. They just wanted what they wanted, whether it was malls or trash pick up or "no hunting" signs plastered on everything.

I don't like Peyton Mayerson, don't trust her one bit, and that flashy Italian boyfriend of hers is an odd duck if I ever saw one. There was something funny about the way he followed that woman around, unable to speak any English at all, but always giving Donny a look like he knew just what was going on.

Then there was that magazine . . .

Donny dipped his paintbrush into the can and reached for a spot that he'd sanded only minutes before. He'd been thinking about the magazine all day, and just couldn't seem to make sense of it.

It had happened the night before, when

195

Donny was still shaken up over finding that murdered doctor at Fairview. He'd gone back to his house, taken a little nap, and woke up still picturing those shears protruding from the guy's stomach. That's what had bothered him the most, he realized now, those stupid shears. *I probably dreamed about them too,* he thought. *Sticking right up like a toothpick in a turkey club sandwich, for crying out loud . . .*

He shook his head to clear away the image, remembering what he did after his nap. *I drove over to the Eye,* he thought, *'cause I wanted a little whiskey to steady my nerves.* The Eye of the Storm was the island's only bar, and that afternoon it was busier than ever. Everyone was talking about the murder, and of course Donny had to tell and re-tell his story of the discovery. Each time he told about the body, his horror lessened a little, or maybe it was the whiskey that was helping him to forget. At any rate, he'd just finished recounting the tale for the third time when a figure in the corner of the bar caught his attention. It was a man in a baseball cap, nursing a beer and reading a magazine. Nothing unusual about that — Donny knew that guys liked to hang out in bars, especially the married ones who needed breaks from their wives. Donny saw the man glance at his watch, then get up, looking around the bar as if he did not want to be noticed. He threw some money on the table and turned to leave.

Donny saw the man head on. Curly hair, puffy lips . . . It was the Italian guy, Peyton's boyfriend, but he hadn't noticed Donny. Without making eye contact with anyone in the bar, Emilio left the Eye and walked hurriedly down the street.

Donny decided it was time for him to get going as well. He was due to pick up some passengers that evening, a party of four who were having dinner on Manatuck. Donny downed the rest of his whiskey and said goodbye to his buddies. Before leaving, he decided to visit the bar's bathroom. No sense in using the boat head if he could go right here, he reasoned.

On the way he walked by the table where the Italian fellow had been sitting. He saw the wad of bills waiting for the overworked waitress, and the magazine left behind on the bench. Curious, Donny leaned over to see what kind of European crap the foreigner had been looking at. Maybe a girlie rag, or one of those fancy race car publications. A moment later he stood up, puzzled. The man who couldn't speak a word of English, who had been sitting and reading so intently, had left behind the latest issue of *TIME* magazine.

After punching in Helen Near's phone number, Darby climbed carefully into the truck and drove to Lucy Trimble's little farmhouse, listening to the rings and anticipating an answering machine. She was surprised when a strong, clear voice answered the phone just as she pulled into Lucy's rutted driveway. Darby introduced herself, gave the information about Jane Farr's service, and sat in the parked car to listen to the Florida woman's grief.

"It doesn't seem possible," Helen said softly, her voice breaking a little. "Tina called me yesterday morning and told me Jane was dead. She was definitely getting on in years — I am, too! — but Jane — your aunt — she was such a strong force that it didn't seem like anything would extinguish her." She gave a big sigh. "Oh, I'll miss her. I'll miss her, all right. I spoke to her last week, you know. She sounded fine." She sighed again. "Is the service this weekend?"

"Saturday. I understand if you can't be there . . ."

"Of course I'll be there! Jane Farr was not only my business partner, she was my best friend. Oh, we go back a long way." She chuckled, and then her voice became businesslike once more. "I'll be there, and I would like to read a passage or two."

"Wonderful." Darby made a mental note to call Laura Gefferelli as soon as she left Lucy's house. "Do you need a place to stay, Helen?"

"There's a house I've stayed in before, but I believe Jane told me she'd rented it for the winter. The Hurricane Harbor Inn will be fine, and don't worry, I can give them a call." She paused. "How about you, Darby? How are you holding up?"

"I'm okay," Darby answered, glad the other woman could not see her tears.

Although it was Darby's first visit to Lucy's home and studio, she could tell that Chief Dupont and his deputy had been through the property. Drawers were partly out, papers were scattered, and clothes spilled from the bedroom closet. Even the studio looked as if it had been searched.

Darby remembered her promise to inventory the paintings for Mark. After admiring her old friend's talent, she found a list labeled "Finished Works" taped on the wall. By matching the titles with the actual canvasses, she could see exactly what Lucy had intended to sell. When she was about halfway through the list, however, she came across a painting on the list that appeared to be missing.

"Island Respite," read Darby. She looked through the stack of work again, and left a little mark next to the title. Toward the end of the list, a similar situation happened with the painting "Shorefront Foes." Although it was listed as a finished work, Darby could not find it anywhere in the studio.

Puzzled, she checked the other rooms of the house, as well as the closets, without any luck. According to Lucy's list, she had finished two dozen paintings in time for the show. Darby recounted the stack of canvasses. There were twenty-two.

With the list in hand, she left Lucy's house. Before starting the car, she phoned Laura Gefferelli at the church and left a message on her machine, informing her about Helen Near's participation in the service, and asking if she knew where Dr. Hotchkiss might be living. After hanging up the phone, she sat and thought a minute. Had Chief Dupont learned about the rape, and had that piece of information pushed him to arrest Lucy? Had Dr. Hotchkiss contacted the police? Darby Farr was determined to find out.

EIGHT

Darby drove back to Near & Farr in silence. Tina was out on an afternoon errand and the office seemed unnaturally quiet without her presence. The ringing of the phone startled Darby; she answered it and heard the voice of Mark Trimble.

"The judge set a bail amount for Lucy," he said. "I just spoke to her on the phone. She's wiped out, but happy to be going home. I've got Donny Pease and his water taxi lined up to take me over there so she doesn't have to come back on the ferry. He's got a truck at the landing and can drive me to the jail. Do you want to come?"

"Definitely," said Darby. "I'll meet you at the boat."

An air of quiet disbelief hung over the little party of Darby, Mark, and Donny Pease as they sped across the water toward Manatuck. As if to echo their mood, the weather had turned gray and chilly, with dark clouds forming on the horizon. The wind was starting to blow harder, and Darby found herself wishing she'd worn a warmer jacket.

Mark Trimble seemed to be in a daze. Darby began to feel concerned, but just then he cleared his throat and asked Darby whether she'd inventoried Lucy's artwork.

She quickly described the two missing paintings. "Lucy will have an explanation, I'm sure. Perhaps she'd sold them and hadn't had a chance to note it, or maybe she decided to put them in a gallery on Manatuck."

"We'll find out," he said, resuming his brooding air.

Donny Pease opened a locker and offered Darby an oilskin coat.

"Thanks," she said gratefully, slipping it on.

He smiled shyly. "Thought you looked a bit chilly," he observed, deftly avoiding a lobster trap. He seemed to think a minute before saying anything else.

"I helped out at the inn this morning," he offered. "Heard quite a lot of squawking coming from that Miss Mayerson's room around noon."

Darby gave him a shrewd look.

"Peyton Mayerson? What happened?"

"She was shouting at the Italian fellow, so loud I could hear it through the door. Something about things falling apart, and that he wasn't any help. Then she slammed the door and left the inn, alone. She took that fancy car of hers and left him shut up in the room. A little while ago, he was in the Eye, all by himself."

Mark and Darby were silent a moment.

Mark asked, "Do you think it's strange that we haven't heard from her about Fairview? Has she heard anything from her investors?"

Darby hugged the jacket tighter around her shoulders. "My gut feeling is that Peyton Mayerson doesn't have a whole lot of say over this purchase. She seems to be at the mercy of her backers, so if they are taking their sweet time, there isn't much she can do about it."

"You're saying she doesn't have much, if any, control," Mark said.

"Exactly," said Darby. "It could make someone feel pretty desperate. The question is: could it drive them to murder?"

"Hey, someone killed the guy, and I know it wasn't my sister," said Mark, his tone becoming stronger. "Do you think the police have even questioned Peyton and

Emilio? Asked them their whereabouts? Maybe Peyton knew about Emerson Phipps all along." He thought a moment. "What if Phipps contacted Peyton, hoping to flip Fairview for more money? Or maybe he called her to rub it in her face? He was arrogant enough to do something like that."

"I wouldn't discount anything," said Darby. "I'm planning to visit Peyton Mayerson as soon as I'm back on the island. In my book, she had a very strong motive to want Emerson Phipps dead, and there's something bizarre about that doting boyfriend of hers."

Donny nodded. Darby watched as he seemed about to add to the conversation, but instead picked up his handheld radio. Advising the Manatuck marina that he was pulling up to the dock, he readied the lines and slowed his engine.

"The Italian fellow is an odd one," he muttered, shaking his head.

"In what way, Donny?" asked Darby.

The captain shook his head again and Darby knew he would not elaborate. Moments later, he was tying them up to the dock.

Darby and Mark climbed into Donny Pease's truck and he drove them in silence to the jail. After waiting for a few minutes in a dingy reception area, they spied the frail figure of Lucy Trimble emerging from a door, accompanied by a female police officer.

She practically collapsed into her brother's arms.

"I'm sorry," she said, her eyes ringed with dark circles. "I am so sorry for everything."

"It's okay, Lu, it's okay," Mark murmured. He turned to the police officer. "Are we free to go now?"

She nodded and pointed toward a plastic shopping bag sitting on a metal table. "Those are her things," she said curtly.

"I've got them," said Darby, picking up the bag.

Donny hustled to open the door for Mark and his sister. Darby was sure he was thinking the same thing she was: Lucy seemed to have become an old woman overnight. She was hunched over and shuffled her feet as she tried to walk the few steps from the jail door to Donny's truck.

Donny's face showed concern. "Here, now, Miss Trimble, you just come right over here. Can you climb up okay? Dang truck, it's so high off the ground. I can give you a boost if you like?"

"That's okay," Lucy managed, giving a

weak smile. "I'm not an invalid, I just look like one."

After she was settled in the front seat with Donny, Mark and Darby climbed into the back of the cab. *Avoiding the ferry was a good idea,* Darby thought. Lucy would never have been up to the inevitable questions of the islanders, however well-meaning their comments may have been.

Donny drove them to the Manatuck dock and soon they were speeding through the water to the island.

It was Lucy who brought up her drug use first. "I don't remember anything about this," she said. "I don't remember doing any drugs. How would I have gotten them? The whole thing is lost to me."

"When you were using drugs before, would you have remembered things?" Darby saw the wind whip her friend's blonde hair across her face.

"No," Lucy admitted. "I often had total blackouts. But I swear to you, I wasn't doing drugs. I was clean. Unless I have a Dr. Jekyll and Mr. Hyde kind of split personality, I didn't do it."

"If you didn't take the drugs, they must have been given to you somehow without your knowing it. Did anyone visit you in the hospital?"

"I had a few visitors from Coveside yesterday afternoon. Today was the day I normally ran the group."

"Group?"

"A support group for those struggling with addictions. A few of them came over to see me."

"Who are the members of your counseling session?"

"I'd rather not say. Client confidentiality and everything."

Darby thought a moment. "Could one of those people have given you something? Injected you?"

"They wouldn't do that! None of them would do that." She frowned. "I don't see how or why any of them would want to hurt me, Darby."

"Did any of them give you anything to eat or drink?"

She shook her head. "Darby, these people are my friends! None of them gave me anything." She leaned back in the truck, exhausted.

After a moment, she cleared her throat. "I need to get some legal advice . . ."

"Lu, don't think about it today," her brother advised. "I've already made some calls. We'll deal with all that tomorrow." He gave Darby a quick glance, his expression grim.

"Mark is right. Get some rest so we can figure this all out tomorrow."

Lucy nodded at Darby, her eyes filling with tears. "I didn't kill Emerson Phipps," she whispered.

"I believe you." Darby cleared her throat. "Lucy, I have a different question for you. When I was in the studio, I noticed that you had a list of twenty-four paintings to hang at the art show. By my count though, there were only twenty-two. 'Island Respite' and 'Shorefront Foes' are missing. Any idea what happened to them? Did you give them to a gallery, or sell them privately?"

Lucy shook her head once more. "No. I suppose I could check with the arts festival coordinator — perhaps she needed a few for a photo?"

"Do you have the name of the festival coordinator?"

"I've got it at home, but it's on the town website as well." She shook her head. "What a giant mess."

"It'll all work out in the end," said Donny Pease, placing a reassuring hand on her shoulder as he expertly docked his boat. "You listen to me, Miss Trimble. It'll all work out just fine in the end."

■ ■ ■ ■

Peyton Mayerson navigated the narrow streets of Westerly in her Mercedes, scrutinizing the numbers on the little shops. Already the streets of this touristy town were thronged with people shopping and eating ice cream cones, and Peyton felt her impatience growing. *She said it was on this street,* she fumed. *She said it was past the whale watching dock . . .*

Peyton glanced toward a narrow building with a hand-carved sign and smiled. The Beals Gallery. There it was, finally, with a parking space right in front.

She parked, leaving Lucy Trimble's paintings safely stowed in the trunk. The sun was warm and for a brief moment she envied the tourists eating their mint chocolate chip cones with such oblivious delight.

She locked the car and went inside the building's cool lobby.

Immediately a woman in a tailored silk dress with upswept blonde hair appeared at her side. "May I help you?"

Peyton pursed her lips. "I'm looking for the gallery owner."

The blonde woman smiled. "You must be Ms. Mayerson. Come right this way."

Peyton was taken to a room off the main gallery. The woman closed the door behind them and indicated a glass table with several modern chairs. A towering flower arrangement in the center of the table dominated the room. "I'm Camilla Beals," the woman said smoothly. "Please, sit down. Care for some iced tea?"

"No, thank you," said Peyton, taking a seat. "I'm on a rather tight schedule . . ."

"Of course." Camilla glided into a chair. "I understand. Have you brought the paintings?"

"That was our deal, wasn't it?"

Camilla gave a small smile. "Then I'll ask Joseph to bring them in. Where are you parked?"

"In front of the building."

"We do have a back entrance. Unless you'd like us to bring them in through the front door . . ." She arched an eyebrow and waited.

"The back way will be fine." Peyton stood, tossing her hair. She gave the gallery owner a level gaze. "You'll be selling these paintings out of the state of Maine, correct?"

Camilla rose and nodded. "That was our deal, wasn't it?" She handed a business card to Peyton. "We spoke about the Manhattan store, but I've made some calls and I prefer to place them in our Miami Beach location." She tilted her head to one side. "I trust that will be fine with you, Ms. Mayerson?"

Peyton pretended to consider the question. *The bitch knows I want those stolen paintings as far from Maine as possible,* she thought . . . *She's toying with me, and yet, I need that money . . .*

"I suppose," she said airily, removing the Mercedes' keys from her Gucci clutch. "I suppose Miami Beach will be fine."

Once off Donny's boat, Darby stopped at the office for a quick update from Tina.

"You had a visitor," she announced. "Alicia Komolsky. She's the dead doctor's sister. Seems nice enough, even with the shock of it all. Came by to talk to you about the contract and whether she needed to do anything. I told her to come back at five P.M."

Darby consulted her watch. "That's in two hours. Perfect. I'm going to head over to Chief Dupont's office, see if I can find out anything more regarding the evidence he thinks he has on Lucy. Any word from Peyton Mayerson?"

Tina made a face. "Her highness has an appointment for tomorrow morning. She

211

said 'first thing,' which to her means nine o'clock."

Darby grinned. "Well, if we can get her to buy Fairview after all this, it will be worth dealing with her eccentricities. I'll be back at five to meet Alicia. Will you be here?"

Tina coughed. "Actually, I have a date with Donny."

Darby gave a little smile. "Fine. I'll see you tomorrow then."

Miles called while Darby was en route to the police station.

"How is the rest of your day going? Any developments?"

"Yes, but nothing good so far. I'll tell you about it at the cabin. How's my dinner coming?"

"Dinner? What dinner?" Miles joked and laughed. "So far, my humble palate is pleased, but you'll be the real judge."

Police Chief Charles Dupont was seated at his desk, his round belly bulging in the blue uniform shirt. A broad grin broke out on his features when Darby entered his office.

"Little Darby Farr, come to pay me a visit," he said. "Take a seat." He indicated a faded plastic chair into which Darby settled. "How's the foot?"

"Better."

"I remember your mother sitting so delicately in that very same chair," he said. "That glossy black hair, just like yours, twisted up off her neck. She always looked so fresh and clean, her hands folded just so on her lap . . ."

His eyes grew dreamy. "And could she ever cook! Do you remember that chicken dish she would whip up with the mushrooms and tomatoes, what was it, pulley something . . ."

"Poulet Sauté Chasseur," said Darby.

"That's it! Boy, I have tried to remember that name for years. Was it ever delicious. She was one fabulous cook, that Jada."

Darby knew that Chief Dupont wanted her to ask more about her mother's acquaintance with him, and although it made her uncomfortable, she complied.

"I didn't realize that you and my mother were friends."

"Oh no? We were certainly friends. She needed help with a few things —" he coughed delicately — "and I was happy to oblige. I like to think that if it hadn't been for your father, we would have been more than friends."

Darby felt her heart racing and struggled to keep her composure. "Chief, I wanted to ask you about Emerson Phipps' murder," she said carefully. "I don't think Lucy Trimble had a motive to kill him."

"Heroin addicts don't need a motive," he said, his eyes narrow. "She might have wanted his cash or his car. She could have been looking to take some kind of drug-induced rage out on him. Everyone in town knew she didn't want to sell him that house. She told a friend at the clinic that she wanted the wedding lady to get it. Something snapped and the next thing she knew, she was whacking Emerson Phipps with the garden statue." He paused, a sly look on his face. "Besides, more evidence may come to light very shortly, I'm sure."

The phone rang and Chief Dupont took the call. He made a few notes on a pad of paper, and hung up.

"Lorraine?" Chief Dupont buzzed his secretary in the outer office. A thin woman with black-rimmed glasses appeared instantly, as if she had been waiting outside the door. "Find the parking ordinance and send it off to the dingbat who runs the charter fishing boat."

She nodded nervously, glanced at Darby, and backed out of the room.

"Remember her? Lorraine Delvecchio? She was in your class, wasn't she?"

Darby tried to remember the secretary, but failed.

"Can't recall her? It was only ten years ago. Ten years is nothing." He picked up a pencil and tapped it on the desk. "Lorraine graduated and got a job as a medical transcriptionist. Pretty good at it too, from what I hear. She worked until last summer for the same employer, and he was very satisfied with her performance. That's a rare thing nowadays, wouldn't you say?" He tapped the pencil again and leaned closer to Darby. "Maybe you remember the man Lorraine worked for? Important doctor in town . . . Theodore Hotchkiss?"

Darby's quick intake of breath wasn't lost on Chief Dupont. He rose from his desk and gave a smug grin. "Your friend Lucy Trimble's got a good lawyer, right? Because I'll tell you what, Darby Farr, she's going to need one."

Darby's pulse was racing as she drove back to Near & Farr Realty. *He knows about the rape,* she realized with a sinking heart. *That secretary of his, Lorraine Delvecchio, knew Lucy's secret and has told the chief. All he needs now is evidence . . .*

Evidence. Not for the first time, Darby wondered where the old records from Dr.

Hotchkiss' practice had ended up. *If I could find them first . . .*

Darby grabbed her cell and called the Congregational Church, hoping that Laura was working. The calm voice of the minister answered on the second ring.

Darby explained what the chief had said and Laura groaned. "That's all Lucy needs!" She paused. "Darby, I think I may know where those files are kept. And if I'm right, your aunt had a key!"

Laura pulled into Near & Farr Realty at the same time as Darby. She gave a small smile as she exited the car.

"Your aunt managed a property over on the cove. It's rented by Dr. Hotchkiss' daughter and her little girl. There's a storage shed on the property, and I believe that's where the doctor's records were unloaded when he went into the nursing home."

"Terrific." Using her key, Darby opened the door of Near & Farr. Tina had already left and the place was quiet. A blinking light on her phone caught Darby's attention.

"The keys are on that board, right there," Darby indicated. "Maybe you'll recognize the name? I'm going to check this message quickly."

216

She listened to the voice of Alicia Phipps Komolsky explaining that she was delayed and would arrive on the island first thing in the morning. "I'll find your office and plan to be there at ten A.M.," she said.

Darby groaned.

"Anything wrong?" Laura inquired gently.

"No, just back to back appointments first thing tomorrow morning." She hung up the phone and crossed the room to Laura. "That was Emerson Phipps' sister, Alicia. She's coming to see me in the morning."

Laura nodded. "She's coming to the church as well. Wants to have her brother cremated and wondered if I could suggest some appropriate words to say goodbye." She sighed. "God, what an awful business. Can you believe the police would even suspect Lucy of something like this? It's ludicrous."

Darby was surprised to hear anger in the normally calm woman's voice. "Who do you think killed Emerson Phipps?"

Laura shot her a look as she pulled the key from a hook. "Given my position on the island, I shouldn't speculate, but I know you won't repeat this." She lowered her voice. "I'm convinced that Soames Pemberton is behind this. Not only is he one of the most dangerous people I've ever met, but

he was one of Lucy's counseling clients."
She looked Darby in the eye. "I believe he's
stolen drugs from the clinic as well."

"Prescription drugs?"

Laura nodded. "I'm sure they help support his heroin habit." She sighed. "I'm telling you this because I trust you, and I know
you are trying to help." She paused. "Please
don't quote me."

"Understood. Now let's go find that file."

Donny Pease gave his boat a final spray with
fresh water and nodded. She looked good
and clean, ready for the next pile of people
wanting a ride somewhere. So far, business
was good. This water taxi thing would sure
help, especially if the Trimble place ever sold
and he was no longer the caretaker.

For the most part, he enjoyed ferrying
people back and forth in his vessel. He'd
earned his captain's license as a young man,
and he never tired of blasting over to the
mainland. Each day was different. The sea
had a thousand stories to tell, and so far,
he'd heard only a handful.

Donny took a look down below to make
sure the cabin was shipshape. He saw a
white bundle in the corner of the berth and
picked it up. Lucy Trimble's sweater. She'd
forgotten to take it when he, Mark, and

Darby brought her home from the Manatuck jail.

His face hardened. Jail! That pretty little thing, locked overnight in a jail. The thought made him so angry he wanted to punch something. *Calm down,* he said to himself. *Think about your old ticker . . .*

He felt his pulse slowing and went back above deck. The image of Lucy Trimble, sitting numbly on his boat, came back to him. *She looked like a skinny little ghost,* he thought. *A ghost who's seen terrible things.*

The memory of Emerson Phipps' dead body flashed before his eyes. Lucy had seen it too, had been right there. She'd reached down with her little hands and tried to pull those shears out of the surgeon's stomach. Then she'd lifted her bloodied arms to the heavens and run, horror struck, from the shed. *I saw her running from him, and who can blame her?* he thought. *I would have run, too, if my stomach hadn't sent me into the bushes.* Embarrassment washed over him. *What a sissy, getting sick like that. Tina won't want to have anything to do with me.*

And yet, Tina had called just a few minutes earlier, inviting him over to her place for supper. Donny grinned. Tina was an excellent cook, and his mouth watered just thinking of her home-cooked meals. Last time, she'd fixed some sort of beef Stroganoff, with the curly noodles he loved, and a fresh strawberry rhubarb pie for dessert. *Strawberries are still in season,* he thought. Just that morning he'd passed an old-timer selling some by the side of the road. *Perhaps she'll have that pie again.*

Donny Pease closed up the companionway and climbed off the boat. Tomorrow he was going back to Fairview, back to the scene of that murder, but he wasn't going to let it stop him. Spruce the place up: that's what he was planning to do, and haul off some of the trash piled up in the woods by the garden cottage.

Donny knew it would feel good to putter around the old estate again, to be useful to the Trimble family, and he was thankful to Mark for giving him the work. *After all, I'm still the caretaker. I'm the one who needs to make sure it is in top condition.*

He clutched Lucy Trimble's sweater in his hand and thought again of all she'd endured. Parents who started drinking martinis at noon. Her brother Wes' suicide. And now being blamed for a murder she surely didn't commit. *I'll drop this off on the way to Tina's,* he thought, feeling the softness of the fuzzy material. *Poor girl, it's the least I can do.*

■ ■ ■ ■

With Laura seated next to her, Darby Farr drove her aunt's truck past Long Cove. "What's the address?" she asked Laura.

"Two-twenty Cove Road," she replied. "It's a cute little Cape."

Darby shot a look at Laura, but the minister was gazing at the cove. "That was my parents' house."

Laura turned to look at Darby, her gray eyes showing concern. "Darby, I had no idea. Let me go alone."

"I can handle it. It's just a funny coincidence."

Darby pulled off the road and parked the truck.

The tricycle was still on the grass. Next to it was a brightly colored plastic lawnmower with a smiley face sticker on the handle. Despite the toys, the yard looked well kept. The lawn had been recently mowed and trimmed, and someone had planted pansies along the foundation.

It hasn't changed at all, thought Darby. She remembered the fanlights on either side of the door, where her dog Rex always pressed his wet nose. There was the pear tree, laden in late summer with ripe Bartletts. She smiled at its graceful branches, even taller now, reaching toward the upstairs bedrooms, the one on the far right that had belonged to her parents . . .

She swallowed painfully and got out of the truck. The same mailbox, perhaps a bit more rusted, leaned at the edge of the driveway. There were the twin sugar maples, so flamboyantly orange come fall. Darby looked up at the front door. It led to the kitchen, she knew, and memories of opening that door and seeing her parents were almost more than she could bear. She saw her mother wearing a polka-dotted apron, standing at the stove concentrating on a complicated recipe. She pictured her father, seated at the little table, browsing happily through a sailing magazine. She shut the truck's door.

The house represented the final straw, she realized. The tipping point that had led her to exile from Hurricane Harbor for a decade. Darby Farr thought back to that June night when she'd confronted Aunt Jane. Something had unhinged inside her, something furious and wild that had been bottled up for far too long.

"You sold my house!" she'd screamed.

"Darby, really, it's just a house," Jane had said, her tone condescending. "And I made you money, for God's sake! Surely you are old enough to realize that it is simply a building, nothing more!"

The voice of Laura Gefferelli broke her memory.

"The shed is over here." She pointed to a small structure on the property line. *That's new,* Darby thought. *Something the current owners must have erected . . .*

"I'll go and ask for permission," Darby said.

The door was opened immediately by a slim young woman with chin-length dark hair. A little girl sat coloring at a table, a box of sixty-four crayons open and waiting. Darby remembered sitting in the same spot and felt her knees grow weak.

The little girl stopped coloring. She smiled up at Darby and showed her a picture of some kind of animal with stripes. Darby complimented her and turned to the girl's mother.

"I'm Darby Farr, from Near & Farr Real Estate. Your father had a patient, Lucy Trimble, who is a friend of mine. I'm helping Lucy, and she needs her medical records. I wondered if I might have a look for her file."

The woman looked relieved. "I was afraid you were coming to tell me we needed to move or something." She shrugged. "Sure, you can look at his stuff. That shed is full of boxes." She opened a door and pulled out a key chain. "The little one undoes the padlock."

Darby thanked her and took the keys. She crossed the grass to where Laura was waiting.

"I tried the key from your office — no luck," Laura said.

Darby produced the keys she'd been given and tried the small one in the padlock. The lock unhinged and the door swung open, revealing stacks of cardboard banker's boxes. Fortunately, they were arranged alphabetically with the "T" labeled box in plain sight.

Darby knelt and opened the box. She flipped through the files, searching for one with the name "Trimble." *It has to be here,* she thought, rifling through them again, this time more slowly.

"Nothing," she said. "Perhaps there's another 'T' box? Or it could be misfiled, I suppose . . ."

Laura frowned. "It will take us all night to look through these boxes. Truthfully, I have some work I need to do at the church."

"I guess the good news is that it's not going to be easy for Chief Dupont to find

Lucy's file either," said Darby.

A bark of a laugh echoed outside the small shed. "Nothing's easy for me," said the chief, his bulky form blocking the light. "Nothing at all, Darby Farr."

Two hours later, Darby was seated on a comfortable upholstered chair in the cozy Kendall cottage with a bag of ice on her ankle. She'd showered, dressed, and driven the truck to meet Miles, and was now describing to him how Chief Dupont had caught her and Laura rifling through the files from Dr. Hotchkiss' practice.

"I swear he followed us there, Miles," she fumed. "He made a point of telling me his secretary used to work for Hotchkiss. He wanted me to go looking for that file and he followed us."

Miles handed her a glass of Merlot. "The chief is no dummy," he said. "He may look like one, but he's not." He lifted his glass. "Cheers."

Darby lifted hers halfheartedly and took a sip. She leaned back in the chair. "I'm just so discouraged about the whole thing. Lucy didn't kill Emerson Phipps, I know that, but the evidence is starting to stack up against her."

Miles sat in a chair across from Darby and

took another sip of wine. "What do you say we try to recreate the crime? Our dinner is simmering gently on the stove, and this kind of thing is right up my alley, so to speak."

Darby smiled. "So I'm to see Miles Porter, Investigative Journalist, in action?"

"That's right." He grinned. "Now — the murder took place on what — Sunday, right?"

"Yes."

"Okay. Here's Fairview." He picked up a coaster and placed it on an ottoman. "And this pack of matches is Emerson Phipps." He placed the matches on the coaster. "Phipps drives his shiny BMW over to Fairview and parks it in the front. Maybe he goes in the house, maybe not."

"The chief has found no evidence that Phipps entered the house."

"So, he parks and then walks around the back, right?"

"Right. He circled the property and went to the garden cottage, where quite possibly, the murderer was waiting." She thought a moment. "The chief has found no evidence of tire tracks, so that person —" Darby picked up a pencil, "— came on foot."

"Or flew," joked Miles.

She took the pencil and placed it by the coaster and matches. "We need something to represent the cottage."

"See, you're getting into it," said Miles, reaching behind him for another coaster. "This one's different, will it do?"

"I guess it will have to." Darby placed the pencil atop the coaster. "So the murderer is waiting in the cottage. Emerson Phipps enters the cottage and is killed. The murderer leaves, perhaps taking the time to plant evidence first."

"Such as?"

"The jumpsuit and the cigarettes. The killer left no fingerprints on the garden shears nor on the statue, and none were found on the cottage door. Obviously the killer touched these things, so he must have been wearing gloves."

"Good point," noted Miles.

"Now, the killer left only those things. Why?"

"Because they incriminated only one person: Lucy Trimble."

"Right."

"Do you think we should be looking for someone who hates Lucy Trimble?" Miles asked.

"I thought about that, but I sense that Lucy was just a convenient scapegoat for the killer, a way to throw the police off the track. I think we need to concentrate on the people who want Fairview."

"Besides Phipps, there's Peyton, right?"

"Peyton Mayerson, and the money men behind her. Peyton was pretty desperate after the planning board meeting. She needed to see her way out of that situation. She might have felt desperate enough to kill Phipps to ensure her position as the buyer."

"But how would Peyton have known about the back-up? That planning board meeting didn't occur until the next day. On the day Phipps was killed, Sunday, Peyton still assumed she would be Fairview's owner."

"Someone might have told her," Darby said. "Someone who knew what was going to happen . . ."

She snapped her fingers. "Soames Pemberton knew what would happen the next day. He had the old deed prohibiting liquor and he knew that would keep the planning board from granting the zoning change. Suppose he made Peyton Mayerson pay for the information, and when she realized that her plans were in jeopardy, she killed Emerson Phipps."

"And framed Lucy?"

"Exactly. She could have easily gone to her studio, stolen a jumpsuit and a pack of cigarettes, worn the suit to kill Phipps, and then planted the evidence."

"When did Peyton arrive on Hurricane Harbor?" asked Miles.

"Saturday morning. That gave her plenty of time to find out about Phipps, hatch a plan, and execute it the next day. Then when the planning board meeting denied her the changes, she put on a big act about how angry she was."

Darby thought a moment. "Do you have a pad of paper? I need to write a few things down."

Miles handed her a legal pad and a pen.

"We need to see if anyone noticed Peyton going into Lucy's house on Saturday. That's when she would have stolen the jumpsuit and cigarettes."

Darby looked at Miles. "And the paintings! Two of Lucy's works are missing from the studio. I wouldn't put it past Peyton to have helped herself to a little artwork while she was there."

"Where was Lucy on Saturday? Wouldn't she remember if Peyton came to her house?"

"I don't know." She added another note to her list. "We'll find out Lucy's whereabouts for Saturday.

"Now Miles, the other suspect in this murder is Soames Pemberton. Fairview was built on property that was once his family's land. He lives in the woods that abut the estate, and I think the pending sale enraged him."

"Is he the kind of person who would not only bash someone else's head in, but try to ruin the life of an innocent person in the meantime?"

"Exactly," said Darby. "A person with nothing to lose." She stopped and sniffed the air. "Dinner smells fabulous. Are you sure we're not ready to eat?"

Miles Porter smiled and rose to his feet. "We're ready," he said, proffering a hand to Darby. "Dinner is served."

NINE

"I've never tasted such delicious chowder," Darby exclaimed, sitting back in her chair in the Kendall cottage's cozy dining room. "Haddock, right? And this bread is terrific, too. So moist."

"I'm glad you like it," Miles said, smiling. "I must confess, I felt under some pressure, what with your being a gourmet cook and all . . ."

"My mother was the gourmet cook," Darby corrected. "I can barely boil water." She took another sip of her wine and felt it warm her body. Outside it had started to rain, but in the cottage, she felt warm and safe.

"Remember what you said about some mysteries being unsolvable?"

Miles nodded. "Are you thinking that we won't figure out who killed Emerson Phipps?"

"No. I was thinking about my parents and

the mystery of their disappearance." She shifted slightly in her chair and met his earnest gaze.

"I'd like to hear what happened, if you want to tell me," he said.

Darby let out a long sigh. "It's been awhile — a long while — since I told anyone about that day. But I think somehow I need to. With the murder of Emerson Phipps I feel like my past is coming back at me, and I need to face this mystery before I can prove Lucy Trimble is innocent."

She took a last spoonful of her soup and thought back to the day her world had changed, and then she began her story.

"The summer I was thirteen, I was on top of the world. My dad ran the sailing program, my mother showed up with picnics of wonderful French delicacies, my parents were in love with life and with me, and I was the happiest kid in the world. It was a beautiful August afternoon. Classes were finished at the club and my dad asked me if I wanted to go with him for a sail. We had a sleek boat — an Alden 48 — just gorgeous. But I was meeting Lucy Trimble to go swimming, so I said no. Just then my mother arrived. I remember she was wearing a pair of white shorts and a red-checked blouse. She was laughing and smiling, and when my dad mentioned that they could have a date, she said, 'Why not?' They got in the dinghy and waved goodbye, and I pedaled off on my bicycle to meet Lucy. I never saw my parents again."

"My God."

"That afternoon, the winds picked up and the National Weather Service issued a small craft advisory. I was home by five o'clock, but I didn't begin to worry until six P.M. I called the harbor master and he called the Coast Guard. Chief Dupont must have heard the call, and he took me to stay with the Trimbles at Fairview. The next day Jane Farr flew up from Florida. I'd met her only once before. The Coast Guard searched for a week and recovered parts of the sailboat. But my parents' bodies were never found."

Miles exhaled. "That's rough at any age, but at thirteen . . ." He shook his head. "So Jane stayed here with you?"

"Yes. She had a real estate company in Sarasota, Florida, with her friend Helen Near. They opened a second office here and for a while Jane flew back and forth. Then they came to some sort of an agreement, I guess. Jane stayed with me and ran the office here, while Helen took care of their old clients in Florida." She thought a moment. "I haven't seen Helen Near in ages, but she's coming up for the memorial service."

Miles reached across the table and put his hand on Darby's. "I can't imagine the shock of that day. It must have been awful."

She nodded. "I felt numb for so long. My whole world collapsed without any warning, you know? One minute you're pedaling off to go swim in the quarry, the next you are hearing these men tell you that your parents are never coming back." She shuddered. "I think I got used to the feeling of being emotionless, and as I got older I looked for ways to anesthetize the pain. Alcohol and pot worked pretty well. Even so, there was a part of me that wanted to feel something, so I would push myself to do risky things, probably in the hope that I would snap out of the state I was in."

"No one helped you through it? No grief counseling, no therapy?"

"No." She squared her shoulders. "To tell you the truth, I wouldn't have participated even if it was offered. I felt so guilty." She took a deep breath. "I still do."

"How could you feel guilty? What could you have done?"

She turned to Miles and there were tears in her eyes. "I could have gone sailing with them. My father asked me. I should have gone, and then perhaps . . ."

"Darby, you were just a child! Whatever happened to that boat would have happened regardless of whether you were aboard or not. Your dad was a world-class sailor! You would have been killed as well."

"There were times I wished that's what had happened, believe me. I wanted to be dead for years after they died. And maybe it's foolish to think I could have saved the situation. But my mother was not a sailor. She'd worked on a tall ship, but purely as a decorative feature. My father used to say she couldn't tell the mast from the mizzon." Darby sighed. "So whatever situation they encountered, my father was alone. If I had been there, I might have made a difference. And maybe we all would have survived."

Miles shook his head and smiled gently. "The 'what-ifs' are the worst, aren't they?" He reached out and held Darby's hands in his, offering comfort in his touch that she welcomed. After a long moment, she rose and reached for Miles' dishes.

"Sit down, I'll take care of it later," Miles said.

"After such a great dinner? Not a chance."

"Fine, then I'll help you and we'll see if we can work on solving this Hurricane Harbor mystery while we work, shall we?"

As Darby washed the dishes, she told

Miles about her appointments for the next day. "Alicia Komolsky, Emerson Phipps' only sibling, is coming in at ten A.M. And before that, at nine A.M., Peyton Mayerson plans to make an appearance." She thought a moment. "I'll check back in Jane's files, see if she has any more information on Peyton's partners. It might be worth it for me to drive down to Boston and talk to them."

"Really?"

"Sure. I mean, we can't count on Chief Dupont to do anything other than try Lucy. He is convinced she did it and isn't going to spend any energy or resources exploring other avenues." She paused. "I'll meet with Ms. Mayerson tomorrow and see where we stand on her purchase of the property now. I'll use that meeting to get more information about her and, most important, her whereabouts Sunday morning."

"Peyton was the only one who really wanted Fairview, besides Phipps, that is," mused Miles.

"Yes. Unless there's someone we don't know about. Someone who wanted Fairview so badly they were ready to kill for it." She grew thoughtful a moment. "I suppose someone could have paid Soames to do it. Someone like Peyton."

"That's a thought. The sticking point is: how did Peyton know about Emerson Phipps?"

"I don't know." She rinsed the last dish and handed it to Miles to dry. "Let's think for a moment. Who did know about Phipps? Mark, for sure, and my aunt. She was the one who drew up that backup offer. Lucy says she never looked at the documents, so she didn't know about Phipps until after the planning board meeting on Monday. But Jane knew, and Mark knew. Now, would either of them have wanted to tell Peyton Mayerson that there was another buyer waiting in the wings?"

"Wouldn't that have been counterproductive? I mean, if Peyton found out, she might have backed right out of the contract."

Darby turned to Miles, her eyes alive with excitement. "What if they wanted her to back out of the contract? Jane may have even offered Peyton money to back out. When Peyton refused, Jane had to think of another way to force her. She made sure that planning board approval by a specific date was a condition of the contract, by getting Peyton to sign that index-card amendment. Miles, that's it. Jane knew about those old restrictions — she must have, she was such a stickler for research that she would have found those deeds herself. She used them as a way to guarantee that the planning board would not grant that permit, and Peyton's contract would be void. She did it so that Emerson Phipps could be the buyer."

"So you're saying that old deed wouldn't have come to light if your aunt hadn't found it?"

Darby nodded. "I'm certain she was the one. It's unusual for a bank or lawyer to look back that far. I have a hunch that Jane Farr knew from old-timers about that long-forgotten prohibition, and all she had to do was find proof."

"But why? Why kick Peyton out and introduce a whole new buyer?"

Darby smiled. "Money. The classic root of all evil, Miles. I can't go into specifics, but let's just say Emerson Phipps was offering a substantially higher amount for Fairview than Peyton and her investors. Enough to make a difference. Rather than tell him 'no dice,' Jane Farr found a legal way to get Peyton out of the picture."

"And where does Soames Pemberton come in?"

"I don't believe his story that he found the deed on his own. I think my aunt found it, and needed someone to deliver it to the planning board."

"Why not do it herself?"

"Too obvious. Chances are she paid him off for his little theatrical scene."

Miles motioned towards the living room, where a small fire was ready to be lit. He touched a match to the tinder and it crackled to life. They sat on the sofa before the fire, and Miles watched the flickering shadows on Darby's thoughtful face.

"I wonder if Mark knew about the old deed as well," she said slowly. She looked at Miles. "I'm trying to remember what he said at the planning board meeting — something very cavalier. He wasn't really surprised, Miles. Now that I think of it, he was the only one in that room who wasn't shocked by Soames Pemberton's revelation."

"How do we find out if Mark knew?"

"I'm going to use an old-fashioned method. I'm going to ask him."

"Capital idea." He rose to poke the fire. "All this sleuthing has made me want dessert. May I interest you in a coffee drink and an assortment of chocolates?"

"Perfect. I'll have Bailey's if you have it."

Miles emerged from the kitchen a few minutes later with coffee, liqueurs, and a beautiful box of chocolates. "I know, I know, they look like the kind you see in hospital . . ."

Darby sprang to her feet. "Miles, you've made me think of something. When I went with Mark to pick up Lucy, I took the bag of her personal items, things she had used at the hospital. The bag brushed against my leg in the truck and I felt something hard, like a rectangular box. What if it was a box of chocolates? Suppose that's how she was poisoned? Someone brought them as a gift . . . a gift intended to kill."

She grabbed her cell phone and called Mark. A moment later he had checked his sister's items from the hospital and was back on the phone.

"Darby, you're right. There is a small box of chocolates among her items, and two are missing." He paused. "Do you really think they're laced with heroin?"

"I do, Mark, Lucy was adamant about not abusing drugs herself, and I believe her. There simply is no other explanation."

"What should I do? She's sleeping now, and I hate to wake her."

"Get them to the police so Chief Dupont can have them analyzed. If we can prove that Lucy was poisoned, perhaps he'll stop trying to pin her as Emerson Phipps' murderer."

Miles looked incredulous as Darby hung up the phone.

"Lucy Trimble . . . poisoned? Who? Why?"

Darby's face wore a grim expression. "I don't know, Miles. But I have a hunch it was the murderer."

Darby rose early the next morning, feeling as if she needed some exercise before her appointments. Gingerly she tested her ankle; it was still tender. *I'll take it slow,* she told herself. Five minutes later, she had laced up her sneakers and was trotting carefully down the winding roads. Determined to face her fears, she forced herself to head to Fairview.

Even under the cloud of a murder, the grand old house retained an almost majestic air. Darby jogged around to the side of the house, hearing the waves crashing against the rocks below. She rounded the corner of the building and her eyes could not help but stray to the garden cottage, where the door was ajar.

Darby stopped and walked cautiously toward the cottage. A man emerged and Darby froze, expecting the malevolent force of Soames Pemberton. Instead, she was greatly relieved to see Donny Pease.

The caretaker looked up and smiled.

"Got my old job back," he said, indicating the house and estate. "At least until somebody buys the place. Any takers, or does the thought of a murderer on Hurricane Harbor scare 'em all off?"

"It's not helping sales, that's for sure," said Darby. "What are you up to?"

"Cleaning up the property, that sort of thing. There's a pile of junk behind the cottage I've been meaning to get to. Those police detectives made a mess of the landscaping over here, and I'm just getting it all shipshape again." He smiled happily. "Did you know my father worked for the Trimbles way back? I grew up helping him. I can remember as a little tyke watching him build that stone wall over there. He was quite a gifted stone mason. Knew just where to place the rocks so it would last forever." He gave a wistful look. "Now who knows what'll happen with the old place. You don't suppose the Trimbles would decide to keep it, do you?"

Darby shook her head. "I don't believe so, Donny. I think they've decided that they need to move on."

He shrugged. "Time was when a family kept a place, and passed it on, you know? Nowadays it's all about the money." His grim expression became cheerful once more. "Still, I don't think they'll sell it all that quickly. Not with a murderer on the loose." He glanced at his watch. "Gotta close up and run to the harbor. Don't see your vehicle . . . You want a ride anywhere?"

"That would be great, actually. Could you drop me off at Aunt Jane's house?"

He seemed glad for the errand and whistled as they made their way around the yard to the old truck. Darby noticed the back of the vehicle was full of old bottles, rusted pieces of machinery, and several old tires.

"Mark asked me to work on the old junk pile, you know, get rid of some of the trash piled up in the woods," he said. "Used to be that islanders didn't have a landfill to put their castoffs, so they made their own dumps at the edge of the property."

"Have you found anything interesting?"

"At times I have. Mostly, though, it's just a lot of beat-up junk."

They drove the winding roads to Jane's house in silence. When they reached the driveway, Darby thanked Donny for the lift and he smiled.

"I hear you're trying to help Miss Lucy, and I'm grateful," he said. "She wouldn't kill anyone, that girl. Just plain nonsense is what it is." His expression grew grim. "That idiot police chief . . ."

"I take it you don't think he's investigating thoroughly enough?"

Donny Pease snorted. "I know he's not investigating anywhere near enough. He's fine when it comes to vandalism or a parking ticket, but he's in way over his head on this murder. Hate to see Lucy suffer 'cause Chief Dupont doesn't have a clue."

"I'll do my best to help her, Donny. Thanks again for the ride."

An hour later, a freshly showered and dressed Darby met Tina at the door to the Near & Farr office. Tina clutched a bag from the Hurricane Harbor Café in hand.

"Bet you didn't have breakfast," she said, wiggling the bag before Darby's face. "I've got muffins and coffee, so help yourself."

"Actually, I am hungry, and that coffee smells wonderful. Thanks."

"You can't solve a murder on an empty stomach, is what I always say."

"Why does everyone think I'm trying to solve the murder? I'm trying to sell a house, that's what I'm trying to do."

"Well, Lucy was a good friend of yours, maybe still is, and you know she's not getting much help from anybody else." Tina bit into a blueberry muffin and munched for a few seconds. "Hey, how was your little dinner with Miles?"

"Very nice."

"No more details than that? What did he make?"

"Haddock chowder."

"Okay, I get it. Despite this wonderful breakfast I've prepared, you aren't going to tell me about your love life. I'll just go back to my typing, I guess."

Darby checked messages and e-mails for a good forty-five minutes while Tina worked in the other room. *It's liberating to think about something other than Emerson Phipps' murder,* she realized. She saw that the Costa Brava mansion, her newest waterfront listing for Pacific Coast Realty, was still available, although ET had made progress with a few of their lower-priced listings.

Darby stood and stretched, checking her watch. Nearly ten minutes after nine, and no Peyton Mayerson . . .

The door opened with a rush and in flounced Peyton.

"Whew!" she exclaimed. "They've started setting up for that art show by the hotel. I could hardly walk on the sidewalk! And the first boat is in from Manatuck and it was full of tourists. Full! Too bad Lucy Trimble can't sell her paintings. She'd make herself a bundle."

"Lucy will be selling paintings," said

Darby. "She's free on bail and is looking forward to working in her booth."

"What?" shrieked Peyton Mayerson. "They're going to let a murderer sit in the sun at the art show? What kind of justice is that?"

Tina stood up. "Lucy Trimble didn't kill that man. Everyone on this island knows that."

"Well somebody sure as heck did, and they wore her little painting outfit to do it!"

Darby glanced at Tina, who took the hint and turned on her heel. Once Tina had stomped back to her desk, Darby indicated a chair. "Please sit down, Ms. Mayerson."

Somewhat mollified, Peyton Mayerson sank into the chair. Darby gave her a few moments to cool off before continuing.

"Now, Ms. Mayerson, as you know, Fairview is no longer under contract. My clients have asked me to convey their willingness to enter into another contract with you as soon as possible on the same terms. We are prepared to grant you the time you need for proper approval concerning your plans for the property."

Peyton snorted. "What about that idiot Soames and his rantings? Is it true I can't have a gin and tonic on the premises?"

"I've looked into that issue, and I think

your attorney can make a good case that the old restrictions were meant to only benefit the original Pemberton homestead, a structure that was once located where Soames' shack is now. I'm hopeful it can be cleared up so that you'll be able to get approval for a liquor license and zoning change after all."

Peyton Mayerson waved her arm impatiently. "I don't really care about that anymore," she said. "My plans for the property have changed — but so has my offering price." She smiled coyly at Darby. "I'm not willing to spend $5.5 million for the property any longer. We'll give you $4.9."

"And your reasoning?"

"A murder took place in the backyard! An as yet unsolved murder. Imagine the advertising I'm going to have to do to overcome that stigma! Surely you can't expect me to pay the same amount when Fairview is now damaged goods."

Darby held her tongue. Peyton Mayerson had a point, and if she were her buyer's broker, she would advise her to do the same thing.

"I will convey your verbal offer to my clients and see what they say. Thank you for your time, Ms. Mayerson."

Peyton Mayerson rose and glanced toward the conference room, where Tina was still sequestered. She lowered her voice.

"I admit, it is hard to imagine that Lucy Trimble killed that man. It's worked out awfully well for me, but still, what a drastic thing to do!"

Darby stood as well and looked Peyton Mayerson squarely in the eye. "Lucy Trimble didn't kill him," she said. "I believe she was framed." She paused a moment. "Just out of curiosity, where were you on Sunday morning?"

"You think I had something to do with the murder! How ridiculous!" Peyton Mayerson laughed. "You Mainers can be so strange." She cocked her head and thought a moment. "Let's see. Sunday morning . . . oh yes! I was in bed with Emilio, and as I recall, neither one of us were sleeping . . ." She chuckled. "Well, if that's all the questions you have for me, Detective Darby, I'm off to see how things are coming for the art show." She paused a moment. "I hope your friend Lucy Trimble keeps painting in prison. Her work is becoming quite valuable, you know."

No sooner had Peyton Mayerson sashayed out the door than Tina burst out of the conference room.

"That little . . . !" she seethed. "I heard every word out of her nasty mouth. Painting in prison! I'd like to smack her, Darby, really I would. Don't let her buy Fairview, no matter how badly the Trimbles want to sell. That woman doesn't deserve to live on Hurricane Harbor."

"I know what you mean, Tina. Believe, me, Peyton Mayerson is not my favorite person either." She thought a moment. "I'm going to call Mark and let him know about Peyton's offering price for Fairview. Why don't you go over to the hotel and see if you can catch Emilio alone? Maybe you can find out from him whether Peyton and he were really so cozy on Sunday morning."

"I'm on it." Tina stood and grabbed her turquoise purse and was about to exit when a pale, petite woman stepped into the office. She wore a linen suit that was wrinkled and large dark glasses, which she removed as she looked at Tina and Darby.

"I'm looking for Darby Farr," she said quietly. "I'm early for our appointment. I'm Alicia Komolsky. Alicia Phipps Komolsky. Emerson was my brother."

Darby introduced herself and offered a chair. Tina gave a discreet little wave and left the office.

"I'm so sorry," Darby murmured.

249

"Thank you," Alicia Komolsky whispered, her voice quavering. "I'm still — I still — I can't believe it."

"I understand."

"Did you know my brother?" She looked up almost hopefully.

"I met him many years ago. Our agency was helping him to purchase a property."

Alicia nodded. "I know. Fairview. It was all he could talk about, from the moment he saw it was for sale." She managed a weak smile. "He was like a little kid about it. So excited. He said it would be a place for me and the boys — my sons — to spend the summer. He told them they could learn how to sail." She brought a tissue to her eyes and dabbed at them, struggling to regain her composure.

Taking a steadying breath, Alicia went on. "I'm on the island to bring home his personal things, and I thought I would see if he had paid any money for the house, you know, any deposits."

Darby pulled a file from her desk. "Yes, he did give us an earnest money check with his agreement to buy Fairview," she said. "And I see now that it was never deposited." She frowned. *Why hadn't Jane deposited the check in the company trust account?* That was a violation of state laws, to say the least . . .

She handed Alicia Komolsky a copy of the contract and the check.

"This is for one hundred thousand dollars!" she exclaimed.

"That's right. But as I said, it was never deposited. Are you the executor of his estate?"

She nodded. "I am. It was just us — Emerson and myself — and my two sons. He left everything to them, well, except for a donation to SWS."

"SWS?"

"Surgeons Who Serve. It's a charitable group that travels to Third-World countries to operate on the underprivileged. Emerson went on three or four trips to the Caribbean with them every year, Haiti mostly. He'd come back so invigorated. Once he showed the boys and I photos of the work they were doing, the people they were helping." She paused and looked down at her hands. "He had faults just like anyone, but he was a wonderful man."

Darby touched the woman's shoulder gently. "Would you like me to come with you to the police station to get your brother's things?" she asked.

"I hate to put you to the trouble," Alicia Komolsky said, "but I would be so grateful for the company. As you can see, I'm not functioning very well right now."

"Did you drive up here alone?"

She nodded. "A friend of mine is watching Sam and Michael — those are my sons — and I just got in the car and drove. It wasn't too bad, really."

Darby grabbed her purse and escorted Alicia Komolsky to the door. "Would you like to ride with me?"

"Yes, thanks," she said. "I'd hate to subject you to the horror show in my car." She indicated a dark blue minivan with a dented rear fender.

"I'm afraid it's a little messy. I'm sort of a soccer mom, transporting the boys back and forth to all of their activities, and I guess I don't clean up the car too often." She sighed. "I've had to raise them alone since they were in diapers. My ex took off with a waitress and I haven't heard from him since. I guess I didn't choose too wisely, but at least I got Sam and Michael." She glanced back at the minivan. "It's a convenient car, though. When my old station wagon bit the dust, Emerson said I should get a minivan, and he was right. He helped me pick out this one and even helped with the financing." She choked a little and Darby knew she was close to tears.

"The police station is up this road, by the town office," Darby said, opening the truck's door and starting the engine. Once Alicia Komolsky was inside, she began driving up and away from the harbor. "The police chief is a man named Charles Dupont. Have you spoken with him?"

"Yes, he's the one who called." She blew her nose and looked blankly out the window. After a few moments, she gave a deep sigh.

"I used to worry about my brother, when he went on these trips to all these dangerous places. And I worried about him in Boston, too, because he had such a high profile, and not everyone liked him. You know, he was famous, and that makes some people jealous. But I never thought I had to worry about him up here."

"Who didn't like your brother in Boston?"

"Oh, I don't know if there was anyone in particular. He used to tell me there were other doctors who were envious of his talents, and patients who didn't understand how trivial appointments and things were to a skilled surgeon. Nobody specific, though, nothing like that. Just, you know, he was a brilliant and handsome man, one of the city's most eligible bachelors, and that was bound to make some people dislike him."

Darby thought of the newspaper stories

Miles had found on the Internet. She hadn't yet taken the time to read them, but perhaps they would shed light on Emerson Phipps' enemies in Boston.

"These people who were jealous of your brother. Did they dislike him enough to kill him?"

Alicia Komolsky's face was vacant. "I don't know," she said dully. "I don't know anything anymore."

TEN

Emerson Phipps' effects fit in a small duffel bag. He had brought a few changes of clothes, a medical thriller novel, some toiletry items, and a manila file folder labeled, "Fairview."

"We've gone through it, of course," Chief Dupont said conspiratorially to Darby. "There's nothing out of the ordinary. A copy of the contract, the deed, and the listing packet on the property — that's about it."

Alicia Komolsky signed for the items and spoke with the chief about returning her brother's body to Massachusetts. He discussed plans for transporting the BMW to Boston, and Alicia nodded as if under heavy sedation.

Chief Dupont consulted his watch and Alicia jumped.

"His watch — is that in this duffel?"

The chief frowned. "What watch?"

"My brother wore a very expensive watch called a Vacheron Constantin. It was pink gold, made in Switzerland. He never went anywhere without it."

The chief scribbled a note on a small pad of paper. "We haven't located it yet," he said. "When we do, I'll give you a call."

Again she gave a slow nod and followed Darby back to the truck.

"I guess I should be going back to Boston."

"Would you like some lunch first?" Darby offered. "We could go to the local place in town."

"No, I don't feel up to being in public."

"I understand. How about a sandwich on the ferry? They make a mean chicken salad. We can dine in your minivan."

Alicia Komolsky smiled. "Okay. But how will you get back?"

"On foot. We islanders do it all the time."

The two women drove back to Near & Farr and fetched Alicia's minivan. Darby tried not to smile as Alicia bundled school papers, candy wrappers, pencils, and small sweatshirts and tossed them hurriedly in the back.

Once on the ferry, the two women ate their sandwiches in silence. Alicia took a drink of her water and turned to face Darby.

"Do you think the police chief will solve Emerson's murder?"

"I think the murder will be solved, yes." She paused. "Would you mind if I had a look at your brother's things?"

"Of course not."

The two women walked to the back of the van and opened the hatch where Emerson Phipps' duffel bag sat. "ESP," said Darby. "His initials stood for Extra Sensory Perception?"

Alicia giggled. "Yes, I used to tease him about that when we were kids. He, of course, claimed he had ESP because his initials spelled it out. His middle name was Samuel. My oldest boy is named after him." She was quiet a moment, then clapped her hands. "Oh! I think I have a photo of Emerson with the boys. I picked up some copies the other day and I think they are still in the glove compartment. Would you like to see my sons?"

"Definitely."

While Alicia Komolsky hunted for the photos in the front of the car, Darby looked at the contents of the duffel bag. The clothes were clean and folded, with nothing in the pockets. His toiletry bag held the standard items — toothbrush, toothpaste, shampoo, razor. She opened the file folder and checked the documents. There was the contract, along with a copy of the earnest money check, the deed, and the property's listing packet.

There was nothing else in the file, and Darby returned it to the duffel bag. Idly she opened the medical thriller. There was nothing written on the inside cover, and Emerson Phipps' bookmark was a receipt from a bookstore in Boston. He'd read only the first chapter.

Darby turned over the receipt and saw a handwritten phone number. From the first three digits, Darby guessed it was for a Manatuck residence. She pointed it out to Alicia Komolsky.

"I have no idea," the other woman said. "You can use my cell phone and call it, if you'd like."

"Thanks. I have my own." Darby punched in the numbers and waited. The phone rang and was answered by a man saying, "Manatuck Agway."

Darby confirmed that it was the Agway store just a few blocks from the ferry landing and hung up.

"Interesting," she said. "Your brother took the time to look up the number for the local hardware store. Maybe he was planning to do some repairs on Fairview."

Alicia Komolsky laughed. "That would be the day! My brother was fine when it came to fixing people, but he could barely flip off a light switch inside a house. He didn't lift a finger to do repairs on his condo in Boston. He had a guy who took care of even the easiest things, and a cleaning lady too, of course." She pulled a 3 by 5 photo out of an envelope. "Here's the picture. This one is Samuel, and this is Michael. Isn't that a great shot? Look at the way Michael is grabbing his arm. The boys just adored their Uncle Emerson. He was like a dad to them." Her eyes filled with tears. "Do you want one? There are some wallets."

"Sure." Darby accepted a photo and gave Alicia a hug. The sound of the ferry docking brought both the women back to the present. Darby zipped up the duffel bag and closed Alicia's minivan hatch.

"Are you going to be okay to drive?"

"I am. I find it helps, actually. Gives me something to do. And I need to prepare myself to deal with the boys. You know, be strong for them."

Darby squeezed her bony shoulder. "Take care of yourself. I'll do my best to find out who did this, and I'll keep you posted, okay?"

"Thank you. And good luck."

Alicia climbed into the minivan and drove carefully off the ferry and onto the mainland. Darby watched as she turned toward the coastal route to drive south, back to Massachusetts. Her heart ached for Alicia and her sons. *Emerson Phipps may have been a total bastard,* she thought, *but he had a sister and two nephews who will miss him terribly.*

Once Alicia Komolsky and her minivan were out of sight, Darby pulled out the photo and studied it carefully. Phipps had been a handsome man, no doubt about it, and she thought his younger nephew Michael, with his thick sandy hair and square jaw, looked like him in miniature. Michael was clutching his uncle's arm, and Darby thought she glimpsed the pricey timepiece that was now missing. *Perhaps I'll get a better look with magnification,* she thought.

Darby tucked the photo back in her pocket and began walking the block or so from the ferry terminal to the Manatuck Agway store. Why had the surgeon scrawled down the number of a hardware store if he was not a handy person? Had it been a place to rendezvous with Jane Farr, or Mark Trimble?

A gangly teenager in the midst of restocking lightbulbs answered her inquiry about the manager. "He's not in," he said. "But he'll be back in an hour, 'cause that's when I go on break." Darby thanked him and pulled out the photo of Emerson Phipps and his nephews.

"Do you recognize the man in the middle?" The boy looked at the photo and shook his head.

"Nope. Don't think he's a regular customer, not that I've seen anyway."

Darby looked around the store for a few minutes, hoping that the manager would come into work early. Finally, she left her cell phone number with the teenaged clerk and left the store. She knew the Manatuck Public Library was only a block away, and she hoped to get more information on Surgeons Who Serve.

"May I use a computer?" she asked the desk clerk, once inside the handsome brick building. The librarian pointed to a machine and within minutes, Darby was logged on.

She typed in Emerson Phipps.

The first entries dealt with Phipps' murder in the small town of Hurricane Harbor, Maine. Darby glanced over them and found they contained the usual information, but no useful facts. Her eyes lit on an entry from Boston Memorial Hospital's website. Knowing this was the hospital where Emerson Phipps had privileges, Darby clicked on the link. Someone in the public relations department had written a flattering article about Dr. Phipps' involvement in Surgeons Who Serve. Darby learned that Phipps had participated in three missions with the group, all to a remote part of Haiti. A photo showed the surgeon smiling beside a pretty Haitian girl. Her spine had been severed, and with the help of SWS and Emerson Phipps, she was now able to walk. "The good doctor did a miracle," the girl's mother was quoted as saying.

There were several entries from professional journals, mentioning Phipps' work as a surgeon and his pioneering technologies. Darby flipped through them quickly, wishing she knew more medical terminology. The rest of the stories were easier to understand. They dealt with the surgeon's brushes with hospital disciplinary boards for actions related to tardiness, absence, and misconduct. Alicia Komolsky was correct: there were angry patients and frustrated administrators who had been unable to rein in her brother. Darby figured that a few of the articles were the ones Miles had already found and given her; nonetheless she forwarded them all to her computer at

Jane's house.

She checked her watch. If she hurried she would have time to speak to the Agway manager and make the next ferry back to Hurricane Harbor.

Darby jogged back to the hardware store, grateful that her ankle was feeling stronger all the time. Once inside, she spotted an employee she guessed was the manager, checking over a clipboard by the paint department.

To her surprise, he glanced at the photo and recognized Emerson Phipps almost immediately. "He came in here once," he said. "About a week ago. Left a few things for me to hold for a customer."

"Is that something you normally do? Hold things for other people?"

"Oh yeah. I'm like the frigging post office for some of these people, you know?" He chuckled and pointed to a shelf under the counter. "I'm in a good location, near the ferry and all, and it makes it easy for people to drop stuff off. Keys to their house or car, a bill they want paid, things like that. Been doing it for islanders for years, and I don't mind at all. Makes them loyal customers, is how I figure it."

Darby couldn't recall her parents ever using the Agway's unusual service, but she recalled Tina's comment about her aunt.

"What did this man leave here?"

"Couple of envelopes. Two, I guess. One was 8 1/2 by 11, the other just a normal size envelope. They were numbered one and two."

"Who were they for?"

"Who needs to know?"

"I do." She gave a sweet smile. "I was working with him, as his real estate agent. We were getting along so well and then he was murdered." She paused. "I suppose I could ask the police about this . . ."

The manager squirmed visibly. "There's no need to get them involved," he said. "The envelopes were initialed 'SP'."

"Soames Pemberton?"

"Guess so. At least, he was the one who opened them up. He picked up the big envelope on Sunday, and the small one on Monday, just before I closed. Soames had a big smile both times, like he'd won the lottery or something."

"Maybe he thought he had," murmured Darby, as she left the store and hurried to the ferry.

Miles Porter called on Darby's cell phone as she sat watching the water churn behind the ferry. She told him about Emerson

Phipps' drop-offs at the Manatuck store.

"He left envelopes for Soames Pemberton. I bet the large one was the old deed, which Soames picked up on Sunday. The small one was undoubtedly a check, which Soames picked up on Monday, after he'd made his little scene at the planning board meeting."

Miles whistled under his breath. "How in the world did Emerson Phipps know about Soames? Or the Agway store for that matter?"

"I'm betting Jane Farr," Darby said. "I think she made the suggestion to use Soames to present that old deed. If Soames grew greedy after one payment, maybe he killed Phipps when he wouldn't pay more."

"But Phipps was killed before the planning board meeting, right?"

"True. Maybe Soames contacted Phipps before the meeting and demanded more money. When Phipps said no, he killed him in a fit of rage."

"Then why would he have gone through with presenting the deed? And why frame Lucy Trimble?"

Darby was quiet for a few seconds. "You're right, it just doesn't fit. Maybe I'm trying too hard to make Soames the murderer. It just seems like it has to be him, Miles. After all, he knew Lucy had a drug problem from the stories they'd shared at the counseling group. She was trying to help him kick his habit, but maybe in doing so, she gave him all the information he needed to frame her."

Miles nodded, "Soames is a dangerous man. He's got to be found, and fast."

Darby sighed. "I haven't heard anything more from Chief Dupont. If Lucy is still his prime suspect, he's wasting valuable time not pursuing Soames. He must have had those chocolates analyzed by now."

"I'll try to find out. Are you coming back to the island?"

"Right now." She consulted her watch. "I'll be there in five minutes."

"Meet you at the dock and we'll go see the chief together."

Chief Dupont gave Darby a frosty look as she and Miles entered his office.

"You again? What is it you want this time? I don't mean to be rude, but I'm a busy man." He shuffled a stack of papers on his desk as if to reinforce his words.

"There are a few things involving Lucy Trimble that I'm not sure you're considering."

"Oh really? So, you're not just an expert

on real estate, eh? You've come all the way from California to tell me how to do my job?"

Darby pressed on. "Have you tested those chocolates? What if Lucy was poisoned?"

"The chocolates are still at the lab in Manatuck. So what if she was poisoned? She still could have killed the guy."

"What if someone was trying to frame her?"

Chief Dupont snorted. "Look, we've got ourselves someone who always thought she was above the law. It's a typical mentality of the summer people. She didn't want to sell her big fancy house, but her brother did. And then she didn't like the guy buying it. So, she puts on her jumpsuit, and goes over to Fairview, and smashes in his skull. And just because she's a Trimble, she thinks she can get away with it."

"Lucy Trimble's not a 'summer person'," Darby said. "She grew up here just like I did."

"You know damn well she's not one of us," Chief Dupont sneered. "She's never had to worry if she could pay her heating bill come winter. She's never had to clip coupons, or cook for somebody because her husband was scraping by . . ." He stopped abruptly and sank back into his chair.

Darby leaned forward. "What are you saying?"

"Nothing." His voice was tired.

"Are you talking about my parents?"

Miles touched her hand gently. "Darby, let's go, we can . . ."

"No! I want him to tell me what he's talking about." She glared at Chief Dupont. "You've been hinting at something ever since I set foot on Hurricane Harbor. Now's your chance to get it off your chest."

"It doesn't have anything to do with this investigation," he said gruffly.

"It has to do with how you're treating me."

The chief was quiet for a moment, regarding Darby under bushy eyebrows. He cleared his throat.

"Your mother cooked for me twice a week," he said quietly. "For a year or so. My wife was useless, half in the bag, and Jada said she could use a little extra cash."

Darby stood up, stunned. "She never said anything about cooking for anyone."

"She didn't want your father to know."

Darby turned and walked toward the door.

"I'm just trying to tell you," the chief called after her. "Your friend Lucy Trimble is not one of us."

Darby was reeling as she and Miles left the

police station. She made her way to Jane's truck and climbed in, wordlessly. Miles got in beside her and they sat quietly for a few minutes. Finally, Darby turned to Miles.

"I don't want to believe what he said, but it makes sense," Darby said. "I remember her making large quantities of food, and I always wondered who she packed it up for."

"There's nothing wrong with what your mother did," Miles said. "She was a personal chef, making some extra money for her family."

"I know. But she kept it a secret from my father. Why?"

"Maybe she didn't want to tell him she needed more help with the household finances. A lot of couples don't like to talk about money, even people who seem very savvy."

Darby thought a moment. "Now I know why the chief has been acting so strangely toward me. Miles, I think he had a crush on my mother — I don't think it was more than that — and for some reason I make him uncomfortable."

"Do you resemble your mother?"

Darby glanced in the mirror at her almond eyes and glossy black hair. Her features were softer than her mother's, but there was an undeniable family resemblance. "Yes." She took a breath, wanting to change the subject, hoping to keep the pain at bay.

"He's dead set on pinning this whole thing on Lucy Trimble. If he were to get his hands on that medical record . . ."

Miles nodded. "That would be the nail in her coffin, if you'll forgive the terrible cliché." He paused and looked Darby in the eye. "What next?"

She caught the scent of his soap, something woodsy and clean, and felt her face grow warm with the force of his gaze. Why did he have to make it so hard for her to concentrate?

"Well, I think we need to find out where Soames Pemberton is holing up." She made a major effort to focus on something other than his rugged face. "I'm going to see Laura Gefferelli. She may have some ideas as to Soames' whereabouts. What about you?"

"I want to be with you, naturally, but I do think I need to plug away on this article, for a little while at least. Are you going to be okay?"

Darby nodded.

"Then I'll head back to the cottage. Promise you'll stay in touch?"

"Promise." Darby was glad he couldn't see the flush in her cheeks as he climbed out of Jane's truck and waved goodbye.

The church was hushed and quiet as Darby made her way through the sanctuary and back to Laura Gefferelli's cramped office. Despite its small size, the minister had made the little room cheerful and pleasant. A neat row of books lined a shelf, a few framed pictures hung on the walls, and Laura's diploma from seminary school was on the wall.

She looked up with pleased surprise as Darby knocked on the open door.

"Come in, Darby. Great to see you." She stood and moved a few things off a chair and indicated she should take a seat. "I assume you're here to do some finishing details on Jane's service . . ."

"No," Darby admitted. "Actually, I'm looking for Soames Pemberton."

"A difficult person to find. Has new evidence come to light?"

"Not really, but I believe he killed Emerson Phipps and framed Lucy."

Laura Gefferelli shook her head. "I can't say that I'd be surprised," she said quietly. "Soames Pemberton is a very troubled man. A brilliant, but deeply disturbed man. Did you know he was a Navy SEAL?"

"I'd heard something like that."

"I've pieced together the gist of his story. He was in the Persian Gulf when Iraq invaded Kuwait in August of 1990, retrieving downed pilots and taking part in mine hunting missions. Then he was sent to patrol the water border between Kuwait and Saudi Arabia, and one of the mines he was detonating exploded. Soames was hospitalized for months. He came back dependent on painkillers. Added to the post-traumatic stress from his missions, it makes it nearly impossible for him to function in everyday society." She closed her eyes and murmured something, which Darby assumed was a quick prayer. "It hurts me to see a soul that troubled," she said with feeling.

Darby nodded, but she found it difficult to feel anything approaching sympathy for the man who'd attacked her twice.

"I really tried — we all tried, especially Lucy — to break through and touch his humanness," continued Laura. "But Soames operates in combat mode — he won't let anyone in. In the past year, his behavior's become even more erratic, and his rantings at therapy make less and less sense. And now if he has taken a life . . ." She rose from her desk and became businesslike. "What you have to remember is that Soames Pemberton is an extremely dangerous man.

You've seen some of that, right, Darby?"

Darby nodded. "He's a time bomb."

"Exactly. I think you should let Chief Dupont deal with him."

"I will tell the chief, but I'd like to know his whereabouts."

Laura sighed. "I know there's an abandoned cabin over by the Powderkeg quarry where he's lived before. Do you know where that is?"

"By the transfer station?"

"Yes. I could drive you by it, if you'd like. Or you could follow me in your truck."

"I'll come with you," Darby said. "I left the truck at the office and walked over."

Darby watched as Laura closed her office door and led her through the church.

"Pastor Thompson is still recovering from his illness," she said, pointing to a much larger office where the senior minister worked. Darby could see the harbor through the office's large picture window. "He's been out for several weeks now. I'm kind of getting used to the quiet." She smiled. "Actually I miss him quite a bit. He's a brilliant man, especially when it comes to a few books of the Old Testament. His writings on the book of Isaiah are very well received." Her face clouded with concern. "I understand that his prognosis isn't too good though. He has lung cancer, I believe. I'm not sure how much longer First Congregational will have him."

"What happens to your position if he can't return to work?"

"I don't know," Laura said thoughtfully. "I'm willing to do whatever the congregation needs. I love this island and my parishioners."

"Might they promote you as the senior minister?"

Laura smiled. "Anything's possible."

They exited the church and Darby saw Laura's Subaru parked a few steps away. The two walked to it, but Laura paused before opening the door and gazed at the harbor. "I always stop and thank God for this amazing place," she said.

"What brought you here?"

"The sea and the job. I grew up on Cape Cod, and the coast is definitely in my blood. I'm learning how to sail, did you know that?"

"Yes, I saw your boat moored next to Mark Trimble's."

"He's my instructor, and a great one at that. So what do you think of *What's in a Name*? Isn't she a sweet little boat? Sturdy, stable — I'll have to take you out for a sail."

Darby said nothing and Laura's smile faded.

"I'm sorry. Is sailing a painful subject, given your parents' accident?"

Darby climbed into Laura Gefferelli's car and waited for the older woman to join her. "I guess it is. I don't have any desire to sail now, but at one time, I absolutely loved it."

"Loss of loved ones can do that to you," said Laura gently. "I myself lost my sister a few years back. It was an accident, just like your parents' deaths. I know how hard it is to go on when you miss someone so much." She touched Darby's hand. "I realize you aren't staying on the island for much longer, but if you ever want to talk, my door is always open."

Darby nodded but kept her feelings to herself. They were too thorny to untangle, like the beach roses she'd tried to gather as a girl. She hadn't counted on how difficult it would be to face the loss of her parents all over again, more than fifteen years later.

They drove in silence into the interior of the island, heading toward the transfer station. Just before the entrance to the dump, Laura took a sharp left. It was a dirt road that ended at a series of quarries once mined for granite. A few hundred feet down the road was a rough path, so overgrown it was nearly invisible.

Laura pointed at the rocky trail. "That winds down to a small quarry that the locals call Powderkeg. Just before the quarry itself is a small structure, so rough it's barely standing. It blends into the surrounding brush so well you really have to be looking for it. I know Soames stays there on and off." She turned to face Darby. "There is no one — and I mean no one — down there. So promise me that if you go, you'll take someone with you."

"I will," Darby pledged.

Laura backed up the car and turned back onto the road where the transfer station was. "I'm worried about Soames doing harm to himself. He's tried it before, you know." She slowed as a flock of wild turkeys skittered across the road. "In my years of working with addictions, I find heroin addicts the most challenging. It's an evil thing. I look at poor Lucy and her struggles . . ."

"She has no recollection of yesterday afternoon," Darby said. "I think Soames Pemberton could have drugged her by poisoning a box of chocolates."

Laura shot a quick look in Darby's direction. "My God, if he's gotten to that point — where he would actually have planned this whole thing out — he's worse than I ever could have imagined."

Laura Gefferelli drove Darby back into town where she checked in with Tina at Near & Farr. Darby told Tina about the cabin where Soames Pemberton might be hiding.

"What do you say we take a ride out there this afternoon?"

Tina shuddered. "I really don't want to go anywhere near that lunatic, but if it will help Lucy, I'm game."

"That's the spirit. It's four P.M. now. Shall we meet back here in an hour?"

"Nah, let's go now, before I lose my nerve." She saw Darby eyeing her open-toed sandals and chuckled. "Don't worry, I've got sneakers in my truck that are perfect for tromping around the dump."

"And I've got a flashlight." She tried calling Miles at the cottage and left a quick message. *Maybe he'll call back before we get there,* Darby thought. *Not only would I like to see him again, but it wouldn't hurt to have another person along . . .*

Fifteen minutes later they slowed down by the rutted path.

"This is where we start," Darby said. "I'm not sure how far we go until we see the cabin, but let's give it a shot."

277

The two women began walking down the path, trying to be as quiet as possible. In the distance, Darby could hear the dull throbbing knock of a woodpecker searching for insects in a rotten tree. The brush was thick; a few mosquitoes buzzed around their heads. The edge of the quarry came into view, and Darby scanned the overgrown trees for signs of a dwelling.

"There it is," she pointed, indicating a tumbledown old structure half hidden behind an enormous pine. "Be ready to bolt if Soames comes at us."

"Don't worry," Tina hissed.

They crept toward the cabin, hearing nothing. Cautiously Darby pulled open the rotting door and peered at the darkness within. Suddenly a whoosh of wings made them both scream and fall back.

"Bats!" cried Darby. "You all right, Tina?"

"Never been better," said Tina, sweeping dead leaves from her legs. "Even though they scared the beejeesus out of me. Anything else in there?"

Darby switched on her flashlight and looked around. "I don't see anything," she said. "And it doesn't look like anyone has been here recently, either."

She began backing out of the cabin when several small plastic bags caught her eye.

"Tina, is that . . . ?"

"Smack," Tina answered, her voice hollow. "He's at it again."

Darby poked at the bag with the flashlight. Beneath it was a file folder.

"Trimble, Lucille," was typed neatly on a label. She picked it up and leafed through, reading the notes as fast as she could. The rumble of a truck made Tina look out the window.

"Shit! Someone is here! Darby, we have got to get out of here!" Darby flipped through another page as if she had not heard Tina.

"Darby! Now! Whoever's out there is fiddling in his truck. If we go now he might not see us! Take the damn file with you for God's sake!"

Darby looked at one last page and put the file back. "Let's get out of here."

They opened the door and crept around the rear of the cabin, then into the woods. They walked a short distance through the brush until they came to Tina's truck.

"Tina, could you tell if it was Soames?"

"I'm not sure. If it was, he probably recognized my truck."

"He's not stupid," agreed Darby. "Hopefully, he's in an altered state thanks to some of that heroin in the cabin and didn't know

279

it was us."

"Let's hope." Tina started the truck and quickly turned around. When they were barreling down the road, she asked, "So what was in the file? Why didn't you take it with you?"

"I don't want Chief Dupont accusing me of tampering with evidence," she explained. She took a deep breath.

"I think you need to know what happened to Lucy. She was sexually assaulted the summer she was sixteen. She went to Dr. Hotchkiss for treatment, but no one ever pressed charges. They called it 'molestation' back then, but Lucy was raped."

"My God . . ." Tina breathed. "Soames! That animal!"

"Tina, this time it wasn't Soames Pemberton who did the attacking. The doctor's notes confirm what Lucy herself told me: her rapist was Emerson Phipps."

"Emerson Phipps? No wonder she didn't want to sell her house to him! Do you think Mark has any idea?"

"Lucy told Mark and me on Monday."

"It's too awful to think about. Wasn't he a college buddy of Mark's? I knew from the moment I saw that Emerson Phipps that he was a slimebag." She slowed the truck to turn onto the harbor road. "How did

Soames get that doctor's file? And why would he even want it?"

"I can't imagine how he knew about the attack, but Soames Pemberton is a clever and dangerous man. Somehow he found out about this incident in her past, and knew Lucy would be the right person to frame."

"So what do we do now?"

"Truthfully, I don't know. If the chief finds out about that file, he's got even more of a reason to keep Lucy Trimble as his number one suspect. But that heroin could help explain how Lucy was poisoned." She paused. "I know one thing: I need to speak to Lucy. I think it's only fair that she prepares herself for the rest of the world knowing her secret."

"I'll drive you over there and wait in the car," Tina said. "Take as long as you need." She turned the wheel of the truck around a long turn. Darby could see the tension around her coral-frosted lips.

"That poor girl," Tina muttered. "That poor, poor girl."

ELEVEN

It was nearing five o'clock when Darby and
Tina drove over to Broad Cove, where Lucy
Trimble's studio was located. Tina stayed in
the truck while Darby knocked on the
weathered old door. Lucy, holding a canvas
in her hands, answered after only one
knock. Dark circles ringed her eyes, but her
grin seemed genuine.

"Being accused of murder may have its
perks," she said. "Who knows what will happen once the art show actually starts, but I
had at least a dozen calls today from poten-
tial buyers. Maybe the publicity will be good
for business."

"I hope it's good for something positive.
What are you doing now? Can I help you
load paintings into your car?"

"That would be great." The two women
made several trips carting canvasses from
the studio to Lucy's vehicle.

"I haven't seen your brother around,"

Darby commented. "What's he up to?"

"Oh, he hates all the tourists invading the island," she said. "He took off on the boat with this guy he met — Ryan somebody. He runs an island preservation organization and loves to sail. I'm not sure if they'll be back tonight. What's up?"

"I have a few things to talk with you about, Lucy. Can we go inside?"

"Sure."

Darby didn't relish the idea of bringing up such a painful part of Lucy's past. She knew all too well the anguish she would inflict on her old friend. *Still, I have to tell her that Soames knows everything and is the real killer,* she thought. *I have to bring up the past so that we can save Lucy's present.*

The lupines in Lucy's yard had faded and scattered their blossoms. Beside them, day lilies rose from the rich soil, their buds just beginning to form. The early summer cycle of the island had begun. Tourists arrived, stayed a few days, then departed. Summer people moved in and the little community bustled. The lupines, then the day lilies, then the peonies bloomed in succession. Life went on and on.

Darby followed her friend into the kitchen.

"Iced tea?" Lucy asked, pouring herself a tall glass. "The mint is from my garden."

283

Darby nodded, the smell of the mint freshening the air in the little kitchen. The two women sat at the blue enameled table and sipped the cool amber liquid. Darby cleared her throat.

"An hour or so ago, Tina and I were at an old cabin by the Powderkeg quarry. Inside, we found heroin, along with a file on you from Dr. Hotchkiss' office. Lucy, that file talks about your rape by Emerson Phipps. Somehow Soames Pemberton obtained it."

Lucy Trimble set down her glass with a shaking hand. Her blue eyes searched Darby's face. "Soames?"

Darby nodded. "It's true, Lucy. Somehow Phipps paid Soames to disrupt the planning board meeting and bring the old deed to light. Later, Soames must have demanded more money, but Phipps wouldn't pay it, so Soames hatched a plan to kill him. I don't know how he knew your medical history, or how he got that file, but he decided to make it look as if you killed Emerson Phipps. He then tried to kill you, by pushing you over the cliff, and when that didn't work, he laced the chocolates with heroin."

"No," Lucy breathed. "It can't be . . ."

"It all fits. He knew you were a former user from the counseling sessions, right? And if you ever mentioned the attack . . ."

"I didn't. No one knew about it — no one. My mother and Dr. Hotchkiss were the only ones I told — and my mother took it to her grave, I'm sure." She looked down helplessly.

Darby put her hand on Lucy's. "I can't imagine the pain that's caused you, Lu."

She nodded miserably. "Oh God, I don't want to think about it, but I suppose it will all come out now, right?"

"I honestly don't know. If the chief searches that cabin, he'll find the file. I had to leave it there because I'm hoping somehow it will help prove you were framed."

Lucy nodded again, wiping her eyes with the back of a hand. "I've dealt with it, you know. I've let it all out in my paintings. The shame, the pain, the years of nightmares . . . Of course, if my mother had been on my side it wouldn't have been so traumatic. But for her it was an unbelievable stain on the Trimble name. In her mind, it was all my fault."

"You must have lived through it all over again when Emerson Phipps appeared on the island."

She nodded. "I admit it — my thoughts were full of anger when Mark told me Phipps wanted to buy Fairview. I hated that man for what he did to me. I hated my mother for not protecting me even more. She was always in an alcoholic fog, and when I got up the courage to tell her what had happened, she flew into this rage, denying the whole thing." Lucy exhaled a long breath and seemed to collect her thoughts. "You need to see this." She lifted her shirt and revealed a pattern of burn marks resembling Greek letters. "It's a fraternity symbol. Phipps did it — when he was finished."

"God, Lucy!"

"I spent years hating him, and then — I made peace with it. When he appeared last week, I slid backward for a while, and then the peace overcame me once more. I didn't kill him, Darby. Do you think anyone will believe me?"

"I believe you. Tina believes you, and your brother will, too."

"You're sure it was Soames?"

"I have a strong hunch. I wish I knew for sure. But I do know one thing: you're innocent."

Tears rolled down Lucy's face as she nodded.

Darby rose and faced her friend. "Are you going to be okay?"

"I am."

"Then I'm going to see Chief Dupont. Trust me, we'll get to the bottom of this."

■ ■ ■ ■

Darby was glad Tina was doing the driving as they drove to Charles Dupont's house. Her hands shaking, she could not get the image of Lucy's scarred stomach out of her mind. Her thoughts were churning, her emotions a mix of anger and sorrow. *All these years, all these years . . .*

Darby figured the chief would not be putting in late hours at the station, and her assumption was correct. His police car was parked in the driveway of a new modular home set back from the road. Darby watched as he opened the front door, a puzzled look on his face.

"Miss California and Tina." His joviality was forced. "What can I do for you ladies?"

Darby slammed the truck door and walked toward the big man. "Hello, Chief. Can we talk? I have some information on the Emerson Phipps murder case."

"Is that so? Well, come on in then." He opened the door of his house and ushered Darby inside. "What about Tina? She coming in?"

"I don't think so."

A large golden retriever rose with difficulty from a dog bed by the foyer. She wagged her tail hopefully and walked stiffly toward Darby.

"This is Aggie," he said, bending to pet the old dog. "She's a trooper. Aren't you, Aggie? You're a good old girl." He straightened and said, "She's fifteen. Would you believe it? Fifteen."

He walked toward a small bar area and poured himself a drink. "I'm going to fix myself a whiskey. Can I get you anything?"

"No, thank you."

He continued to linger at the bar while Darby looked around the small house. It was new, with wall-to-wall carpeting that had yet to show signs of Aggie damage. The walls were white and unadorned, the furniture brand new, but sparse.

"Good old Aggie," he said, bending to scratch the old dog's head. "She saw my kids graduate from high school, my mom pass on, and my wife high tail it off to Vegas. Fifteen years is a long time, eh Darby?" He pointed to the couch. "Please, sit down." He lowered himself into an easy chair and took a long drink of the whiskey. "Are you here to talk about what I told you today? I didn't mean to upset you."

Darby shook her head. She didn't want to discuss her parents with Chief Dupont. She leaned in closer and cleared her throat. "I'm here to talk about the murder of Emerson Phipps. Lucy Trimble is innocent. Soames Pemberton is the man you should be looking for."

"Soames? Why in the world would he want to kill some fancy doctor he didn't even know? Soames has had some hard times since coming back from the Gulf, but he's not a homicidal maniac."

"Emerson Phipps paid him to present the old deed at the planning board meeting so he would have a chance to buy Fairview. Soames demanded more money to keep quiet about it and Phipps told him no. I think that Soames decided to kill him and frame Lucy for the murder. He knew she had some weaknesses in her past, and he used those in his favor."

Chief Dupont took a long, thoughtful drink of his whiskey. "Hmmm . . . lots of conjecture. Tell me, you know about this — partnership — between Phipps and Soames how exactly?"

"There was a telephone number in Emerson Phipps' personal effects. I called it, and it was the Agway store on Manatuck. I spoke to the manager there and discovered that Phipps was leaving envelopes for Soames Pemberton at the store."

"And how do you make the jump that

Soames framed Lucy?"

Darby knew the chief was not going to be happy about her breaking and entering into Soames' cabin, but she had to tell him about the file. As she suspected, his face hardened into an unreadable mask as she described entering and finding the doctor's notations.

"That cabin is private property," he said coldly. "You had no right to go snooping around there."

"I know," she said quickly. "I didn't disturb anything."

"Well, you looked at this file, didn't you?" He gave an exasperated sigh. "What did it say that's so important Soames could frame Lucy?"

"Dr. Hotchkiss described an incident that happened when Lucy was sixteen. She was sexually assaulted by Emerson Phipps."

The chief whistled. "Sounds like that gives her a reason to want the man dead, doesn't it?"

"But don't you see it also gives someone a prime reason to frame her? Lucy hated Emerson Phipps for what he did to her, but I know she didn't kill him." She looked Chief Dupont squarely in the eye. "You know Lucy Trimble. You know she's not a murderer."

"Don't be too sure about that. Her motive for hating Emerson Phipps is stronger than ever. This man assaulted her and decides to buy her house? Come on, Darby. Use your judgment. Her painting jumpsuit was found at the scene. Did you forget that it was covered in the victim's blood? And like it or not, your friend Lucy Trimble is an addict. And once an addict, always an addict."

"Lucy is a scapegoat, a convenient person to pin this whole thing on."

"I didn't decide to pin a murder on anyone, young lady. I work with evidence. Material you'd do well to leave alone or you'll get yourself in trouble!"

He was panting, his face an angry shade of red. Darby willed herself to calm down. *My emotions won't help Lucy,* she told herself.

"I'm sorry I lost my temper. Please tell me you'll investigate Soames Pemberton's cabin. Please, Chief Dupont."

"I'll go out there in the morning," he said, sounding mollified. "You said it was by the landfill, right?"

Darby nodded, not trusting herself to speak. *Why is he waiting until the morning to investigate this lead? Just to show me he can,* she thought. Backing toward the door of the chief's house, she nodded curtly and saw herself out the door.

Tina waited until she'd pulled out of Chief Dupont's driveway before asking Darby what happened. When Darby told her, she was frank in her assessment of his abilities.

"That asshole!" she spat. "He has never liked the Trimbles — or anyone with waterfront property for that matter — but I can't believe he'd let his stupid prejudices affect an investigation. Poor Lucy! What do we do now?"

"I'm not sure." Darby's energy was flagging, she was hungry, and the encounter with the chief had sapped her determination.

Tina thought a moment, and then snapped her fingers. "What we need to do is confront Soames. Get him to confess, the way they do on television." She thought again. "Hey! There's a guy who's a regular at that grungy bar in downtown Manatuck, over by the Army-Navy store. The Dip Net. He might know where Soames is hiding."

Tina's enthusiasm was contagious.

"Let's grab the ferry and go over there, see if he shows up tonight," said Darby.

"I'm game. If we hurry we'll be there just in time for the end of Happy Hour, and I don't know about you, but I sure could use a little shot of happy right now."

Peyton Mayerson closed her cell phone and took a long, deep, breath. She exhaled and saw that her hands were trembling. *Breathe,* she reminded herself. *Just breathe.*

God, she wanted a cigarette. She had a rule about not smoking in the Mercedes but dammit, this was an emergency. She pulled a cigarette out of her pack, lit it, and sighed.

Just what had he said? The closing on Fairview was in jeopardy. The whole plan was in jeopardy, and her little wad of cash from the sale of two paintings wouldn't even begin to make a dent in what she owed her investors.

And the investors were starting to circle like a band of hungry sharks.

Peyton inhaled deeply, feeling her heart race despite her efforts to relax. *I can get the hell out of here,* she thought, leaning back against the Mercedes' leather seat. But where? Where could she possibly run that Tony Cardillo and his men would not find her?

The whistle for the ferry back to Hurricane Harbor blew, but Peyton, seated in her car in the parking lot, barely heard it. She tried to quell the feeling of nausea that was starting to build in her stomach.

I need cash, and fast. I need this Fairview deal to work. I need a break from this frigging island and the ferry and people who can't speak English.

Peyton grabbed her cell phone again, punching in the numbers for her lawyer in Boston. *Answer your phone,* she said out loud, hoping this time he would actually pick up. When the metallic voice of his answering machine once more met her ears, she left another message and clicked shut her phone. *He is the key,* she thought. *He can make the Trimbles listen if only he would answer his damn telephone . . .*

From past experience, she knew there was another way to get his attention, involving what she liked to call her feminine wiles. Unfortunately, the accoutrements which had so successfully done the trick once before — a black lace thong and bustier — were back in her room at the Hurricane Harbor Inn.

Screw it, she thought, turning on her car and backing out of the parking lot. *I can improvise.* She thought briefly of Emilio, waiting forlornly in the hotel room. *Screw him, too.* She checked the time on the Mercedes' display. Five o'clock. She would be at the lawyer's house by ten, ready and willing to plead her case.

■ ■ ■ ■

The 5:30 P.M. ferry was more crowded than usual as tourists who'd arrived early for the art show began trickling back to the mainland. Despite the extra passengers, Tina secured a spot for the truck, and both she and Darby breathed a sigh of relief.

"I don't even feel like getting out," said Tina, watching as the throngs of tourists crowded the decks.

"Me neither." Darby opened up a newspaper and pointed at a story. "Looks like the *Island Courier* has a story about Lucy," she said. The two read the several-column story in silence.

"That poor girl," Tina said. "Maybe tonight we'll find something that will help clear her."

It was a short ride to the Dip Net. The parking lot was moderately full for a Wednesday night, with half a dozen cars and pickup trucks parked haphazardly in the lot. Tina and Darby locked the truck and approached the building. Strains of country music and the aroma of French fries assailed their senses.

"Man, I'm hungry," Tina said.

"So am I. Burger and fries, my treat."

"I'm gonna want a beer, too."

"You're on."

Inside, the light was dim but Darby noticed a few heads turning in curiosity. Trophy fish adorned the walls and a huge net hung behind the bar. The bartender gave a friendly nod and Darby and Tina slid into a booth.

Moments later, he was at their side. Darby ordered food and a beer for Tina.

"Aren't you having one?" Tina asked. "When it comes to Soames, I find that I need all the fortification I can get."

Darby shook her head. "I promise, I'll have a beer with you when all this is through."

The women grew silent, waiting for their order and thinking of the dangerous man they were hunting.

"I gotta say, I know Soames is more than capable of killing somebody, and he probably shot a whole bunch of guys overseas, but I have a hard time picturing him smashing that prissy doctor's skull in," Tina said, re-applying her red lipstick.

"You do?" Darby asked, surprised. She could imagine Soames doing just about any violent action.

"Yeah, and I'll tell you why. Soames is into strategy, you know, special ops and stuff.

He's a Navy SEAL, right? If he had killed the guy, he would have done something less bloody. Strangled him, or caught him in a booby trap. We're talking a man who could definitely kill with his bare hands. Why pick up some statue of a garden nymph? That's for sissies."

The bartender brought their order and Tina took a swig of her beer. " 'Course, I could be wrong. I've been wrong about that man since I first laid eyes on him."

"What made you go out with him, Tina?" Darby asked.

"Huh. I've asked myself that a hundred times," she said. She gazed off into the distance. "What makes anyone fall for someone? His looks, for one. He isn't much to write home about now but a few years back, before he went overseas, he was handsome, you know, in that wild, Rambo kind of way. He's smart, too — very smart. I like a man with brains. He listened to me — or at least faked it pretty well. And, I guess I was drawn to his dangerous side. My dad was a bit of a loose cannon and maybe I'm attracted to those types of men."

Tina looked around the bar before continuing. "I never knew what happened to Soames over in the Gulf, but it really messed him up big time." She sighed.

"Before that, he had a tender side. I don't think anyone has seen that part of him for many years."

"If he suffers from post-traumatic stress syndrome, why isn't he getting treatment?" asked Darby.

Tina frowned. "First you have to want to be helped. And that's not our friend Soames." She took another gulp of her drink. "Let's talk about you. Have you made peace with that stubborn old aunt of yours, or what?"

"She's dead, Tina. How do you make peace with that?"

"It doesn't matter what kind of shape she's in, girl. I'm talking about you realizing that she tried to do the best she could for you. Hey, it was a hard situation for her, too. She never asked to come to Maine and deal with an orphaned teenager. She wasn't equipped for it."

"No," Darby said slowly.

"This is the key. You make peace with her, something's going to come over you that helps you with everything else. It's like a magic blanket or something. You forgive her for all the things she didn't know and everything she did wrong."

"I hear you, Tina. I'll think about it."

The bartender arrived with two platters

and placed them before the women. Each had a cheeseburger, a large dill pickle, and a pile of French fries.

"Mmmm, smells good," commented Tina. Darby nodded. "I'm famished."

The two ate in silence, enjoying their dinner and the bar's cozy atmosphere. When they'd finished, Darby requested the check while Tina glanced unhappily around the restaurant.

"I thought for sure we'd see somebody who'd know something about Soames." Tina swallowed the last of her beer and seemed about to say more when she stopped and pointed at a man entering the Dip Net. "Aha," she whispered. "I think that's one of his old buddies. Watch me work my magic on him."

Darby watched as Tina sashayed up to the man, gave him a peck on the cheek, and talked for a few minutes. When she returned to the booth, he swiveled in the bar stool to watch her. Darby noted a triumphant smile on her face.

"Soames is here in Manatuck," she said, "shacked up at an empty building a few miles from here, over near the Rusty Scupper. Remember that place? Anyway, this guy hasn't seen him for a day or two, but he says before that, Soames was buying drinks for everyone like his ship had come in." She grabbed her turquoise purse. "What do you say? Shall we go find him?"

Darby tossed enough money for the bill on the table and grabbed her denim jacket. "I'm ready."

Outside the Dip Net's dingy doorway, the sun was low in the sky and dusk was falling. Tina started the truck and headed away from the coast, driving slowly through unfamiliar Manatuck streets. After a few minutes she slowed down before a dilapidated building.

"There's the Scupper," Tina said. In contrast to the Dip Net's crowded parking lot, the Rusty Scupper was forlorn and abandoned.

"Now, the place where Soames is staying is on the other side of this." She pointed at an old warehouse. "Think it's that."

"We need to be sure before we alert Chief Dupont," said Darby, scanning the front of the darkened building for any sign of life.

Tina opened the car door. "His room is in the basement — at least that's what that guy said."

Darby nodded. "I'll wait a few minutes and then follow you in. I'll be listening and ready to help you out. Be very careful, Tina."

"Don't worry. I know this guy like the

back of my hand." Tina climbed out of the car and closed it quietly. "See you in a few," she said.

Darby watched as Tina made her way across the barren parking lot to the building's front door. She opened it gingerly, and stepped inside, looking toward Darby and the car as she did so.

Darby exhaled slowly and tried to still her thumping heart. Her mind registered all kinds of scenarios — none of them good — involving Tina and Soames Pemberton, but she forced herself to stop the worrisome thoughts and focus on her plan. Assuming Tina found Soames in the basement of the warehouse, she would try to get him to talk about the murder and his reasons for framing Lucy Trimble. Darby prayed that Soames' penchant for bragging, coupled with Tina's presence, would win out and he would confess to the crime.

I've waited long enough, she thought, easing out of the truck and closing the door as quietly as she could. She put the keys in her denim jacket pocket and crept to the front door. It opened quietly and Darby surveyed the dim interior.

Trash lay in piles on the muddy floor and overturned chairs — a few of them broken — littered the space. What looked like an office in one corner of the room was heaped with plastic garbage bags, and Darby saw that gaping holes had been chewed in the bags and waste was spilling out. A door in another corner was ajar and Darby guessed that it led to the basement and Soames Pemberton.

She tiptoed toward the door and soon heard voices rising from the darkened stairwell.

Tina's was a low murmur, but Soames' booming rant was more audible.

". . . knew the money belonged to Phipps, even though it was Trimble who called me," said the voice. There was a pause when Tina murmured something low. "Yeah," Soames continued. "He set it up. But I knew it was Phipps because he wanted that house like a dog wants a bone. I tried to get more cash out of him but son of a bitch just laughed."

Tina said something else and Soames Pemberton swore.

". . . what you think? I could have, if I wanted to, but I didn't."

More murmurs from Tina.

"Yeah, but I'm not telling you. Why should I tell you?"

Darby heard him chuckle at something Tina must have said and the sound stiffened her spine.

"Help me? Get a fucking grip. After the shit I've taken from you and this island? You make me crazy, you know that? Crazy. All that crap I took in the Gulf, this is worse . . . sometimes I hate you, you bitch."

Darby heard the crash of furniture and the sounds of a scuffle. She was down the darkened stairs two at a time when Tina let out a soft scream.

Inside a dusty, half-finished room, Soames Pemberton had his hands around Tina's throat.

TWELVE

Darby grabbed the closest thing she could find: an old mop inside a rusted metal bucket. She brandished the mop at Soames. "Let her go!" she yelled.

"What the hell?"

Darby had taken the huge man by surprise, so much so that he relaxed his hold on Tina's neck. It was only for a moment, but it gave Tina enough time to twist out of his grasp. As soon as he realized she had escaped, he lunged at her, but she avoided his arms and flung herself to safety by Darby. Without thinking, the two women were backing toward the stairs as Soames lurched in their direction.

"So you brought her along," he leered. "Your little Jap friend."

Darby reached down and then threw the bucket as hard as she could at Soames' head and yelled for Tina to run. There was a resounding thud of metal hitting skull as both women bolted up the basement stairs. They dashed across the warehouse and toward the exit, with Soames Pemberton somewhere behind them. Tina yanked open the door and rushed into the night, Darby right on her heels. The two women practically jumped into the truck and Tina fumbled in her pocketbook for the keys. Soames Pemberton was now outside the warehouse as well and only steps away.

"Sweet Jesus, where are the damn keys?" Tina wailed.

Darby hit the automatic lock on the doors seconds before Soames tried yanking hers open. She heard Tina's pocketbook fall to the floor and her heart sank. If Tina didn't find the keys immediately, Soames would smash the glass.

Suddenly Darby remembered shoving the keys in her pocket. "I've got them," she yelled, jamming her hand into her jacket pocket. Her fingers touched a cylinder; she pulled it out as well. "Here!" Out of the corner of her eye, she saw Tina thrust the key into the ignition.

Soames was battering his fist against the glass of Darby's window and she braced herself for the sound of it breaking. His face was contorted with rage and Darby prayed that the truck would move before Soames shattered her window.

There was a tinkling of glass and Soames' meaty hand thrust through the jagged pieces toward Darby's head. She yanked the top off the small cylinder and pressed the top of it. There was a blast and then a yowl of pain. Soames fell back, his now bleeding hand clutching his eyes.

A moment later, the engine roared to life,

"Gun it!" Darby yelled.

Tina stepped hard on the gas and the truck lurched forward, thrusting Soames backward against the pavement. The tires squealed as she sped out of the parking lot and down the road. The two women rode in stunned silence, breathing heavily, putting distance between them and Soames. Finally, Tina found her voice.

"Holy shit. That was close."

Darby nodded. She could not get the picture of Soames' hands around Tina's throat out of her mind. "How's your neck?"

Tina rubbed it gingerly. "Sore. That bastard."

"You're not kidding."

"Did you hear what he said? Mark Trimble paid him to present the deed."

"No!"

"That's what he claims. Mark paid the money, but Phipps was the one behind it.

When Soames tried to blackmail him for more money, he just laughed."

"Who laughed? Phipps?"

"Apparently. When I asked him if he killed Phipps because he wanted more money, he said no. He said, 'I could have, but I didn't want to'."

"Yeah, right. Just like he wasn't going to hurt you. Tell that to your neck."

Tina gave a rueful smile. "I asked him who killed Phipps and he acted like he knew."

"He knows all right: it was him." Darby turned to her friend. "Mark knew from the beginning that the sale to Peyton wasn't going to happen. He lied to me."

Tina nodded. "I can't believe it! With as much money as he's got, what's he going and getting greedy for? Sounds to me like Phipps came along, offered more money, and that was the end of the whole wedding idea." Her face darkened. "Although I never did like that Peyton Mayerson, and there's something fishy about her boyfriend."

Darby heard the rumble of a train in the background and guessed that she and Tina were driving past a seldom-used freight line. The noise only added to the confusion in her brain. She had never felt so mentally or physically exhausted.

"Tina, there's something I haven't considered. What if Mark knew what happened to Lucy way back when? What if Phipps told him about the rape on one of his trips up here this month? Bragged about it over drinks or something?" She paused. "He might have even confessed to Mark in remorse."

Tina's face grew ashen. "What are you saying? That Mark could have killed Phipps as payback for what he did to Lucy all those years ago?"

"You said it yourself: Mark would do anything to help his sister. What if he learned about the deal my aunt concocted with Phipps, even helped her to put Phipps in the position to buy Fairview, and then found out about the rape. When he realized he'd made a terrible mistake, he met Phipps at the property and killed him."

Tina shook her head. "Then he would have known Phipps was already dead when he met you at that planning board meeting. Did he act like someone who'd butchered his buddy the day before?"

"No. But clearly he's a better actor than we thought."

"Guess you never do know what people are really thinking. Look at that old Jane for example! Here she is doing this double deal, and me never knowing. Could Mark have killed that doctor if he found out what he'd done to his sister, all those years before? I guess anybody might do anything if they were provoked enough, but my money's on that loser Soames Pemberton." She touched her throat again and winced.

"You blasted him with my spray, didn't you?"

Darby nodded.

"Good," Tina said grimly. She turned to Darby. "You going to read Mark the riot act?"

"You bet," vowed Darby. "I'm finding Mark Trimble first thing tomorrow morning. And this time, he's telling me the truth."

Miles Porter was waiting when Darby and Tina drove off the ferry and on to Hurricane Harbor. "I left you a message," he told Darby, a concerned look on his face. "Did you get it? I've been worried."

"I'm sorry, Miles. I looked for my phone on the ferry, but I've misplaced it." She turned and hugged Tina. "You're sure you're okay?"

Tina nodded. "Takes more than that to kill me," she said.

"Kill you? What happened?"

Darby sighed. "It's been an eventful day.

Can you drive me back to my aunt's house? I promise I'll tell you what happened."

Miles agreed and Darby climbed into his car. While he listened attentively, she brought him up to date on what she and Tina had found at the cabin and Chief Dupont's reaction. When she told Miles about their encounter with Soames Pemberton at the warehouse, he narrowed his eyes and frowned.

"That maniac could have killed you both," he said sharply. "What did Dupont say about that?"

"He doesn't know yet," Darby said. "I'm going to call him as soon as I get to Jane's."

Miles followed Darby into the house. "I'm going to make you some tea," he said. "After the day you've had, you need a good strong cup."

Darby nodded gratefully and dialed Chief Dupont's home number. After a few rings he answered.

"You're saving me a call," he said, interrupting her mid-sentence. "We searched the shack by the quarry and found the file and the heroin, as well as something else."

Darby waited, her heart beating.

"The doctor's fancy watch. My men will be combing the island for Soames come morning. It's only a matter of time before we find him and bring him in for questioning."

"He's not on Hurricane Harbor," said Darby, trying her best to remain calm. "He's in Manatuck, living in the basement of an abandoned warehouse by the Rusty Scupper Restaurant. He nearly strangled Tina."

"What the hell —" began Chief Dupont. "What about you? Are you all right?"

"Just more convinced than ever that Lucy is innocent. Soames admitted to blackmailing Phipps . . ." She couldn't bring herself to mention Mark Trimble's involvement in finding the old deed or her new suspicions. After all, he was her client. *If I weren't so exhausted, I'd give Mark Trimble a piece of my mind tonight. But I'm in no state to confront him now.*

. The chief promised to call the Manatuck Police Department immediately. He hung up and Darby replaced the receiver, her heart racing. Maybe by the morning, Soames would be in custody. Lucy would be cleared of all charges and life on Hurricane Harbor could get back to normal. *And I can bury my aunt and return to my life in California,* she thought.

Miles asked her how she took her tea.

"Strong," she said wearily. Although it was

only nine o'clock, Darby felt as if it was midnight.

"Why don't you go out to the cottage," Miles suggested. "I'll bring this out to you and then head back to my little house."

Darby complied and walked through the dark garden to the cheerful cottage. She was enjoying the comfort of a chintz-covered chair when Miles appeared with two steaming mugs of tea.

"I used to hate American coffee cups," he said, handing Darby one of the mugs, "but I have to say, they come in handy when you require a nice big portion."

Darby smiled. "Thanks. This is just what I need." She took a sip of the hot liquid. "Darjeeling. One of my favorites." She gestured toward the other comfortable chair. "Take a seat. I need to process out loud a moment." Miles obeyed and waited for Darby to compose her thoughts.

"There's something that's bothering me," she began. "Soames Pemberton is a braggart. He's an ego-driven, highly trained man who thinks he is smarter than everyone else. If he killed Phipps, why didn't he boast about it to Tina like he did the blackmail?"

"Maybe the seriousness of killing someone has actually sunk in," Miles said. "Maybe it dawned on him that this time he's going to prison for the rest of his life."

"Maybe." She thought back over the days since she landed at Portland Jetport. "I arrived here in Maine on Sunday, the day the murder of Emerson Phipps took place."

Miles nodded.

"Tina and I stopped at the ferry terminal in Manatuck and I used the restroom, where Soames Pemberton surprised me for the first time. Thinking back on it, he didn't act like a man who'd killed somebody that day."

"Is Soames the kind of person who ever behaves in a predictable fashion?" asked Miles.

"That's just it. The person who killed Emerson Phipps lured him to his death in that garden shed. They somehow knew he was going to be at Fairview that morning. It was calculating, and premeditated, and our friend Soames the Navy SEAL could easily have carried out that plan. And yet it was a sloppy, bloody mess in that shed. That doesn't seem like a military-type execution."

"I see what you mean," Miles agreed. He looked down at his mug of tea and then back at Darby. "Couldn't the whole thing have been a coincidence that worked to Soames' advantage? You know that Soames loitered about Fairview, living in the woods where he did God knows what. Perhaps he

313

was there, sleeping off a drunken binge, and heard the BMW roll up the road. He guesses that it is Phipps — maybe he even recognizes the flashy motorcar — and sneaks into the shed. When Phipps comes in to investigate, Soames uses the first thing he gets his paw on and smashes in his skull."

"Maybe. I keep thinking about Soames' combat missions, but all he seems to do of late is blunder into situations in which he tries to destroy everything in his path."

Darby took another sip of tea and leaned back against a cushy pillow. Should she bring up Mark Trimble? She wanted Miles' reaction, but she was so tired . . .

"I am so comfortable, I might actually doze off," she said, sighing.

"With all you've been through the past few days, I won't take it personally if you do nod off," he said.

She turned toward him and smiled. "Another hot date with Darby Farr."

"Indeed." Miles' gaze became more intent. He touched her arm lightly and a tingle went up Darby's spine.

"Your life isn't always so dramatic, is it?" he asked. "I mean, setting traps for murderers and making multimillion dollar deals . . . surely there are times when you catch your breath, so to speak?"

Darby laughed. "I live a much quieter life in California, that's true. I'm sure things will settle down after Jane's funeral."

"That's Saturday morning, correct? And you fly back on Sunday?"

"Yes."

"And once you are back in Mission Beach, may I visit you and see your peaceful West Coast life?"

Darby took a sip of her tea, feeling it warm her right down to her toes. "I'd like that very much," she said lightly. "I think you should plan on it."

Moments later, after she'd said goodbye to Miles and thanked him for the tea, she sat wrapped in her bathrobe, making a few last minute notes for the next day. First on her list was to see Mark Trimble. *Soames said that Mark put up the money for him to present the old deed,* she thought. *He's been lying to me all along.*

And then there was the sale of Fairview. Peyton's verbal offer was much lower than what Mark and Lucy expected, and yet she was still willing to buy it, even with the archaic deed restrictions. *The closing is supposed to take place tomorrow,* Darby thought. *What are the chances of that?*

Written in large letters at the bottom of

the list was the single word JANE. *I'll call Laura Gefferelli as soon as I wake up,* she thought, *and make sure we are all set for my aunt's funeral.* She needed to touch base with Jane's attorney as well, to be sure she was correctly executing her duties as personal representative. With that resolved, she padded over to the comfortable bed. A wave of tiredness overtook her and she eased against the pillows, falling into a sound sleep.

A vivid dream, fueled perhaps by the caffeine in the tea, filled her thoughts.

She was alone in the woods behind Fairview and had lost her way. As she wandered through the brush, she came to a clearing where a huge easel was set up. A large canvas was propped on the easel, and Darby drew closer to see what it depicted. As she approached, a hooded figure appeared silently from the back of the easel and began painting using broad, sweeping strokes.

Darby was certain that Lucy Trimble was the hooded artist, and she continued to walk closer to the easel. When she was close enough to touch the canvas, the hooded person slowly turned, laughing, and the hood slid away. Darby drew back in horror. It was Soames Pemberton, laughing maniacally, his face painted in desert camouflage.

He lunged at her and Darby screamed. As she sprinted through the woods and away from danger, she heard a strange noise. Against her better judgment she glanced backward.

Soames was reaching into the hood to pull something off his face. *A mask,* Darby realized. *He is wearing some kind of mask.* She watched, mesmerized, as a new set of features peeked below his own. *Someone else is behind Soames,* she realized with dread.

She woke with a jolt, her heart pounding, and thought about the dream. Who had been under Soames' mask? Emerson Phipps? Mark Trimble? Peyton Mayerson? Or someone else entirely?

Donny Pease drove his truck through the darkness to the Hurricane Harbor Inn. He'd been asleep when the night manager phoned, asking if he'd help with an emergency water leak. "Right there," he'd answered, his voice groggy with sleep.

He couldn't resist a grin as he pulled into the inn's parking lot. The islanders knew who to call when an emergency happened — Donny Pease. With his ability to fix just about anything, he was an invaluable part of the community fabric. Over the years he'd been summoned to repair everything from boat engines to washing machines, and had been quizzed for advice on the finer points of carpentry, tree trimming, and landscaping. Why, he'd even helped the new lady minister, Laura, deliver a baby who came during one of last winter's worst snowstorms. And the little tyke was doing just fine.

The night manager, a young kid with a worried look on his face, met him in the lobby.

"Mr. Pease, I'm so glad you're here. There's water coming down and I don't know what to do." Donny saw little drops of perspiration beading the boy's forehead, and had to suppress a chuckle.

"Easy, son, just show me where the problem is."

The boy took him to the first floor hallway and pointed up at an elaborate chandelier. The plaster around the fixture was dark gray with moisture, and Donny saw a steady stream of drips falling from the ceiling and onto the carpet, where a soggy circle the size of a beach ball had formed. Serious water damage was occurring; that much Donny knew.

"What's up above this?" he asked. "Laundry room?"

The boy shook his head. "Second floor suite."

Donny imagined the layout of the second floor and realized the boy was right. "What did you find when you went in there?"

The boy blushed a deep crimson. "I didn't go in," he confessed.

"What? Why the heck not?" Donny strode toward the stairs, hating to reprimand the boy, but unable to keep quiet. "That suite's where the problem is, any fool can see that."

He turned to face the boy. "You can get me the key at least, can't you?"

The boy nodded and raced to the registration desk. He returned a moment later and handed Donny the key.

"Is it vacant?"

The boy shook his head. "No. It's occupied by that lady with the Italian man." He squirmed. "Usually they have their 'Do Not Disturb' sign out . . ."

Now Donny understood why the boy had chosen to avoid Peyton Mayerson's suite, water damage or not. The night manager, barely old enough to shave, was petrified of catching the amorous couple in an intimate act.

Donny held out his hand for the key. "Come with me. I may need you to fetch something."

The boy and Donny ascended the stairs and found the suite. Donny rapped hard on the door, asking "Ms. Mayerson? Ms. Mayerson?"

No noise came from the suite. Donny knocked again.

Hearing no answer, he took the square room key and used it to open the door. It swung open and Donny said loudly, "Housekeeping . . . we have an emergency."

Again there was no answer. Donny and the night manager crept into the room. "Turn on the light," Donny told the boy, who did as he was directed.

The brightness of the overhead fixture startled Donny, and it took him a few moments to adjust to the light. The boy, meanwhile, had ventured toward the bedroom suite and returned with a relieved look on his face.

"They're not here," he said, pointing toward the bedroom.

The room had not been cleaned, that much was for sure. Plates with half eaten muffins were stacked on the coffee table, and newspapers and trash overflowed the waste basket. Glancing inside the bedroom, Donny caught a whiff of perfume still lingering on the air. He noted that the bed was a rumpled mess.

Donny moved toward the bathroom, searching for the source of the leak. The gurgling of running water stopped him short.

The Jacuzzi tub, the focal point of the suite's bathroom, was filled to overflowing, with water gushing out of the faucets and splashing over the edges onto the pale pink tiles. *One of those idiots was going to take a bath.* Then he looked in the tub.

There, stuck into the drain, was some sheer black material. *Women's lingerie,* Donny thought. Not that he'd had much firsthand experience with it, but he'd seen those racy catalogues just like all the other men on Hurricane Harbor. Donny turned off the water and yanked the lacey fabric out of the drain. There were two pieces: the tiniest pair of ladies underpants Donny Pease had ever seen, and the fanciest brassiere he'd ever dreamed existed.

"Most likely they were drying and fell into the tub," Donny surmised. "Ladies like to wash little things like this by hand, and then hang them up to dry."

"But the water — why was it on?" stammered the boy.

"Who the heck knows. You just get your butt down to the utility room and bring the big shop vac up here lickety split. We gotta get this floor dried up and quick."

The ringing of the cottage's telephone woke Darby Farr. It was seven; far later than she usually slept, and she fumbled for the receiver and said hello.

"Darby, this is Chief Dupont. There's something you need to know right away. The Manatuck police found Soames Pemberton an hour ago. Looks like he threw himself in front of the old freight train by the Industrial Park. He's dead."

Darby was too stunned to reply. She stood for a moment, absorbing the news that Soames Pemberton had ended his life in such a horrific way.

"The train hardly runs anymore, except for a late-night delivery of gravel," continued the chief. "Soames obviously knew the train's schedule."

"Did an engineer from the train find him?"

"No. The guy felt a bump and knew they'd hit something, but he didn't stop the train. Apparently there are quite a few deer that roam out that way, and he figured that's what they'd hit. Wasn't the first time, I guess. He forgot all about it. Some guy going to work at the donut shop down the street saw the body and called it in. That was about five-thirty A.M."

"What time does it look like he died?"

"We don't really have to fix the time of death, because we know the train schedule. It's like clockwork at one A.M. every night."

"I heard the train myself around eight P.M.," said Darby. "I guess that was an earlier run."

"Impossible. That train goes once a day."

Darby heard voices in the background and the chief's barked command to someone. He cleared his throat. "The lab report on Lucy's chocolates came back, too. You were right — they were laced with heroin. The case against Soames Pemberton is still shaky at this point, but I think it's safe to say your friend Lucy Trimble is in the clear."

Darby breathed a sigh of relief, thanked the chief, and hung up.

Hoping that she was already awake, she dialed Tina Ames' number with trembling hands.

A stunned Tina listened as Darby relayed the information. "Who would have thought Soames would do that? Toss himself in front of a train?" She shuddered. "You think he was afraid of going back to prison?"

"You knew him better than I did, Tina. He didn't seem suicidal when he was chasing us around the warehouse, I know that."

"No." Tina paused. "On the one hand, I'm not sorry that he's gone. Me and a whole lot of other people can breathe a big sigh of relief. The guy was unhinged and getting worse all the time. He was obviously lying his head off in that warehouse. Said he never went near the Powderkeg . . . Still, I'm going to remember the few good times we had together and say a little prayer for his soul." She sighed and Darby imagined her cocking her head to one side as she had done so many times before.

"So then it's over?" Tina asked. "Soames is dead, Lucy is in the clear, and Peyton's going to get her dream house after all."

"I don't know about that," Darby said. "I'm headed over to the office as soon as I take a shower. We haven't seen an amended purchase and sale from Peyton or her lawyer, so it's going to be tough to have a closing today."

"I'm keeping my fingers crossed. I'm on my way to the office now in case you need me to do anything special."

"I'll see you in a half an hour then." Darby was about to hang up when she posed one more question. "Last night, after we escaped from the warehouse, did you hear a train go by?"

"A train? Hell no. The only thing I could

hear was my heart pounding away, reminding me I was lucky to be alive."

Darby made a pot of coffee before calling Miles Porter at the cottage. His phone rang several times, but Miles did not pick up. *Probably taking a shower,* Darby thought, her cheeks growing hot as she began to picture his muscular body. He'd asked to visit her in Mission Beach. *Maybe then we'll finally move beyond the little pecks on the cheek,* she thought. She imagined his reaction to her little bungalow and smiled. He'd like the beach, and the little restaurants they could walk to together. *Who knows, maybe he'll like California enough to relocate . . .*

She poured a cup of coffee and the strong taste snapped her out of her reverie. *Enough daydreaming,* she told herself sternly. *I've got work to do.*

Darby drove straight to Near & Farr, where Tina was waiting with an envelope in hand and a triumphant smile on her face. "A courier delivered it," she explained. "It's from Peyton's lawyer. Do you think it's the contract for Fairview?"

Quickly Darby tore open the envelope and

surveyed the contents. Sure enough, it was an offer to purchase Fairview at the original price, with a closing date of Saturday. Planning board approval of zoning was to be handled by the buyer once she owned the property. Darby smiled and nodded.

"Hallelujah!" shouted Tina. "That's a good way to start a Thursday, or any day, for that matter."

"You're not kidding. I'm off to get Mark and Lucy to sign this. Do you think they know about Soames' death?"

"It's the top story on the news, so I don't know how you'd miss it. That and a big storm headed up the coast tomorrow. I hope Helen Near doesn't have any problems with her flight."

Darby headed out the office door and noticed her denim jacket hanging on a hook.

"Where'd that come from?"

"You left it in the truck yesterday," Tina said. "I think your phone might be in one of the pockets."

Darby reached in and pulled out her cell phone. The battery was dead but she was relieved nonetheless. "I'm glad to have that off my mind. Thanks, Tina."

"Don't mention it. Hey, Donny called this morning with some interesting news. Looks like Peyton's left the island and her boyfriend, the Italian guy? He's gone missing."

"What do you mean?"

"Donny had to go to the inn last night to fix something in their room. He said it looked like Peyton left the hotel in a hurry with most of her things, but Emilio just plain left. All his clothes are still in the room, but no sign of him."

"Strange. This offer from Peyton is dated yesterday, so she must have been available to her lawyer when he drew it up." She thought a moment more. "I'll try giving Peyton Mayerson a call, just to let her know we're on track for Saturday. In the meantime, keep me posted."

Darby drove Thelma over to the dock where the *Lucy T* was tied up. With the new Fairview offer in hand, she knocked on the side of the boat, listening for Mark Trimble. Hearing nothing, she climbed aboard and looked below deck. The cockpit was closed and the vessel seemed empty.

"Dammit," she swore softly. A blonde head poked from the neighboring vessel and looked around curiously.

"Darby? I thought that sounded like you." Laura Gefferelli emerged from the bottom of *What's in a Name* with a broad smile. "It's nice to see you down here. Please, come aboard and see my little piece of heaven."

Darby hesitated for a moment but then swung a leg over the side and hopped nimbly onto the deck. Laura smiled and indicated a boat cushion and Darby sat down.

"I was just about to have another cup of coffee," Laura said. "Would you join me in a cup?"

Darby agreed and Laura emerged with two plastic cups full of coffee. "Cream? Sugar?" asked Laura.

"Black is fine," Darby said, catching the rich aroma of the coffee.

"To Lucy's freedom," Laura said, raising her coffee cup.

"To Lucy's freedom," echoed Darby. She took a sip. "So you've heard the news?"

"By now the whole island has. I'm praying that Soames didn't suffer." She took a sip of her coffee and looked out over the harbor. "What a sad and troubled soul. At last he's at peace." She sighed. "Is Tina okay? I know they had some history . . ."

"She seems to be. At least for now."

"Good." Laura set down her plastic mug and gave Darby a small smile. "So what brings you over here? Were you looking for Mark?"

"Yes. Any idea when he went out?"

"He sailed in early this morning and left about an hour ago."

Darby tried to hide her irritation.

"What is it?" asked Laura. "Something wrong?"

"Yes. I have a hard time with the fact that his sister's been a murder suspect, and he takes off on his sloop for a few days."

Laura gave a gentle grin. "Darby, we can't judge what others may do under stress. This whole thing has affected Mark in ways we can't even imagine. Going off for a sail may have been exactly what Mark needs to do."

"Time alone to sort things out," Darby said.

Laura smiled again. "I didn't say he was alone." She took another sip of coffee. "He has a new friend, a man named Ryan Oakes. He introduced me to him this morning. He works with an island preservation group. The two of them went out yesterday, I think." She took a look at the sky. "Good thing they came back today. Tomorrow we're going to get some weather."

Darby nodded. "So I hear." She took the last sip of her coffee. "I don't want to bother you on your time off, but is there anything else I need to do for Jane's service?"

"I think we're in good shape," Laura said. "But my notes are at the office. Can we go over the last-minute details this afternoon? Then I can get the program together in the morning and have the church secretary print it in the afternoon."

"Okay," Darby agreed. "I'll call you or come by today." She paused. "If you do see Mark, will you ask him to call me?"

"Sure."

Darby jumped from *What's in a Name* to the dock, noting that her legs remained remarkably steady. *I'm making progress.* She waved goodbye to Laura, still seated in the stern, and contemplated calling Miles on her cell. *Dead as a door nail,* she thought, using one of Aunt Jane's expressions and tossing the phone on the seat. *I need to charge it back at the office.*

Darby drove to Lucy's studio, wondering if she would still be there or setting up for the art show. She was relieved to see Lucy's old sedan in the driveway, the trunk open and waiting for more paintings.

Darby jogged up the rutted pathway and knocked on the door. Lucy opened it with a smile.

"Hey! I was hoping I'd see you. Did you hear about the chocolates? You were right."

"Chief Dupont told me. You must be so relieved."

"I am. I don't like the fact that heroin was in my system again, but at least I know that I didn't ingest it myself, and that's a huge relief." She frowned. "Too bad about Soames. I wish I could have helped him." She indicated the little kitchen table. "Want to sit down?"

"Sure, just for a minute. I know you're busy with the art show."

"Yeah, but I have to say, I feel so free. The burden of knowing there were people who thought I might have killed someone . . ."

"Very few people thought that, Lucy."

"Thanks. So what's up? I know my friend Darby Farr. You're on a social call, but with an agenda."

"You got me there. I just received a new offer from Peyton. She still wants to buy Fairview, at the same price, and close on Saturday. I haven't seen your brother yet, but what do you think?"

"Terrific. What about those restrictions?"

"She and her lawyer are going to worry about it once they've purchased the property. My guess is they've already been assured that they can be changed."

"Wow. Mark will be thrilled. Where do I sign?"

Once Lucy had looked over the agreement and signed it, Darby helped her carry a few

331

canvasses to the car. "I'm off to find your brother now," she said.

"He may actually be at Fairview," Lucy said. "I can't make myself go over there, but he said he was going to check that everything was okay."

Darby drove Thelma over to Fairview, wishing as she was driving the winding roads that she was out for a run. She looked uneasily at the woods in which her dream had taken place. It had given her the creeps to see Soames' face like that, especially now that she knew he was dead.

She wound her way down the driveway and came around the bend to see the grand old house in all its glory. Mark Trimble's car was parked in front, along with a small compact car bearing a bumper sticker for the "Maine Island Association."

She slowed to a walk at the front door, hearing voices.

"Hello?" she called out.

"Hey, we're in here," yelled Mark Trimble. He was talking animatedly to someone and sounded very cheerful. A moment later he greeted her at the door.

"Darby! You're up bright and early! I was just going to call you. You heard the news about Soames? Lucy's totally in the clear.

It's great." Grinning, he pulled her from the hallway into the living room of his old home. "There's somebody I'd like you to meet. This is Ryan — Ryan Oakes. He's the head of the Island Association. Have you heard of them? They work to keep islands like ours from becoming too Disney-fied, right Ryan?"

Ryan Oakes smiled and shook Darby's hand.

"Actually, we try to help keep what is special about working islands functioning," he said. "I'm pleased to meet you, Darby. Mark has told me so much about you. I know he's very grateful for what you've done for his sister." Ryan looked at Mark who shook his head emphatically.

"Absolutely. She's off the hook. Soames Pemberton killed Phipps and now the radio's reporting that he's killed himself to boot." He clasped his hands together, reminding Darby of a little boy with too much energy.

"So, thanks to you, Darby, Lucy's back to her normal life on Hurricane Harbor. I've got to say, there was a little too much action for a small place like this."

Darby wanted to question Mark concerning his role with providing Soames Pemberton with the deed, but knew that now was not the time. Instead she said, "I have some news about the sale of Fairview, Mark. Can we talk?"

Mark looked at Ryan and then back at Darby. "I told Ryan all about it, so shoot. What's up?"

"A courier delivered an offer from Peyton and her partners this morning. Same terms with a closing on Saturday. I've just come from Lucy's studio; she reviewed the offer and signed it. I've brought it along for you to take a look at and sign as well." She added, "I'm sure you and your sister will be happy to see this chapter close."

Mark Trimble squirmed and again Darby was reminded of a child.

"Umm . . . yeah. So Peyton is definitely buying the house? On Saturday?"

"That's the plan. Why?"

Mark gestured toward Ryan. "I've been thinking this would be a great headquarters for Ryan's organization," he said. "You know, a place for them to have meetings, retreats, and entertain rich donors." He laughed. "People like me, right?"

Ryan Oakes smiled. "As I've already explained to Mark, we don't have the funds for our own building, much less one like Fairview. Our current office is in Manatuck, over the Natural Foods store. Someday, though, a place like this would be ideal. It's certainly fun to dream about."

Darby nodded. "It's a lovely spot." She fixed her attention back on Mark. He needed to understand that he had a deal with Peyton Mayerson. She didn't like his thinking he could switch gears now and dangle Fairview in front of some brand-new friend who couldn't afford a rundown ranch, never mind an estate. Unfortunately, Mark was far too adept at changing buyers. *Not this time,* she vowed.

"Let's take a look at this together." She pulled the offer from the envelope and moved closer to Mark.

He glanced at it quickly. "She let go of the old deed restrictions?"

Darby nodded, not trusting herself to say more. She was still angry over Soames' revelation that Mark had known all about it, but wasn't going to bring it up in front of Ryan Oakes.

"Same money she was originally offering?"

"That's right."

Mark reached in his pocket for a pen and scribbled his signature on the last page. "Hard to believe it's really going to happen this time."

"I know."

Darby extended her arm toward Ryan Oakes and shook his hand. "Nice to meet you. Good luck with the Island Association."

"Thank you," he said.

Mark gave Darby a wave. "See you," he said breezily.

Mark's dismissive goodbye couldn't dampen Darby's spirits. She felt the surge of adrenalin she always experienced when she put a real estate deal together. *It's going to happen, Aunt Jane,* she said silently. *Even if I have to stay here until next week.*

She drove back to Near & Farr and called Miles with the news of Soames' death.

"The dragon has been slain and the village is safe," he said. "Not exactly slain, but close enough."

"There are certainly people who will sleep a little easier knowing he can't darken their door again," Darby agreed. "Tina Ames, for one." Darby looked out the window to the street where Tina was emerging with a coffee and a Diet Coke. "I had a strange dream last night."

"Was it about me?" Miles teased.

"No."

"Then I don't know if I want to hear about it. Well, all right, you may tell me."

Darby laughed. "No, I think you're right.

It isn't worth retelling. Instead, I'm going to ask you to a meal for once. How about lunch with me today?"

There was a pause from Miles. "I'm afraid I must decline, Darby. I've been summoned to Boston, on business, and am leaving in a few minutes. I'll be back late tomorrow night or very early Saturday for your aunt's service."

"Oh," Darby said lightly, as a wave of disappointment washed over her. *Get a grip,* she told herself sternly. *You've got work to do.* She made an effort to keep her tone as light as possible. "See you Saturday, then, Miles. Drive safely."

THIRTEEN

After hanging up with Miles, Darby checked her watch and decided it was a good time to call ET in California. It was just after eleven A.M. in Maine, so with the three-hour time difference, her able assistant would be up and working, most likely in his silk bathrobe and slippers.

The phone rang only once before she recognized his melodic voice on the other end.

"Darby! I was hoping it was you . . . have you sold the lovely Fairview yet?"

Quickly Darby filled him in on the events of the past few days, concluding with the good news she'd received via courier that morning.

"We're scheduled to close on Saturday afternoon," she said, "with Aunt Jane's service in the morning. I'm changing my flights to Monday. I didn't plan on staying here so long, ET, but I've got to see this through."

ET made a sympathetic noise. "I understand completely. How about the sister of Mark Trimble — Lucy? — is she cleared of murder charges?"

"Yes, thank goodness." Darby sighed. "She's free, and the man who killed Emerson Phipps is no longer a threat to anyone. Last night he committed suicide."

"Quite a lot happening on such a small island. The service for your aunt can now proceed without the shadow of an unsolved murder, correct?"

"I hadn't thought about it that way, but you're right. I guess it is finally time to put the murder at Fairview in the past and focus on my final duty here." She paused. "Enough about Maine. What's going on at the office?"

ET told Darby that several of her listings were seeing increased activity, and that he expected an offer on at least one home by the weekend. "I have signed up a new client, a couple from London, and they are scheduled to meet with you next week. And now are you ready? I've saved the best piece of news for last," he teased.

"I could use some good news, ET. Tell me it's the Costa Brava property?"

"It's the Costa Brava property, all right.

That buyer who was nosing around early in the month has decided to put in a full-price offer. The sellers are thrilled and it looks like this is one mansion that will definitely be sold."

"Fantastic. I really should go away more often."

After saying goodbye, Darby decided on impulse to try Peyton Mayerson's cell phone again. *If she's not on the island, then where is she? She needs to know that Lucy and Mark have signed that purchase and sale . . .*

Darby searched through her contacts and found Peyton's number. Soon she heard the recorded voice of Peyton asking her to leave a message, which she did, along with her own cell phone number. Moments later, to her amazement, her phone rang.

Darby expected the caller to be Peyton Mayerson; instead, it was a man's voice who asked for her.

"Ms. Farr? We've been trying to reach you at your aunt's home."

"Who is this?"

"I'm sorry — this is Special Agent Edward Landis, FBI."

"FBI? What's this about?"

"It's a long story, one that's best explained off island. We'd like to pick you up, Ms.

Farr. To talk."

"Pick me up?"

"We have a helicopter waiting at a private airstrip on the island. Do you know the Merewether estate?"

Darby was dumbfounded but still able to speak. "Yes. I know it."

"You can leave your vehicle on the property. Agents Cooper and Cardazzo are waiting for you there. Bring an overnight bag — we've reserved a hotel room at the Ritz Carlton in Boston for you."

"Just what is this about?"

"I really can't explain over the phone. My agents can come and get you at your office, or you can meet them here. Either way, we need your cooperation."

"How do I know this is legitimate?"

"Good question. The agents will have their credentials and you can verify them on site."

Darby said she would arrive at the Merewether estate in ten minutes. She hung up, the strange conversation replaying in her head. *Had the FBI contacted her because of her message to Peyton Mayerson?*

Tina opened the office door, her hands full of containers. In addition to the beverages she'd purchased at the store, she'd gone to the Café and bought a few sandwiches.

"Are you as hungry as me?" asked Tina. "Hope so." She looked at Darby and gave a look of concern. "You okay?"

"Well, I thought I was fine — that is, until that last phone call. You're not going to believe this, but I'm on my way to the Merewether estate where a helicopter is waiting to take me to an FBI meeting in Boston."

"No way!" said Tina. "What in the world is that about?"

"I don't know, and the agent wouldn't say over the phone. If I had to guess, I'd say it has to do with Peyton Mayerson."

"Should I work on those closing documents?"

"Absolutely. Until we know otherwise, the sale of Fairview is on. And until we know why I'm headed to Boston, please don't say anything about this trip. No sense in getting Mark or Lucy upset when we don't have a clue what's happening."

"Agreed."

Tina placed the sandwiches on a nearby desk and snapped her fingers. "I nearly forgot — the Café owner said she's all set with the food for the memorial service." She paused. "You will be back from Boston, right?"

Darby nodded. "I'm staying over tonight,

but I'll be back tomorrow. Good thing we made the service for Saturday and not Friday." She thought a moment. "I'm staying at the Ritz Carlton if you need me, although I don't have my room number." She frowned. "What about Helen Near? Have you heard when she's arriving?"

"Tomorrow. Don't worry, I'll send Donny to Portland to get her if she needs transportation." Tina lowered her voice. "Do you think this means that Peyton Mayerson is a genuine crook? I can't say I'd be surprised . . ." She reached for a sandwich, tore off the wrapping and bit into it. Glancing back at Darby while she chewed, she made a sheepish face. "Sorry, but I'm starving." She reached for the other sandwich and thrust it at Darby. "Do me a favor and bring this one with you. You're turning into a skeleton!"

The Merewether estate was on the opposite end of the island from Fairview and was not, in Darby's estimation, as impressive a structure. Built in the same time period but "renovated" in the 1950s, the building sported several ungainly additions that obscured its once graceful lines. A cedar playset in the yard along with a sandbox made Darby pause. Perhaps Merewether wasn't beautiful, but it looked well-loved.

Darby drove the truck to the rear of the property where a black car and two dark-suited men wearing sunglasses were waiting. A helicopter waited on the lawn behind them. Darby parked and walked toward the car. The men introduced themselves as Special Agents Cooper and Cardazzo and each showed her a wallet-sized leather case that held their badges.

Darby scrutinized the badges. They certainly looked authentic, with the imposing Federal Bureau of Investigation insignia. Nevertheless, she was not about to get in a helicopter with two strange men just because their identification looked plausible.

"I need more proof, fellows."

The men glanced at each other and produced their FBI identification badges. Darby scrutinized the photos and handed them back. "I'm still not going," she said.

The agent called Cardazzo shuffled his feet impatiently and frowned. Agent Cooper looked more sympathetic.

"Here," he offered, handing her his cell phone. "This is the number of the bureau. Give them our credential numbers." Darby took the phone and called. Soon the voice on the other end verified that George Cooper and David Cardazzo were indeed

FBI Special Agents.

Darby frowned. She called directory assistance for the bureau's number and waited to connect. She then asked for the field office location for the two agents. Moments later, she spoke with someone named Thomas Gray, who verified the agents' whereabouts on Hurricane Harbor, Maine. Satisfied, Darby handed back the phone and allowed the men to escort her to the helicopter.

The machine's pilot waved as Darby got in and signaled that they were about to take off. Darby buckled her seat belt and felt a sensation she'd experienced previously only in elevators or at carnival rides as the chopper lifted. She saw the Merewether estate become smaller, and then watched in wonder as the coastline of Hurricane Harbor came into view. She saw the cove where she'd played as a girl, the Yacht Club, the harbor, and even the ferry going across the water to Manatuck. Seen from above, all of it was beautiful.

"Great view," she shouted to the agents. They remained quiet, seemingly content to accompany Darby to her mysterious meeting and no more. When she tried to ask them about Peyton Mayerson, they shook their heads politely and frowned.

"We're not at liberty to discuss anything," said Agent Cardazzo. The helicopter's whirring blades made a deafening roar, and Darby decided she wouldn't be able to hear him even if he did have information.

An hour later Darby spotted the winding Charles River and Boston Harbor, flanked by tall silver skyscrapers. The chopper circled by a building and landed smoothly on the rooftop. Agents Cardazzo and Cooper helped Darby out, carrying her duffel bag, and indicating that she should follow them into the building. The quietness of the carpeted hallway was in stark contrast to the noise of the helicopter, and when Darby spoke, her voice sounded very loud.

"Where are we going?"

"Right here," said one of the men. "We appreciate your patience, Ms. Farr. We haven't been able to give you any information, but I think you'll have all your questions answered by Agent Landis."

They opened the door of a conference room and Darby stepped inside. Two men were talking quietly but both stopped as she entered. One of them came forward and introduced himself as Thomas Gray from Washington, D.C. "We spoke only minutes ago. And I believe you already know Agent Landis?"

Darby was about to correct him when the other man turned and faced her. He flashed a boyish grin and Darby recognized Peyton Mayerson's handsome Italian boyfriend.

"Signor Landi," she said. *"Come sta?"*

He gave a little bow. *"Bene, grazie."* He then added, without a trace of an Italian accent, "At your service."

"So you're not . . ."

"Italian?" he asked. "Actually I do have some Sicilian blood back there somewhere. I'm afraid I learned the language just for this assignment. Luckily Peyton's mastery of Italian is even worse than mine, so she never caught on to my obvious grammatical mistakes." He shook Darby's hand. "Ed Landis, Special Agent, FBI. My focus is Organized Crime."

He indicated a table with a pitcher of water, four glasses, and four chairs. "Please, have a seat."

As soon as Darby was seated, Thomas Gray and Ed Landis settled themselves. Darby noticed that Agents Cooper and Cardazzo had disappeared.

"Now that you know who I am, I'd like to get straight to the point." He opened a file and showed Darby a photograph of a woman with blonde hair who bore a striking resemblance to Peyton Mayerson.

"We've been following this woman — her real name is Penelope Mancuzzi — for five years, but it wasn't until I went undercover and met her in Rome that we made any inroads. She's the sister of a mob boss in New Jersey but has made all her connections on the North shore of Massachusetts, in the Charlestown area. Penelope — you know her as Peyton — is in so deep that her life is in danger."

He paused, as if to let the seriousness of his words sink in.

"We know that Peyton believes she is buying a property in Maine known as Fairview from your clients Mark and Lucy Trimble." Agent Landis looked to Darby for clarification and she nodded.

Here we go again, she thought. *Another Fairview deal out the window . . .*

To Agent Landis, she said, "I was informed through her attorney that the closing would take place on Saturday. I imagine that's not going to happen, given what you're telling me."

"On the contrary," said Ed Landis, shaking his head emphatically. "It's imperative that Peyton Mayerson purchases that property on Saturday and that she suspects nothing." Beside him, his companion Thomas Gray concurred and cleared his throat.

"Basically, Ms. Farr, our whole case collapses if she does not buy Fairview. But if you can keep this deal together, we'll not only have her as the accomplice of these mob guys, but we'll get them on money laundering and racketeering, possibly even counterfeiting."

Darby shook her head. "What about Mark and Lucy Trimble? Will they in fact have sold the property, or is this one big sting operation?"

Ed Landis gave a quick glance at the other man before speaking.

"Technically, the sale of Fairview will not have occurred, unless you want the property seized by the federal government."

Darby exhaled. "You're saying that we should prepare all the documents for Saturday's closing. Then we'll watch Peyton — excuse me, Penelope — and her cronies leave my office in handcuffs, and then we'll head back to Fairview and put out another 'For Sale' sign? What about my time? What about my secretary's time? What about my clients?"

Ed Landis paused and gave Darby an appraising glance. "Believe me, your clients are lucky this deal will not get a chance to go through. In fact, the whole island is fortunate. Mancuzzi and her so-called investors were planning to push through the bridge to the mainland, which, as you know, would have made the Fairview property a prime commercial location."

"Commercial?"

"Yes. They had plans for all kinds of development — shopping centers, a water park, some sort of casino — and whether it would have succeeded or not wasn't even something they considered. It was all an elaborate scheme to launder funds from other, illegal operations in the Boston area. Luckily for Hurricane Harbor, the sting operation will end before they get a chance to irreversibly change the island."

"So the wedding idea . . . ?

"Pemberton Point Weddings? It's total baloney. A front. Believe me, the last thing these guys think about is running any kind of viable business. Given the chance, they'll sell off the lots and split, just like they have done in other places. They don't let anything stand in the way of their dealings, either."

He frowned. "Listen, I don't like the way this is going to impact you or your clients either, but I thought you should know the facts. For obvious reasons, I couldn't make this meeting happen on Hurricane Harbor." He sighed. "We're not interested in owning Fairview, so I hope your clients will understand the need for this charade. Although, like everyone else but you, they won't know it is a charade until it's over."

Darby grabbed her pocketbook and prepared to leave. "I don't like duping anyone, Mr. Landis, particularly not my clients. I've got a fiduciary relationship with the Trimbles, my chief duty to them being honesty. How can I let them think their property is selling when it isn't?"

"I'm sorry." Ed Landis' voice had a hard edge. "I think when you've had a chance to reflect, you'll see that this investigation takes precedence over your duties as an agent. That's all I can say."

He thrust a business card into her hand. "Don't hesitate to call me with any other questions," he said gruffly. Then his voice softened. "My condolences on the death of your aunt. She had a keen intelligence, and had she lived, I think she might have guessed that I was not a genuine *paisan*." He smiled and reminded Darby of his portrayal of the affable Emilio Landi. "Enjoy your night at the Ritz — you've certainly earned it. We've got a rental car at the hotel for you to use while you are in Boston, and you can drive it back to Hurricane Harbor, too." He lifted his hands. "Unless you'd like to go back to the island now via chopper."

Still frustrated, Darby walked toward the door. "No, I'll take my night in Boston, thank you. Just one more question, Mr. Landis: could Peyton Mayerson — or Penelope Mancuzzi — have killed Emerson Phipps?"

Ed Landis shook his head. "Absolutely not. I tracked her every movement while she was on that island, and there is no way she was involved in the murder."

He paused. "We do know she was in Lucy Trimble's home the day after Phipps died, and we know all about the paintings she stole. They are on their way back to Lucy Trimble and should arrive next week. She's a thief, all right, and a heck of a lot of other things, but so far at least, Penelope Mancuzzi is not a murderer."

Darby had to admit that her suite at the Ritz Carlton was topnotch. *It's the least that Ed Landis can do,* she thought. She stretched out on the silk covers of the king-sized bed, the daily paper spread before her, and replayed her meeting with the FBI agents over in her mind. The idea of keeping the "charade" a secret from the Trimbles or Tina was repulsive to Darby. And yet there seemed no other way.

She flipped through the newspaper in a

halfhearted manner, taking occasional bites of the somewhat-squished sandwich Tina had supplied her with hours earlier. In the Society Section, she spotted a short mention of a dedication taking place at Boston Memorial Hospital the following morning. *Boston Memorial was where Emerson Phipps had practiced,* she remembered. She browsed through the rest of the paper, and before she realized it, she'd fallen asleep.

Forty-five minutes later she was awakened by the ring of the hotel telephone. She cleared the cobwebs from her head and answered the phone.

"So the rumor is true! You're on my turf tonight."

"Miles! It's nice to hear your voice. How did you find me?"

"I tried to reach you in Maine, and Tina told me about your helicopter ride to the Ritz."

Darby laughed. "I didn't take the helicopter to the Ritz, and Tina's supposed to keep her mouth shut. I have to say, though, this whole thing gets more and more confusing as time goes on."

"Why don't you tell me all about it over dinner? I'd love to take you to my favorite French restaurant here in Beantown."

Darby agreed and Miles offered to meet

her in the hotel lobby at 7:30. "What will you do in the meantime?" he asked, "It's only three o'clock."

"I think I'll give Alicia Komolsky a call. She was Emerson Phipps' sister, and I just want to touch base with her. Perhaps I can meet her for tea somewhere."

"That's a nice gesture. I'm looking forward to hearing all about your adventures tonight."

Darby found Alicia Komolsky's phone number and her cell phone. Groaning, she realized it was still dead and that she had forgotten to bring her charger. Tossing it back into the overnight bag, she used the hotel's phone to call Alicia. An answering machine picked up and Darby left a message with the Ritz Carlton's phone number. She then treated herself to a long, hot shower in the hotel's luxurious bathroom. When she emerged, refreshed and energized, she felt like a totally new woman.

The phone rang as she was toweling off her long hair.

"This is Alicia," a hesitant voice said. "Alicia Komolsky."

Darby explained that she was in Boston for the evening. "I was thinking about you and your boys. How are you doing? Perhaps we could meet for tea somewhere and chat?"

Alicia sniffed. "That's very kind of you, Darby. I am — we are — we're coping, that's about it. The boys miss their uncle so much already, and I — well I lost a good friend as well as a brother." She swallowed. "It's definitely very hard."

Darby mentioned that she had been on the hospital website and read a tribute to Emerson Phipps.

"Those words have given me a lot of comfort. Several of his patients have called me as well, describing what a wonderful doctor he was. And tomorrow, Friday, they are having a ceremony and adding Emerson's name to the hospital's Remembrance Wall." She paused a moment. "Did you say you are in Boston?"

"I did. I'm here overnight at the Ritz Carlton."

"This may be too much to ask, but I would love for you to come to the ceremony honoring my brother. Of course — if you are too busy —"

"What time is the ceremony?"

"Eleven o'clock."

Darby thought quickly. If she left the ceremony by noon, she'd be back on the island by late afternoon. That would give her time to visit with Helen Near and take care of any last-minute chores before the memorial service on the following day.

"I'd love to come. Shall I meet you there?"

"That would be wonderful. You can meet Sam and Michael, too."

"Great. I will see you at the hospital, then."

Darby hung up, feeling torn. She didn't want to pay tribute to the man who had raped her friend Lucy, and yet she believed that memorial services were really for the living. *His sister had nothing to do with the ugly parts of his personality. And she certainly had nothing to do with his murder . . .*

Darby plugged in the hotel's blow dryer and began to dry her hair. Emerson Phipps was a young college student when he'd forced Lucy Trimble to have sex. *Perhaps he'd regretted that action. Perhaps he had spent his adult life doing good works because of that one evil . . .*

She thought again about Emerson Phipps' sister. Alicia seemed to be truly devastated with the murder. How close had the siblings really been? *She is the only beneficiary of his estate. She stands to inherit not only his money, but his posh condominium, that pricey BMW . . .*

Had Alicia Komolsky known about her brother's obsession with Fairview? Darby thought back. She remembered the tearful woman saying her brother had been fascinated by the property. Was it likely that she'd known about his planned trip to Maine to purchase it?

Darby willed herself to stop her mind from spiraling out of control. *What is wrong with me? Why can't I accept that the case is closed and that the perpetrator is dead. Next thing I know, I'll be pinning this murder on Aunt Jane . . .*

Slowly she put down the hair dryer and looked in the mirror at her reflection. The raw pain caused by thinking about her aunt was etched across her face. *She's dead,* she thought. *She's really gone. And no matter what Tina says, I will never be able to make my peace with her.*

Darby dressed for dinner in a kind of a trance. She wondered if her inability to accept closure with Emerson Phipps' murder was really a way for her to avoid facing Jane Farr's death. In her dream, she'd known there was someone else under Soames' mask. Could that person have been Aunt Jane? Was the dream not about Emerson Phipps' murder, but about the true underlying demon Darby Farr had to face?

She pulled a rose-colored sweater set over her head and paired it with a slim gray skirt and gray flats. Surveying herself in the mirror, she thought she could detect a new calmness that she hadn't seen in days. *There's one more thing to do,* she thought, finding her cell phone. *I need to call Laura Gefferelli and make sure my aunt's memorial service is a fitting tribute.*

With her cell phone still useless, Darby dialed out on the hotel phone. *The FBI is paying the tab,* she realized. *I ought to see what's in the mini-bar . . .*

Laura Gefferelli offered several suggestions of readings and passages that complemented Jane Farr's character. "This will be a large gathering," she warned Darby. "Your aunt touched the lives of so many here on the island. She really was a legend. And after what you've done to help catch Soames Pemberton and solve this murder, well, the whole island and half of Manatuck are likely to come."

Darby smiled, thinking that her aunt would have loved being the center of a huge gathering. "I've prepared something to read," she said. "Maybe after Helen does her tribute?"

"Of course."

Darby and the minister discussed several other aspects of the service, including flowers, music, and the program. Darby told her that the Café was catering a simple lunch that would take place in the church's gathering room. When she and Laura Gefferelli finished, Darby was satisfied.

"Thank you so much for all of your help, Laura. I think it sounds like it will be a lovely service. I'm in Boston, but I'll check in with you when I get back tomorrow."

"Boston? What are you up to there?"

"It's a long story, but I'm here overnight and on the road tomorrow by one P.M. or so. I'm having dinner with Miles Porter, and tomorrow I'm meeting Alicia Komolsky, Emerson Phipps' sister, at the hospital where he worked. They are having some sort of memorial service for him and I told her I'd attend."

"I see," said Laura. "Did you drive down? Be careful coming back tomorrow — there's bound to be traffic and stormy weather is on the way."

"Good point. I'm in a rental car, and I'll be sure to take it slow."

They said goodbye and Darby grabbed her purse and locked her room. It was not quite four P.M., but she wanted to walk around the Public Garden before meeting Miles. Feeling more peaceful than she had since leaving California, Darby Farr went out the hotel's revolving door, intent on tak-

359

ing a leisurely stroll through the heart of Boston.

Miles was waiting in the lobby as she re-entered the hotel. He glanced up and smiled.

"Where have you been?" he asked with a grin.

"Taking a walk and window shopping," said Darby.

"I see. Ready to fill me in on all the details of your mysterious helicopter trip?"

"No," she said. "Actually, I'm ready to forget all about that and have a good time with you."

"I get it. Mum's the word. I can definitely deal with that."

Darby and Miles laughed, ate, drank, and talked their way through a marvelous meal, capped off by a perfect crème brulee.

"Well? Is my little restaurant as good as the home-cooked fare you remember?" teased Miles.

"Definitely. My mother would have loved this place. I can just imagine her asking to meet the chef, and then questioning him about his techniques . . ." She smiled. "She was always trying to unlock the secret of the perfect crème brulee." She grew pensive.

"You know Miles, some mysteries are just not meant to be solved, are they?"

"Are you thinking about the murder of Emerson Phipps?"

"No — my parents' disappearance. I've spent years wishing that someone, somehow, would tell me how and why they vanished on that August day all those years ago. In some ways, I think I hung on to the hope that they would actually reappear."

"That's a normal reaction to death, isn't it?" he asked gently. "What about your aunt? Did she try to help you with your grief?"

"My aunt knew that I wasn't accepting it. Today they call my behavior 'denial,' right? In Jane's blunt and straightforward way, she tried to get me to face the fact that they were gone. Of course, I hated her for that."

"Maybe it was easier to hate her than to accept your loss?" Miles' voice was very kind.

Darby nodded. "I think you're right. It hurt less to be angry with Jane Farr than to grieve for my parents." She sighed. "I realized this afternoon that I was doing it all over again."

"What do you mean?"

"Avoiding the pain of a loss, only this time it is Aunt Jane's death that I'm trying to evade."

Miles placed his hand over Darby's. "In the newspaper business, we say knowing is the first step. Now you know. You'll figure it out. I know you will."

Darby smiled. "Thanks."

Miles walked Darby back to the Ritz Carlton while a warm June wind floated the scent of roses from the nearby Public Garden. Darby looked up at the beautiful old hotel and then back at Miles wistfully. "Miles, I would ask you to come up, but —"

He reached and very tenderly put a finger against her lips. "Our time will come." His voice was as soft as the breeze ruffling the flags outside the lobby. "This evening was a wonderful surprise for which I'm extremely grateful. This was a perfect gem of a night."

He kissed her on the cheek. "I'll be in touch with you, Darby Farr. We'll take it slow."

"Slow," she murmured. "Slow would be good."

"I'm coming up to Maine for the day early on Saturday, for your aunt's service. I'm happy to help you with anything you need."

"You don't have to drive up for that, Miles."

"I know I don't have to," he said. "I'd like to."

She nodded, feeling a rush of gratitude for the handsome, intelligent, and caring man who'd somehow dropped into her life. "I'll see you Saturday, then. It will be wonderful to have a friend there."

FOURTEEN

Cocooned in her quiet room and comfortable bed at the Ritz Carlton Hotel, Darby slept deeply and dreamlessly. She arose feeling refreshed, looked at the clock on the bedside table, and decided she had time for a quick run around Boston Common.

The air was warm and soft. *A perfect June Friday,* Darby thought, enjoying the warmth of the sun on her face and bare arms as she ran. The swan boats in the Public Garden were gliding back and forth, and a few mothers were already out with their babies, pushing strollers down the winding paths.

After logging three miles through the Common and around Beacon Hill, Darby bought a muffin and coffee from a little shop by the hotel. Once back at her suite, she took a quick shower, gave her room a once-over to be sure she'd packed everything, and took the elevator to the lobby.

The desk clerk handed her a key to a

rental car and indicated which part of the parking garage she would find the vehicle. "Pretty nice one, too," he confided. "Not a scratch on her."

Darby accepted directions to Boston Memorial Hospital and took the elevator to the parking garage. She located the car — a brand-new Chrysler Sebring — without much difficulty and was soon navigating Boston's old thoroughfares. After only one misstep, she pulled into the parking lot of the hospital by the visitor's entrance. Out of habit, she thought of checking her cell phone for messages, frowning as she remembered that it was stuffed inside her overnight bag, useless.

"Rats," Darby said to herself. "No business calls for me today. I'll be listening to the radio on the way home."

She locked the car and entered the hospital's gleaming welcome area. Boston Memorial was massive, a series of old brick buildings connected with newer additions, many of them constructed in an airy, atrium style. Darby paused a moment to admire a striking sculpture in the foyer of the main entrance. It was a tangle of geometric shapes that reminded Darby of an angel bestowing mercy on a patient. She wondered if anyone else would come to this interpretation, especially given that the title of the work was "Working Waterfront." She smiled and thought of Lucy and her paintings back on the island. Perhaps some of Lucy's patrons bought her paintings never knowing they represented a healing from pain.

The lobby was surprisingly quiet, more of a funnel to other parts of the hospital than a waiting room. Darby located a receptionist who directed her toward the ceremony. "We all loved Dr. Phipps," she said sadly. "Such a shame to lose a great surgeon like him."

Darby nodded and took the elevator to the second floor. A brightly lit corridor led to a lobby where a number of hospital staff as well as dozens of well-dressed Bostonians were milling around, drinking orange juice. A woman turned and smiled. It was Alicia Komolsky, flanked by two dark-haired boys in matching suits and ties.

"Darby! You're here. I'm so glad you came." She turned to her sons with pride. "This is Samuel, and this is Michael." Both stuck out their hands for shaking and said in a pleasant, but automatic way, "Pleased to meet you," while their mother looked on, beaming. She gave the boys a nod and they rushed to a table laden with brunch items as if released from jail.

"Your boys are so much more grown-up than in the photo you showed me on the island," said Darby.

"Oh yes," Alicia beamed. "Haven't they just grown a ton! Emerson would be amazed." She paused and managed with difficulty to keep her emotions in check. "This ceremony is going to be so hard," she whispered.

Darby took her hand and thought about her aunt's memorial service, scheduled for the next day. "I know," she said. She glanced around the room. "There sure are a lot of white coats around here."

Alicia nodded quickly and smiled, grateful for the distraction. "Aren't there? Many are doctors who worked with Emerson here at the hospital, and a few of them went on the Haiti trips with him."

"With Surgeons Who Serve?"

"Exactly." A tall man in a tailored suit entered the room and Alicia brightened. "Excuse me, Darby."

"Certainly." Darby watched as Alicia hurried to the newcomer and they greeted each other, then hugged. She saw them talk animatedly and Alicia's quick smile as she pointed out her sons to the man.

Was this a love interest for Alicia Phipps

Komolsky? Darby found herself thinking again of Phipps' murder. Would a lover have given Alicia any more reason to want her brother out of the picture?

Stop it, she chided herself. She walked over to the buffet table and selected a small serving of fruit salad and a bran muffin. *Perhaps if you put something in your stomach you'll stop seeing murderers around every corner,* Darby thought.

After a few moments, the ceremony began.

Several administrators from the hospital spoke about Phipps' career and his surgical accomplishments at the hospital. A gray-haired doctor in a lab coat described an operation he and Phipps had performed on a Haitian girl last year, and read a letter from her mother praising Dr. Emerson Phipps. Darby saw a few of the nurses dabbing their eyes with a tissue at the mother's gratitude.

Moments later, Alicia Phipps Komolsky stepped up to the microphone and pulled out a piece of paper.

She began by thanking everyone for coming and for honoring her brother. She briefly mentioned his career and her pride in his selfless devotion to medicine in the Third World. She then said she had two announcements to make.

"First, on behalf of my brother, I would like to announce a gift in the amount of $100,000 to the Coveside Clinic on Hurricane Harbor in Maine." She smiled at Darby and continued. "My brother loved this remote corner of New England and I know he would have wanted a part of his estate to benefit the good people who live and work on that island."

Impressed, Darby listened to the polite applause. Surely the gift had not been Phipps' idea, but his sister's. *What an act of kindness,* she thought.

Alicia Komolsky waited for the clapping to abate before continuing. "Second, I take great pride in announcing a gift in the amount of $500,000 to Boston Memorial Hospital, earmarked for the new spinal surgery wing. If my late brother were here, I know he would be spearheading the campaign for this new, state-of-the-art center." She paused and again the onlookers clapped appreciatively. "Finally, I would like to introduce my sons, Samuel and Michael Phipps Komolsky, who have another exciting announcement to make."

The boys bounded to the microphone and their mother gave them an indulgent smile. Samuel elbowed his brother for the spotlight. "One million dollars to Surgeons Who

Serve!" he shouted. The audience laughed, and then clapped. The man with whom Alicia had been speaking looked momentarily stunned. He approached the microphone as if in a daze, introduced himself as the president of SWS, and gave Alicia and her boys a big smile.

"I am truly overwhelmed at this generosity," he said. "We will miss Dr. Phipps and his medical missions, but this money will surely continue his good efforts." The onlookers clapped loudly as the SWS president hugged Alicia and her sons.

In her head, Darby tallied up the donations. Alicia Komolsky had just given away $1.6 million of her brother's estate.

A moment later she was at Darby's side, giggling. "That was amazing," she said. "Giving away that much money! What a rush!" She smiled. "Trust me, my brother is probably rolling around in his grave."

"What do you mean?"

She blushed. "He could be generous with his skills and time, but he hated to part with money," she said. "I look at it this way: I'll sell his condo and car and put the proceeds in a trust for the boys. I think that's what Emerson would have wanted. The rest of his estate — what do I need that much money for? I'm happy already."

Darby smiled. "Philanthropy becomes you, Alicia. I'm so glad I was here to see you make those donations."

She beamed. "Me too." Glancing toward the microphone, she said, "The ceremony is almost over. The hospital staff adds his name to their honor roll, something like that."

After a few more moments of elaboration on Emerson Phipps' surgical brilliance, everyone clapped again and the program was over.

"Darby, thank you for coming," said Alicia. "I'm so glad you were here." She motioned toward the window where the courtyard trees were moving with the breeze. "There's a storm coming up the coast. If you leave now, you'll probably beat it."

Darby hugged Alicia and waved to the boys, who were tussling over a plastic chair in the corner. She made her way through the crowd of people, heading toward the door she came in. The administrator who had taken the microphone at one point grabbed her elbow and wheeled around.

"You're going to miss it," she said cheerily. "If you go out that way, you're going to miss our Wall of Remembrance. It's over here."

The woman walked purposefully toward another door, leading Darby by the arm in her direction. In the hallway was a large bronze plaque.

"See?" She pointed with a pudgy finger adorned with peach nail polish. "There's our dear Dr. Phipps."

Darby looked dutifully at the name etched in the metal. Emerson S. Phipps, III.

"Wasn't that fabulous that he gave all that money to SWS?" The administrator had wonder in her voice. "He was quite a man."

His sister donated that money, Darby thought, although she nodded in agreement. *Your dear doctor Phipps was a rapist. A rapist who perhaps did some truly good things in his life . . .*

Darby was happy that Alicia could remember her brother fondly without knowing about Lucy and the pain he had caused her. Instead, she would have the legacy of his involvement with Boston Memorial and SWS, and the joy with which donating his money to worthy causes could bring.

The sound of a throat clearing brought Darby back to the present. The administrator was looking at her expectantly.

Darby thanked the woman for showing her the memorial plaque. Pointing at Emerson Phipps' name, she added, "I know it means a lot to his sister, Alicia, that he is honored in this way."

The stout woman nodded. "That's why we do it," she said. "Means so much to the families." She nodded and made way for others to step closer, among them, a pretty ponytailed nurse in light blue scrubs.

"I was in the ER with him the night before he died," she told Darby, sniffling at the memory.

Darby glanced up. The young woman bit her lip and managed a small smile. "I'm Amanda. Amanda Barnes. I actually thought Dr. Phipps was hitting on me, but then, he did that to all of the nurses."

"Why was he here?"

"I paged him to come in because the on-call doctor was in surgery, and there was a spinal patient needing attention. But he died before Dr. Phipps arrived."

"How did he seem that night? Dr. Phipps, I mean?"

She thought a moment. "Excited about something. He kept looking at his watch like there was somewhere else he wanted to be."

Fairview. He'd wanted to be on Hurricane Harbor, admiring the estate he'd assumed would shortly be his . . .

Darby nodded at the nurse and walked slowly back to the reception room. Alicia was engrossed in a conversation but managed a little wave and smile. Darby waved and then walked toward the exit sign. If Alicia was right about the storm, she needed to get on the highway as soon as possible.

Darby located the elevator and pushed Level 1. As she waited for the doors to open, she thought about the hospital's Wall of Remembrance. It was a way to pay tribute to those who had passed on, similar to the honor rolls found on New England town greens memorializing those who had lost their lives in military service. She hadn't seen something like it in an institution before, but she supposed it did comfort family members and even bereaved staff.

For some reason, the image of the wall wouldn't leave her mind. She felt as if the bronze plaque with its many names was burned on her retinas.

She waited for the elevator to arrive. It was time to drive to Maine, storm or no storm, to deal with her aunt's service and the work that awaited. Nevertheless, she could not shake the feeling that she needed to see the bronze plaque one more time.

Darby gave an exasperated sigh. She made it a point to listen to her intuition, although at times following its lead was darn right annoying. She retraced her steps through the reception area, thankful that Alicia was engaged in conversation. Entering the hallway where a few people were standing and talking quietly, she noted that the pony-tailed nurse was gone.

Once more, Darby studied Emerson Phipps' name.

The "S" — his middle initial — was probably for Samuel. Hadn't Alicia said that one of the boys was named for her brother? She glanced toward the buffet and smiled at the youngsters' antics. Samuel and Michael were chasing each other around the small cocktail tables, nearly knocking down the remaining guests with their exuberance. They needed to be outside, tossing a football or climbing on a jungle gym, whatever it was that boys that age did these days.

Just then, something caught her eye, drawing her gaze once more to the Wall of Remembrance. It was the name etched in bronze two lines above Phipps'. A name she recognized. Her body went cold.

The helpful administrator who had taken her to the wall in the first place was at the buffet table scooping another helping of egg salad when Darby found her. "Oh yes," she said, adding a croissant to an already over-loaded plate. "I remember Linda. She was a nurse in neonatology."

"Did you know her?"

"I'm afraid not."

Darby asked for directions to the neonatology wing and the administrator gave her a curious look. After explaining the quickest route, she turned her attention back to the buffet and Darby turned to leave. She was barely aware of anyone else in the room as she moved through the hallway. She had never sleepwalked, but her body felt as if she were in a dream.

The neonatology wing was off limits to those without an electronic pass. The young receptionist at the desk, however, smiled and buzzed a nurse to come and assist Darby.

The nurse appeared seconds later, a frown on her face.

"Of course I remember her," she said briskly. "Linda was an extremely capable nurse who served at Boston Memorial for years. Her death was a real blow to us all."

"How did she die?"

"Automobile accident."

"Did she have any relatives?"

"I don't really know. We're too busy to socialize in this department."

She gave a dismissive nod to Darby and a reproachful glance at the receptionist and turned abruptly away. The younger woman rolled her eyes as the woman departed. "Nurse Gray is always like that," she confided. "Super grouchy." She smiled. "I'm Tiffany. I'd been here about two months when Linda died. We all took it pretty hard."

Darby nodded in what she hoped was a sympathetic manner. Her throat felt dry and she swallowed with difficulty.

"Water fountain's over there," said Tiffany, noticing Darby's distress. "Help yourself."

Darby walked to the fountain and took a quick sip of water and a deep steadying breath. *Focus,* she told herself. *Find out what you need to know . . .*

She returned to Tiffany's desk, her head clearer. "I'm interested in Linda because I think I may know her sister."

"The one who was in the accident?"

"I'm not sure."

"Must have been. The sister was driving and the roads were slippery. You know, that stuff they call black ice, the kind you can't see very well? They hit a patch and went flying off the road. Linda was on all kinds of machines in the ICU, and her sister stayed right by her side."

"Here at Boston Memorial?"

"Yes."

"Did a doctor named Emerson Phipps operate on her?"

"God, you mean *the* Emerson Phipps? Well if he had, she'd probably be alive today. I don't know if he was involved. But hang on, I can call my friend Mindy in scheduling."

Darby waited, hardly breathing, while the receptionist whipped out a cell phone and pressed a button. "We're not supposed to use them in the building," she said. "But what the hell."

Tiffany spoke quickly into the receiver and nodded, then clicked her cell phone closed. "Mindy checked her computer. Dr. Phipps was scheduled to operate, but Linda died before the operation. She was in very bad shape, I guess. One thing you learn in a hospital: you can't save everyone."

She leaned closer to Darby and lowered her voice. "I'll tell you this about Linda: she was in some kind of trouble before the car accident. A preemie died, and the parents said she'd done something to cause it."

"Wrongful death."

"That's what they called it, all right."

"Were charges brought against her?"

"I don't think they got a chance before that accident . . ." She thought a moment. "The whole thing kind of disappeared after Linda died." She shrugged. "Maybe they settled it with the family." Her face brightened. "Hey! I've got an old recruiting flyer around here somewhere with Linda's picture. Want to see it?" Tiffany rummaged in a desk drawer.

Darby nodded. She took the glossy brochure from Tiffany and looked down at a photo of a smiling nurse holding a baby. The nurse wore pastel scrubs and had short blonde hair. *She looks exactly like her,* Darby thought. *Exactly . . .*

Without meaning to, Darby whispered, "Laura . . ."

Tiffany shook her head. "No, that's Linda. Linda Gefferelli. They looked so alike though, you'd have sworn they were twins. Sometimes her sister came to meet Linda here and none of us could tell them apart. I thought it was cool, you know, the jokes they could play on people? Anyway, after Linda died I heard that Laura left the state and went up north — Vermont, I think. Imagine how awful you'd feel if that was you, driving a car that kills your own sister? Luckily, she's real churchy — a nun I think. That would help."

"Yes," Darby said, handing the brochure back to Tiffany, "that would help."

Donny Pease was battening down the hatches, a job generations of islanders before him had done when a storm was headed up the coast.

He began with his own house, pushing his rusted wheelbarrow into the barn and looking for any lawn tools that could, in high winds, become airborne. Next, he made sure his screen doors were tightly latched and that the windows were down. He regarded an old apple tree that he'd been meaning to prune of dead wood and shook his head. Chances were good that this storm would do the trimming for him.

He recalled his father talking about a hurricane that caused untold damage to Maine in 1938. "You were just a small boy in britches," he'd say, "when that storm swept up from the Connecticut River Valley. Lost half our barn in that gale, although the horses and cows were still standing there later, right as rain."

He knew, as had his father, that preparing for a severe storm took place during the sunshine. It was too late to do much of anything once the storm started. At that point, it was just a matter of waiting it out and praying.

Satisfied that his own house was ready for the storm, Donny headed over in his truck to Fairview. No one was there, which was just fine and dandy. He did not need to find any other surprises, not after what had happened on Monday.

He walked around the old estate, doing the same things he'd done at his farmhouse, securing all of the main house's exterior doors and checking to be sure the windows were nearly closed.

If predictions for this storm had suggested a severe hurricane, Donny would have needed to board up Fairview's many windows. He'd done it before, and it was a time-consuming chore. Back in the day, Donny spent a whole day preparing for bad weather. In addition to boarding up the windows, there would have been about a dozen porch rockers to lug inside, all of Mrs. Trimble's pots of geraniums to shelter, and baskets of hanging impatiens to tuck safely away. Donny would have disassembled lawn games such as croquet and badminton, making any number of trips to the garden cottage with wickets, nets, mallets, and racquets.

He sighed. Those days were long gone, the days of finding a discarded highball glass in the gazebo, its owner having enjoyed its contents while watching the sun sink behind the Manatuck hills. Donny Pease missed those busy times, God knows he missed them, but they were behind him now, mere memories with a hazy, happy edge.

After closing the garden cottage's doors, Donny crossed the lawn to the edge of the cliff, listening to the waves crash against the granite rocks. June was the start of hurricane season, although it seemed that most of Maine's tropical depressions and hurricanes took place in the fall. From Fairview, Donny would head to the harbor, where he'd get his boat ready to ride out the storm and help any other boaters who needed a hand. Donny watched the spray rise from the clash of water against rock for a moment longer. The sea was rougher than usual; the effects of the changing weather were already underway.

Within the cool confines of the rented Chrysler, Darby attempted to make sense of the information she'd just received. While the traffic raced by her on Interstate 95, she once again recited the facts.

Laura's sister Linda worked in the same hospital as Emerson Phipps. She was injured in a car accident and was supposed to be operated on by him.

She couldn't stop thinking about the surprising connection, and yet she didn't quite know what it implied. Was there a link between Emerson Phipps and Laura Gefferelli? She chided herself. There's a good chance the whole thing's coincidental. Linda Gefferelli had been a nurse in neonatology, and Laura, her look-alike sister, had visited her department. If Laura knew Emerson Phipps personally or by reputation on account of her occasional visits to Boston Memorial Hospital, surely she would have mentioned it at the time Phipps' body was discovered. It was the kind of thing Darby could picture Laura saying in her thoughtful, calm, manner. *I've heard of Emerson Phipps. He worked at the same hospital as my sister . . .*

But Laura Gefferelli had never mentioned knowing Emerson Phipps. *That's because she never heard of him,* Darby told herself. It made perfect sense that Laura, a very occasional visitor to Boston Memorial Hospital, would not be acquainted with any of the medical staff. *And yet why hadn't Laura ever commented on the fact that her sister and Phipps had worked at the same institution?*

Darby put on her blinker and moved smoothly into the left lane, passing a car whose driver was chatting away on a cell phone. She thought of her dead battery and groaned. *I wish that I could call Miles or Tina.*

She let a safe distance get between her

and the car and glided back into the right lane. *You need to get back on the island, that's what you need to do.* As if to add to her urgency, she could feel the wind intensifying, the storm beginning its march northward, hot on the heels of the rental car. *With this bad weather coming I won't even stop,* she thought, passing a rest area with a twinge of regret. *I should have used the hospital's restroom when I had the chance.*

The music on the radio was interrupted by a National Weather Service warning for hurricane force winds along the coast within the next twenty-four hours. Darby grimaced and stepped harder on the gas.

Her determination to make good time while the weather remained stable paid off. Darby sped through New Hampshire and straight up the coast, pulling onto the five P.M. ferry at Manatuck. When she finally turned off the car's ignition, she breathed a sigh of relief. Soon after, she felt the boat start to move away from the Manatuck dock.

Darby got out of the car, needing to stretch her legs and find the ferry's restroom.

The restrooms were located up a narrow set of metal stairs on the top deck of the ferry. Darby climbed up, passing a few other passengers who were doing the same thing. The art show was tomorrow and the tourists would descend in full force — that is, unless news of the storm had scared them off. Hurricane Harbor's summer rush was officially underway, and Darby was pleased to see a number of passengers who were clearly visitors to the island.

Once out of the restroom, Darby took her time on the upper deck, pausing to take in the surrounding ocean and outcroppings. Dark, low clouds to the southwest and the increasing chop of the waves foretold the changing weather, and yet the little islands looked serene. Darby felt her mood begin to lighten, despite the ominous skies.

The air was cool on Darby's face, the breeze gaining strength seemingly by the minute. One of the ferry officials looked anxiously at the sky before motioning that it was time for car owners to return to their vehicles. Darby glanced ahead. Sure enough, the boat was fast approaching the Hurricane Harbor dock.

Darby climbed back down the metal stairs to the parking lot, located the rental car, and climbed into the front seat. She reached into the pocket of her jacket for the keys and pulled them out.

Just as she was about to put the keys into

the ignition, she heard a sharp crack, reminiscent of the sound of a sudden summer storm. Like a shove, she felt the jolt of 150,000 volts of electricity wham her in the back. Darby collapsed onto the seat of the car, twitching uncontrollably.

The surprise of the sudden blow and the jumble of the electrical signals in her brain left Darby unfocused and uncomprehending. She saw a lithe figure climb over the seat and felt her body pushed onto the passenger floor of the car. She heard the car start and sensed that it was moving off the ferry and onto the island.

Some impulse told Darby to flee, and she tried getting up from her fetal crouch on the floor, but movement of any kind was impossible. She tried lifting an arm, but that was futile as well. *I'm paralyzed,* she realized. *I can't move at all.*

The car turned to the left and Darby rolled slightly. She was stunned, too stunned to be frightened. She tried to form the words to ask her attacker what the hell was going on, but found she could not speak. The road grew bumpy. Darby's head bounced against the floor of the car, but she felt no pain, even as a red welt began to rise on her cheek.

We're on a dirt road, she thought. There

were more than fifty unpaved fire roads that wove across the island's interior.

Abruptly the car stopped. Darby heard a door open and then the sound of the trunk popping. A moment later the passenger door opened and the face of Laura Gefferelli, normally so calm and kind, looked down at her with disgust.

"Just couldn't leave it alone, could you," she sneered. She clutched what Darby guessed was a large sail bag against her navy striped shirt. She yanked at the bag's metal grommets and reached for Darby's legs.

Helplessly Darby watched Laura stuff her feet into the sail bag. Once her legs were enclosed, Laura grabbed both sides of the sturdy nylon and yanked it upward, so that the sail bag covered her entirely. The top was pulled over Darby's head, shutting out any daylight.

Encased in the bag, Darby heard Laura's muffled grunt of approval. She heard the car door close and the engine start. From the jostling, Darby knew they were driving down the dirt road once more.

After a few more jolts, the road became smooth and Darby sensed the car was back on pavement. *Where is she taking me? Why?* Darby's thoughts were disordered and confused. *Laura Gefferelli shot me with a taser, and now she's stuffed me in a sail bag.* Suddenly the situation became crystal clear. *She's going to kill me . . .*

Several minutes later, the car came to a stop. As horrified as she was feeling, Darby forced herself to listen intently. Was that the sound of waves? Were they at the harbor, where someone might notice something out of the ordinary? *There's nothing strange about a sailor and a sail bag,* she thought, fear seeping into her pores.

The passenger side door opened. With a grunt, the sail bag was heaved upwards. Darby heard a thumping sound as her body landed on a surface, but still she felt nothing. It was as if her physical self was a separate entity from her mind. Her brain and senses were functioning but they were disconnected from the rest of her . . .

The sound of something scraping caused Darby to think she was being dragged. Suddenly the bag lifted again, only to thud down moments later. Darby caught the strong scent of the sea at low tide and guessed she was on a dock. She heard footsteps, and then Laura's grunts of exertion as the bag was hefted up and onto something else. *She's getting tired,* she thought. *If only I could move!* Darby tried to wiggle a finger. Was it wishful thinking, or did it seem to stir? The plaintive cry of a gull echoed Darby's despair.

Moments later, a motor started and Darby knew they were pulling away from land. It was not very powerful — maybe seven or eight horsepower — the size typically used on small sailboats. It seemed to whine in protest against the waves now slapping against the bow of the boat with unusual force. *We're on Laura's boat,* she thought. *What's in a Name.* Her heart sank: the farther they were from a dock, the less likely anyone was to hear or see her.

Darby willed herself to stay hopeful. She knew the effects of the taser were temporary: at some point her mobility would return. She tried again to wiggle her fingers. Yes! She was regaining feeling, although she had no idea how long it would take before she could move more than an index finger. As the motor droned on in the background, Darby forced her brain to keep trying to fire her muscles. She knew it was her only chance.

Now her whole hand could move slightly. Darby felt her toes wiggle. Progress was slow, but she was definitely regaining motor function. She tried to lift her arm. Not yet, but perhaps soon . . .

The sail bag opened with an abrupt tug

and Darby tried to blink. Through blurry eyes she saw Laura peering down at her, her normally relaxed features brittle with rage.

Laura glanced quickly to either side, her hair blowing in the breeze that was quickly becoming a gale. She gave a dismissive glance toward Darby. *This is my chance,* thought Darby. With all the strength she could muster, Darby lifted her arm toward Laura, praying that the stun gun's effects would disappear. Instead, she watched in horror as Laura smiled and lifted a black rectangle, no bigger than an iPod. She thrust it toward Darby, who heard a crack of electricity, then collapsed once more like a deflated balloon.

FIFTEEN

Incapacitated for the second time, Darby Farr slumped in the sail bag, her eyes level with the bag's upper edge. She heard movement around her and the low moan of the wind, but could not summon the energy to care. A strong gust rocked the boat violently; her stomach clenched. *At least part of me feels something,* she thought.

A few moments later she heard the voice of Laura.

"I was hoping we could go for a little sail, but the weather doesn't seem to be cooperating. I think you would have liked that, Darby. Just you and me, a nice little sail . . ."

The boat lurched and Laura hit the side of the boat. The wind was so stiff that Darby knew whitecaps must be forming on the waves. She had never been on the water in conditions like this before, but was certain that a small craft like *What's in a Name* could not survive. And yet she was power-

391

less to do anything.

Laura leaned over the sail bag, keeping one hand on the tiller. She gave an odd little smile. "Who knows whether you even remember how to sail, right?" She studied Darby for a moment.

"You seem anxious about this tropical storm. Are you concerned about the seaworthiness of my vessel?" She threw back her head and laughed. "Look, you really don't need to worry about your safety. You're not coming back alive anyway! So just relax and, as they say, enjoy the ride."

Darby watched as Laura tried to steer the boat through a particularly large swell. Water rushed up onto the deck and she heard Laura swear.

Darby wondered how far out they were going, wondered whether she would be stunned again before being dumped overboard. *Either way, I'll drown,* she thought. She felt warmth between her legs and realized she had lost control of her bladder.

The heavy clouds above seemed to open up and the spitting rain became a downpour. In minutes Darby saw that Laura was drenched, her navy blue and white T-shirt clinging to her body. Laura seemed to notice the worsening weather for the first time and the look on her face darkened.

Darby remained huddled in the bag, praying for time and a miracle.

She told herself that the effects of the stun gun would lessen if she were not shocked again. She remembered reading that victims remained immobile for less than fifteen minutes. If only she could recover the use of her arms, at least, she could fend off an attack by Laura Gefferelli . . .

Laura pushed her wet bangs out of her eyes. "You figured it out at the hospital, didn't you?"

Darby tried moving a finger. Nothing.

"I thought that you'd make some kind of connection if you saw that ridiculous remembrance wall. They don't waste any time getting names up there. But I had to be sure, so I phoned Neonatology. Tiffany was only too happy to tell me about your little conversation."

The rain was beating on the deck of *What's in a Name,* but Laura seemed oblivious to the several inches already gathered.

"She told you about the charges, right? Wrongful death! Can you imagine? In an infant — a preemie no bigger than my fist — with severe intraventricular hemorrhage."

She looked out at the gray sea, the wind whipping her short blonde hair into little frosted spikes. "That's bleeding in the cavi-

ties of the brain. Believe me, it was a bless-
ing to lose that baby. I'd do it again in a
heartbeat."

Her calm, lecture-like style of speaking
chilled Darby to the core. *Laura is insane,*
she thought. *Please let me escape . . .*

A moment later she was peering down at
Darby's face, the rain running in little
rivulets off her cheeks. In the same flat voice
she asked, "You do understand that I'm the
one on that wall, don't you?"

Darby's mind raced with this bit of information. So this was Linda, the neonatal
nurse, who was her captor?

"Laura died on the table, waiting for
Phipps, just like a few of his other patients.
He didn't have one ounce of consideration
or compassion, that man. Never even tried
to keep appointments, or speak to families,
or start a surgery on time." She spat out the
words with a violence oddly in harmony
with the weather. "That's just not good
medicine."

Darby listened, praying Laura — or Linda
— would keep talking and forget that the
effects of the stun gun were bound to wear
off.

"I chose to forgive it all, though, because
Laura was so injured that he wouldn't have
made a difference, even if he had shown up

on time. I mean, she was basically a lost cause. When she didn't survive, I decided to use her life to get a fresh start. She had a new job on this island that she was excited about. I asked myself: How hard can it be to play pastor? I switched our driver's licenses and said I was Laura. I read a few books, did research online, and in no time I became the beloved associate minister." Linda Gefferelli grinned, clearly proud of her deception. Moments later her smile was a snarl.

"The day I saw him here on the island, I was — stunned. That's a good word to be using right now, isn't it? The bastard actually came to one of my church services. Of course, I never knew he had a history here. I saw him and I froze. I said to myself, 'Don't worry, he'll never remember you. You were just an insignificant nurse.' But that son of a bitch, he knew it was me.

"Oh, not right away of course. He gave me an odd look — that was my first clue — and asked where I was from. I made up some lie and thought I was safe. But he came back to my office that afternoon and said I had the same name as someone he knew in Boston. 'She had a sister,' he said . . .

"Again I lied, but this time I knew it was

pointless. Phipps was too smart, too persistent. He was going to destroy everything I'd created on Hurricane Harbor, all the good work I was doing for everyone on the island. He'd take it all away — my position, my projects, my new life — and I would be left with nothing."

The sailboat was pitching helplessly in the storm, the exhausted motor droning uselessly like a fly caught in a fan. Darby sensed that she hadn't much time before Linda tired of talking. She tried clenching a fist, concentrating as hard as she could. She felt her fingers touch her palm and nearly cried out in relief. Instead, she remained as motionless as she could.

"Now this is my plan," Linda Gefferelli announced, raising her voice against the howling wind. "I will dump you into the water and watch as you sink, then turn the boat around and head for shore. I'll need to get you out of that sail bag in case they find your body, but let's face it, sometimes people are never found. You know that better than anyone, don't you, Darby?" She gave a smile that was a sickening blend of sympathy and hatred. "I don't think I'll be stunning you again, not with this weather. I wouldn't want to shock myself and kill us both, now would I?" She scanned the horizon, most likely to assure herself that there were no other boats in sight, but visibility was so poor she could not have seen ten feet away. "I'll have to dispose of the stun gun, I guess, although I've become somewhat attached to it." She warmed to the topic of her weapon. "They sell these things online, you know. Three hundred and fifty dollars for 900,000 volts, and I didn't even have to pay for shipping." A wave crashed against the bow again and Darby was sure they'd be swamped. Linda, oblivious, talked on.

"They call these guns 'non-lethal' but Soames, I swear to God, actually died right then and there. His health was compromised, probably because of all the drugs he consumed. Lifestyle choices can really weaken someone considerably.

"And Emerson Phipps — you'd think that he would have put up more of a fight! Then again, I did come out of nowhere. I stunned him; he dropped to his knees, I zapped him again, then I smashed in his skull."

Darby stayed as still as she could, trying to form a plan while she listened to Linda Gefferelli's rants. She wondered whether there was anything she could grasp and use as a weapon, but dared not move her eyes to see. The only thing she could do, she reasoned, was surprise the woman with an unexpected surge of movement. She had a chance to overpower her, as long as Linda did not realize how much time had elapsed since she'd last stunned her victim.

Linda took one of the sailboat's sheets and stretched it around the tiller and from cleat to cleat so that the tiller stayed on course.

"Automatic pilot." Turning toward Darby, she asked, "Ready for a swim?"

Darby's heart sank. Had she regained enough movement to even put up a fight? She willed herself to stay still as the grim-faced woman approached. Another crack of thunder boomed as Linda yanked down the sail bag's sides. Darby remained motionless, biding her time.

"Ugh," Linda said, noticing the puddle of liquid at the bottom of the bag, "what did you —"

Just then Darby pushed her coiled legs at her captor, using all the strength she could muster and praying it would be enough. The force of the kick caught Linda Gefferelli totally off guard and she slammed backward against the tiller. Darby tried to get up, not sure of her next move, but knowing she had to stand up and fight. Her tottering efforts were met with a powerful punch that caught her in the lower lip, leaving her head buzzing with pain.

She tasted blood and saw Linda about to hit her again. She ducked but Linda's fist managed to connect anyway, propelling Darby down the ladder into the cabin.

"I should have dumped you overboard when you were in the stupid sail bag," Linda fumed. "Now you're going to bleed on my boat cushions." She jumped down the stairs and lunged at Darby, her face a wild mix of fury and hatred. Darby fell back against a berth with Linda on top of her. The crazed woman grabbed at her throat and began squeezing. Tighter and tighter until Darby, still weak from the electrical shocks, felt darkness closing in.

Her father's voice filled her weakening brain. "Clenched fist," he commanded. "Clenched fist, Darby!"

Although it seemed every ounce of energy had ebbed from her body, Darby drew strength from the words echoing in her head. Forming the fist as she had practiced so long ago, she aimed for a pressure point and thrust out at her attacker. At the same time, she drew both her knees up and into Linda's groin area with as much force as she could muster. Knowing she would die if she did not escape momentarily, she put every last ounce of energy she possessed —

plus a hidden strength she never knew existed — into her movements, praying they would work.

Linda gave a grunt as the offensive blows struck, and, for a fleeting second, loosened her hold on Darby's windpipe, letting some much-needed oxygen into Darby's depleted lungs. Darby gasped, and then slammed her knees into Linda's midsection. The other woman let out a yelp of pain as Darby continued with her offense. Linda was now up against the companionway, slumped in pain, but Darby was taking no chances. She grabbed a loose jib sheet and, despite the other woman's flailing arms, tied Linda's hands and feet, using knots she'd learned back in her days as a young sailor. She pushed Linda onto the deck of the boat, hearing a solid whack as Linda's skull hit the deck. *Oops,* she thought grimly. *I hope I haven't killed her . . .*

But the injured Linda Gefferelli was of no concern to Darby now. She climbed the ladder and nearly cried out in anguish at the scene before her.

While she had been below deck fighting off Linda, the storm had reached its violent worst. Foaming waves crashed relentlessly over the sides of the small sailboat, threatening to swamp it with each blow. The tiller, now a jagged mess of splintered wood, was jerking uselessly back and forth in savage rhythm. Worse though, was what lay directly in the small craft's path: the hulking mass of rocks known as the Graves. Rising up from the surging ocean like a mound of rocky icicles, the Graves were to blame for countless maritime tragedies and deaths. Within minutes, Darby was sure *What's in a Name* would be among the wrecked vessels destroyed by these rocks, with she and Linda two of its casualties.

Darby knew that she had to act fast. *What's in a Name*'s tiny motor had died, and perhaps it was useless against the storm anyway. Nevertheless, Darby recognized instantly that it was her only hope. Quickly she pulled the start cord. No sound came from the motor. She tried again. Nothing. She saw the choke button and pressed it a few times, remembering the small crafts she had driven at the Yacht Club as a child. This time the engine made a soft sputter. Again Darby pressed the choke and pulled the cord. Finally, the engine caught and came to life.

Almost mechanically Darby pushed the motor into forward and gunned it. The burst of speed nearly tossed her off the stern of the boat. But she was gratified to see that despite the surging waves and raging wind, she had moved, if only inches. The rocks were only two feet away, close enough that Darby could see a cluster of mussels clinging to the rocks and see the sheen left on their shells after each wave. She swallowed her fear and prayed for the wind to subside, if only for an instant.

It was as if her prayer had been heard and granted. The wind suddenly slowed, and even the rain seemed to slacken. Was the deathly calm the eye of the storm, or the lull before even more violence began?

The little motor revved in a dangerously high whine but Darby resisted the urge to slow it until she was several more feet from the Graves. As soon as she felt she was not in danger of crashing on the rocks, she slowed the motor and surveyed the horizon. She did not know when the storm would intensify, but she was convinced the damaged boat could not weather it. The shore looked hopelessly far away, and Darby knew that swimming in the still frigid water was not an option.

A grunt from her captive brought her back to her immediate surroundings. Linda Gefferelli was alive, although she seemed to be in a state between consciousnesses. Darby resisted the impulse to check her knots.

They'll hold, she convinced herself. Although she had worked in a hurry, her captive appeared to be secure and taut.

Linda Gefferelli moaned, but Darby forced her brain to think of solutions to the predicament of being in a tiny weakened boat in the middle of a storm. She knew Linda did not have a radio to call the coast guard or other help. Her own cell phone was somewhere in the rental car, dead and useless.

Darby pictured the chart of these waters in her mind as she had seen it so many times. She remembered the Graves marked as a clear danger to mariners, remembered the distance from the Graves to the coastline, and racked her brain for other details. There was a bell buoy marking another rocky spot, and behind it, a small island called Sheepscot.

Quickly Darby searched the tossing waves. If her memory was correct, Sheepscot should be in line with the Graves. It was a two-acre or so patch of rocky land, home to spruce trees, bayberry bushes, and an old cabin no bigger than Aunt Jane's tiny cottage. The structure was miniscule, but it represented shelter.

The wind was starting to pick up again and Darby felt her heartbeat quicken. The motor was still struggling valiantly to keep the boat moving, but as the storm once again gathered strength, she knew its efforts would be useless. Darby thought fast. There were binoculars below deck: she remembered seeing them on a small shelf. Quickly she scampered down the ladder. While she was there she looked for a life jacket, finding one in a compartment under a cushion. With the weather turning more and more ominous, personal flotation was a wise idea.

She shoved her arms inside the armholes and buckled the clasps. *If I did fall in, the temperature of the water would induce hypothermia and kill me anyway,* she thought. She pushed the fact from her brain. She had no time for negative thoughts. This was one of those times when her father would have told her to "keep it positive."

The memory of her father describing a particularly grueling sailing race entered her mind. "It was the closest race I'd ever been in," he'd said. "The other guy was a German named Anton Vasser, and he was an incredible sailor. He had me pretty much the whole way, and I was working like a dog to catch up. The other boats were so far behind that it was truly only he and I in the race." Darby remembered him pausing as he recalled that day years before. "Suddenly

I tried a new tack and it worked, and I started gaining on him. I was nearly neck and neck when the thought came to me, 'You can't beat this guy. Give it up and settle for second.' I was so tired that I didn't have the strength to fight back the negativity. It seeped into me like water in a leaky dinghy. Before I knew it, Vasser was too far for me to ever catch and he had won the race." Her father had turned a sober face to her and concluded. "Don't let negativity ever take control, Little Loon. If I had pushed that thought out of my mind, I believe I would have won that race."

Darby climbed back up the ladder. Linda Gefferelli had not moved, and she seemed to have stopped making noises. Darby did not let herself be concerned for the woman's safety. She had to find a way to pilot the damaged sailboat to Sheepscot Island, and quickly.

The sky was darkening with an alarming rapidity and the wind was beginning to howl. Waves smashed against the side of the boat, submerging the struggling motor with each thrust. It was only a matter of time and the motor would be totally useless.

Darby put the binoculars up to her eyes and searched for signs of the island. She recognized the Graves, as foreboding as they had been only minutes before. She peered desperately through the glasses, and spotted the pointed tops of some pines.

Sheepscot! Quickly Darby calculated her course. She would need to steer close to the Graves once more, but if she was successful in avoiding them, she would be able to come close to the tiny island. There, she could swim from the boat if need be.

The wind was moaning like a living thing now, coming from the other direction, and Darby struggled to keep her footing. A large wave crashed overhead, filling the cockpit of the boat with water. Darby hadn't noticed how much seawater had collected. She noticed with alarm that the bow of the boat was leaning precipitously to port. *She's starting to sink . . .*

She grabbed a bailing bucket and tried frantically to remove some of the water, but with the pelting rain it was useless. She peered toward the Graves, finally seeing Sheepscot Island behind the hulking rocks. She prayed she would get there before the boat was swamped and she was tossed overboard.

Concentrating on her course and the rising water, she did not see Linda Gefferelli as she staggered to her knees, preparing to push Darby into the foaming sea . . .

Intuition made Darby glance in the direction of the woman just in time to avoid Linda's thrust with her tied hands. She ducked, but Linda was unstoppable, screaming in a high pitched wail, her eyes wide with fury.

"You're going to die! Just like your parents . . ."

Suddenly the boom of the boat came alive. Darby watched as it was wrenched upward, as if by an invisible hand. With deadly force the wind jerked it to the side. Smack! The steel made contact with Linda Gefferelli's skull, continuing on its path and driving her into the water.

Darby saw the blonde head bob for a moment in the angry waves. Linda's eyes were closed; her head slumped to the side. Blood trickled down her forehead as the water engulfed her and she sank under the churning sea.

Darby looked at where the boom had been and saw more water pouring into the sailboat. She grabbed a boat cushion from the bottom and prepared for the shock of the frigid seawater. *There is nothing more I can do but swim,* she thought, trying to keep herself from panicking. *Maybe I'll get lucky and be washed onto a rock . . .*

A voice on the waves reminded her of her

father. It was a man, yelling something, but she could not focus her eyes to see him. The wind was roaring like a caged animal and it filled Darby's ears with its baleful cries. Once again she imagined the voice. "Hey! Hey! Anyone aboard?"

With an effort, Darby tried to peer through the driving rain. Was that a tug chugging through the churning water toward her? She heard the engine sputtering, and could just make out the shape of a slicker-clad man at the helm. "Hey," he called. "I'll come alongside and get you. Don't worry, you're safe."

The words summoned up strength from deep in Darby's core. A second wind, her father used to call it.

"I'm here!" she called over the moan of the wind. "I'm right here."

The tug came closer and Darby pulled herself up. The water inside the boat was up to her hips; the little craft was nearly underwater.

"Darby?" the tug captain called. "It's Darby, right? Here, grab onto me . . . I've got you . . ."

The strong grasp of Ryan Oakes pulled Darby from the sinking deck of *What's in a Name* and onto his boat, a sturdy steel research tug.

She exhaled. "Your timing is impeccable, Ryan." Together they watched as the abandoned sailboat sunk into the sea, the stern disappearing first and the rest rapidly following.

"Too bad," Ryan yelled over the wind. "She was a pretty little thing." He turned to Darby. "Grab a dry blanket below deck. Then come back up and tell me why in the world you were out here in this weather."

"I could ask you the same thing," Darby replied. "But first I'll grab that blanket."

Chugging back toward Hurricane Harbor, Darby gave Ryan the details of her capture by Linda and her fight for her life. "I'd like to call Chief Dupont, if your radio is functioning."

"Sure," he said, his voice sober. "Channel 23."

Darby contacted the station and asked the dispatch to have the chief call her immediately. She came back on deck, noticing with relief that the storm was starting to lessen in intensity. "You haven't told me why you were out in the storm?"

"There's an old man, Milton Ames, who lives on Sheepscot Island. I come out to check on him every Friday." He shook his head. "I nearly skipped it today, the storm

409

was so bad."

Darby managed a smile. "Lucky for me you stuck to your routine. Is visiting people like Milton part of your job with the Island Association?"

"In a way. I've been trying to convince him for a few years to move to Manatuck, or even Hurricane Harbor, but he loves that little island." He took a look at the sky and pointed to the west. "Starting to clear."

Darby saw the break in the cloud cover and sighed. They were nearly at the town dock, and she had one more question for Ryan Oakes before telling Chief Dupont about the murder of Emerson Phipps.

"Ryan," she asked, pulling the warm blanket more tightly around her wet shoulders, "is the Island Association in the market for a new headquarters?"

He nodded. "We're renting space, but our lease is nearly up, and it's certainly not an ideal location." He turned the boat in the direction of the town dock. "I have to admit, our funding is pretty sparse. It would have to be a heck of a good deal."

Darby grinned, her spirits buoyed by the sight of the island and the little group assembled on the town dock: Tina, Mark, Lucy, Donny Pease, and a very concerned looking Chief Dupont. She turned back to

Ryan Oakes. "Give me a day to figure it out. Trust me, though — what I've got in mind would be the deal of the century."

SIXTEEN

Donny Pease lit a match to the kindling in Jane Farr's fireplace and a bright blaze sprang to life. He added a few slender logs, replaced the fireplace screen, and sat back on his haunches.

The aftermath of the hurricane was more than downed tree branches and power lines. Donny still couldn't believe the news that Laura Gefferelli, the island's minister for more than two years, had stuck those shears in the doctor's chest. Not only that, but she'd killed Soames Pemberton, poisoned Lucy, and tried to drown Darby Farr. Most unbelievable of all — she wasn't even a minister!

Earlier in the day, when he'd been adding extra fenders to his boat, Donny had seen Laura Gefferelli heading out in *What's in a Name*. He'd considered asking her why she was going to sea in a storm. But in the end he'd remained quiet, keeping his thoughts to himself. *She's moving the boat to safer quarters,* he'd convinced himself, although everyone knew Hurricane Harbor's sheltered cove was one of the most protected inlets around.

He'd felt it was strange, and yet he'd said nothing. Meanwhile, Darby Farr was onboard *What's in a Name,* a prisoner trapped in a sail bag.

He stood and felt the fire's increasing warmth. *The Lord works in mysterious ways,* he thought. *And half the time you can't even tell if He's working.*

He turned his attention to the little gymnasium assembled in the living room. Tina wanted several of the machines moved, so Donny dragged a few pieces of exercise equipment into the dining room.

Tina appeared from the basement with several folding chairs and a disgusted look on her face. "These aren't very comfy, but they'll have to do," she said, wiping them off with a rag. "Whatever was that woman thinking, getting rid of all her furniture?"

Donny helped Tina to set up the chairs around the fire. When they were finished, she glanced at the fire and smiled.

"This feels good on a damp night like this, doesn't it?" She looked down at her red-painted nails. "Kind of romantic."

Donny chewed on his lip. Women were such strange creatures, likely to say anything that popped into their heads. He saw Tina look over at him and shyness overtook him.

"Fire's are nice," he managed to blurt out, thinking he sounded like that idiotic night manager at the hotel. He thought about how many times he'd missed opportunities to say things, about how Darby Farr could have died because of his reluctance to open his mouth. Donny Pease took a deep breath and drew himself up to his full height of five-feet-eight inches. " 'Course, I got a nice Rumford fireplace of my own, back at the house . . ."

Tina's head shot up and she smiled. Their eyes met and Donny felt a rush of gratitude toward all of creation, animals, storms, dying apple trees, and people, especially the person standing barely a foot away: a tall, curly-haired lady with fire-engine-red fingernails.

After a hot shower and a steaming mug of tea, Darby Farr felt warm again and reasonably calm. She knew Chief Dupont would be returning to take her statement, and felt sure she was ready to give it.

Tina was waiting for her in Jane Farr's living room. A cheerful blaze burned in the fireplace, and Darby thanked Tina for its warmth.

"Donny took care of it, before he went back to the house. I'll tell him you appreciated it." She turned to Darby and her face filled with anguish. "I can't believe that woman almost killed you. That she came so close to succeeding . . . If something had happened to you, Darby, I —" Tina began to cry, and Darby remembered their first meeting in the Portland Jetport, and Tina's tears over Jane Farr's condition.

Darby hugged Tina while the fire crackled and popped before them. "Tina, I didn't die. I'm right here." She smiled at the still sniffling woman. "It takes more than a homicidal ex-nurse to derail me in the middle of a deal. I'm more determined than ever to sell that darn Fairview!"

Tina laughed and wiped her eyes. "You don't let anything get you down, do you?" She sighed deeply. "We all trusted that woman. Your aunt loved her. I just can't believe she had all of us fooled."

Darby nodded. "I think she had herself fooled, too. I'm not an expert on mental illness, but I believe Linda Gefferelli was unstable for a long, long time. Miles did a little digging and says there were some questionable behaviors when she worked at the hospital; apparently some of her colleagues were wary. And then there was the wrongful death of a premature infant. Linda was on the line for that. When her sister Laura died, I think she saw a way out of a lawsuit, as well as the chance to start a new life."

"Do you think she loved Laura?"

"Everyone says the sisters were close, but I spoke to a good friend of Laura's just a little while ago, and she tells a different story. According to her, Linda harbored some pretty destructive envy. Laura was far more gregarious, had a serious boyfriend, but more important, she was mentally sound and happy. That probably ate away at Linda her whole life."

"Laura — I mean, Linda — seemed fine here. So together and calm."

Darby shrugged. "Who knows? Taking on Laura's career and Laura's persona might have helped her. Emerson Phipps came into the picture and threatened to destroy the life and identity she'd worked for years to create."

There was a knock on the door and the bulky figure of Chief Dupont came into the hallway. He sank into one of the folding chairs and gave Darby a long look.

"How are you?" he asked.

"A little sore," she admitted. "Mostly tired."

He nodded. "I'm not surprised. You fought for your life today, not just against Linda Gefferelli, but also the elements. You used your wits and determination, and you never gave up." He paused. "I'm thinking about your parents. Both of them were pretty special people, I'll grant you that. But more than anyone, Darby, you remind me of another fighter — your Aunt Jane."

He put out a pudgy hand and Darby saw that his eyes were misty. "You're a survivor, Darby Farr. But then all of us on the island have known that a long, long time."

"I suppose I'm every bit as stubborn as Jane Farr," Darby acknowledged. She looked at the fire. "There are so many unanswered questions. Linda killed Emerson Phipps Sunday morning, before she led the church service. She knew he was going to be at Fairview — possibly from my aunt. She never saw Lucy Trimble at the church. Why did she lie and give her an alibi?"

"Near as I can figure, Linda's plan was to incriminate Soames all along. Lucy Trimble showed up on Monday when Donny found the body and that complicated things. I think that's why Linda got her hands on some heroin and poisoned those chocolates.

She figured that would put the blame back on Soames. Everyone knew he was addicted to smack."

"The weapon that Linda Gefferelli used today — any chance we'll find it?"

Chief Dupont made a grim face. "That stun gun is at the bottom of the Atlantic, and I doubt we'll find any record of her having bought it," he said. "But from your description, it was a pretty powerful model. Enough to kill a man — or a woman." He looked at Darby with a meaningful look. "Thank goodness you are in such good physical shape, or the story could have had a different ending."

"It's all that running through the woods, Chief," she responded lightly.

The chief rose from his chair and laid a hand on her shoulder. "Huh. Maybe you've got something there. Anyway, I just want you to know that I am glad you are okay. We'll do the questions some other time." He sighed. "I'm going home to have a stiff drink with Aggie. I'll see you in the morning for Jane's service."

Darby nodded. "Thanks for coming over."

The chief lumbered out of the room and Darby closed her eyes. The moment when she had faced death at the hands of Linda Gefferelli came back to her in a rush. *My father spoke to me,* she remembered. *He told me what to do to stay alive.*

The Clenched Fist. She flashed back to a time when she was nine or ten years old. There had been a karate demonstration at the school, given by an elderly Japanese man who had used his hands and feet so gracefully that it looked like he was dancing. When Darby told her parents about it at the dinner table, her father had shown her a picture of her grandfather with his black belt, and her mother had blushed with pride.

"I didn't know Grandfather Sugiyama knew how to fight," Darby said.

"Karate is not about fighting, it is about becoming closer to God," her mother answered, getting up to clear the dinner dishes. Her father had chuckled and leaned closer to Darby.

"It's about fighting, too," he whispered in her ear. "Come into the other room, Little Loon, and I'll show you something Grandfather taught me.

"This is called the Clenched Fist, Darby, see? Your grandfather could use it to drop an opponent for the count of ten and out! He once told me, 'Do not be fooled into thinking that the Karate Clenched Fist blow is as easy as it looks.' Then he showed me the secret, and I can show you, too . . ."

She remembered him demonstrating the 90-degree angle that the front of her fist and her top knuckles made. "See this line?" he said, tracing his finger along her forearm and bent fingers. "If you want to be powerful, this line must be straight."

She had practiced hitting a pillow, and then he had tickled her, and she had laughed and laughed. As her father had tucked her into bed that night, he'd brushed the hair from her face and said, "Remember, your grandfather was a great karate fighter. If you ever need to use the Clenched Fist, you think of him and he will give you extra power."

Darby smiled at the memory. It was one bright spot in what had been a terrifying and exhausting day. Her body ached, her mind was a swirl of storm-tossed images, and she felt overwhelmed from the sheer effort of processing all that had occurred. Try as she would, she could not reconcile the memory of the helpful minister with the deranged Linda Gefferelli.

Alicia Phipps Komolsky took the news hard. "It's like the wound is being opened up again," she sobbed to Darby when at last they connected. "How could a trained medical professional — a nurse — do that to my brother? She worked with him! Why did she have to end his life?"

Darby agreed that there was no understanding such an action. Her words were of little comfort to Alicia, she knew, and yet the truth — that Linda Gefferelli had murdered Emerson Phipps — needed to be told. *Just like I need to tell Mark and Lucy the truth about Peyton Mayerson and tomorrow's bogus closing . . .*

She closed her eyes and had an inkling of an idea.

Darby was still sitting before the fire when Tina Ames checked in a half-hour or so later.

"Everything is all set for tomorrow," she said, poking one of the logs with a tong. "The service will be held at the Island Community Center, and all kinds of people have stepped forward to help, including Helen."

Tina saw Darby's look of consternation. "Now don't you worry about Helen — she's fine. Lucy Trimble took her for dinner and made sure she was comfortably situated in the Inn. Helen's all set. She said she'll give you a big hug in the morning." Tina gave a reassuring nod. "Tomorrow is going to be a wonderful tribute to Jane, you'll see, and I don't want you to worry about it at all."

She paused. "Darby, are you going to be okay?"

Darby nodded. "I'm just thinking, trying to sort it all out. There are so many loose ends. That man who lives on Sheepscot — he's an Ames. Is he any relation to you?"

Tina smiled. " 'Course. He's my dad's cousin. Crazy as a coot for staying on that little patch of nothing, but I'm sure glad for your sake that fellow from the Island Association was in the habit of checking on him."

She gave Darby a quizzical look.

"I don't mean to nag, but have you called that Miles Porter back? He tried you again about a half hour ago."

Darby rose from her chair and stretched. "I'll call him right now, Tina. You go home and get some rest. Thanks for everything and I will see you in the morning."

Back in the cozy cottage, Darby pulled on pajamas and crawled under the bed's down comforter. Feeling snug and safe, she dialed Miles Porter's phone.

The moment he answered, Darby knew why she had waited to call. The sound of his voice — the care, the concern — was too much for her, and she broke down, sobbing, like she had never cried in her life.

He waited a moment or two, and then he asked her if she wanted company. "I'm on the island," he said simply. "But I don't want to intrude."

"You're here? On Hurricane Harbor?"

"Yes."

"Please come over," Darby said. "I'll be waiting."

Seated in a tiny restaurant on the north shore of Boston, Peyton Mayerson took a bite of her veal scallopini and pronounced it perfect. Her dining companion and attorney, Arthur Toussaint, gulped down his glass of Chianti and scowled.

"This is the last time these guys are gonna help you out, Pen," he said, looking around the little restaurant with an air of indifference. "It's like that story my mother used to tell us, about the boy who cried wolf, you know? You've cried wolf one too many times, you know, and they're not putting up with it anymore."

Peyton put down her fork and looked at him with narrowed eyes. "You've got some nerve threatening me," she spat. "Those guys — Tony, Reggie — they wouldn't be getting anything if I hadn't held this together. The bridge contract, the lots, the construction loans — it's all my doing."

"I'm not threatening you, Pen! I'm your friend, for Chrissake. One of your few real friends," he said pointedly, stabbing a forkful of ziti and bringing it to his lips. "Not to mention I'm your lawyer," he added.

Peyton watched him eat the pasta with smoldering eyes. *There's something going down,* she thought. *Something's happening, I just don't know what.*

Struggling to keep her tone light, she said, "Well, it will all be over tomorrow, right?"

He nodded, spearing more of the hapless tubes on the tines of his fork. "The docs are all in Maine, with that real estate agent. What's her name?"

"Darby Farr."

"Yeah, that's right, Darby Farr. Some big hoopla with her today. My guy up there told me she nearly got popped out in the bay by some other broad."

"Really?" Peyton thought a moment. *Who could that have been?*

She dabbed at her lips with her napkin. So that's what it was, nothing more — a little excitement on the island. "None of that concerns us, I suppose, as long as she's able to close the deal." She took a sip of her wine. "As far as logistics, you'll have my money, right?"

"It's already there and waiting." Arthur

motioned for the waiter and ordered another bottle of wine. "We can celebrate early," he said, grinning broadly.

Inwardly Peyton groaned. She knew what was on his mind and had no intention of spending another night with him. Instead she smiled and said gaily, "By all means, Arthur. More Chianti."

The Island Community Center was full to capacity, and Darby Farr found herself greeting people that she had not seen for a decade. Old friends of her parents; retired teachers she'd had in school; and a robust woman with white hair who turned out to be Jane Farr's attorney, Claire Doyle.

"My condolences, Darby. Your aunt was quite a woman. Still had some surprises up her sleeve, right to the end." She winked. "We'll talk later."

Helen Near was tanned and healthy: a walking advertisement for the Florida lifestyle. She gave Darby a big hug, as promised, and then looked her over with tears in her eyes.

"I never met your mother, but Jane told me you resembled her," she said. "And yet I see some of your father — and Jane — in your face." She gave a sad smile. "Everyone is so friendly and caring. No wonder your aunt loved this island so."

"She didn't care for it at first, but the community definitely grew on her." Darby looked around the room. The service had yet to start: everyone was still milling about, finding seats and swapping stories. "I never really thought about it before, Helen, but when my parents died, and Aunt Jane came to live here, you went out of your way to make that transition smooth. I'm grateful."

"Why, what else would I have done?" Helen asked, surprised. "Jane needed to be with you. That's what you do for family. Jane knew that as well as anyone." Helen lowered her voice slightly. "Your aunt wasn't perfect, I'll grant you that. She didn't know a thing about raising children, never mind a grief-stricken teen. But she did her best, and by the looks of you, I'd say she succeeded rather nicely."

Darby smiled. "Thank you." She saw the Island Center's director make a hand signal that they should begin, and she nodded. Helen gave Darby a final squeeze, wiped a tear from her eye, and took her seat in the front row. Before long, more than a hundred islanders and friends had followed suit.

Darby cleared her throat and went up to the microphone.

"Friends, thank you all for coming," she began. "Today is the day we celebrate the life of Jane Jenson Farr, our friend and fellow islander. I'm her niece, Darby, and I want to tell you personally how much it means to me that you are here to honor someone we all knew and loved."

As she said the words she'd rewritten that very morning, Darby realized that at last she truly meant them. She loved her aunt and wanted to celebrate her legacy as well as her flaws. Perhaps coming so close to death had made her realize the fragility of life, or perhaps she was finally ready to grow up.

She saw the smiling face of Miles Porter seated in the second row. The night before, after his phone call, he'd wasted no time in arriving at the cottage, bringing with him a tenderness and gentleness that Darby's battered body required. She smiled back and hoped the rest of the audience did not see her blush.

When the service was over, and the last of Jane Farr's friends had shared their memories before departing into the bright afternoon sun, Darby looked across the Island Community Center at the cleanup crew of Tina, Donny, and Miles. She watched as they chatted together, tossing away paper plates and cups, covering food that could be kept for later, and restoring order to the large gathering room. A lump formed in her throat. *It's been an emotional couple of days,* she thought, swallowing hard. *And it's not over yet . . .*

The door to the Community Center opened and Ryan Oakes, accompanied by Mark and Lucy Trimble, entered. Lucy came up to Darby and placed a hand on her forearm.

"It was a lovely memorial, Darby." She paused. "You ready to head out?"

Darby nodded and called a "thank you" over to the others.

"Our bill is in the mail," said Miles with a grin.

Peyton Mayerson and her attorney, Arthur Toussaint, were already waiting outside Near & Farr when Darby, Lucy, and Mark arrived.

"Glad you decided to show up," Peyton sang out, as the three emerged from Mark's car.

Mark muttered under his breath, "That woman really gets under my skin."

Darby managed a smile. "Oh really?"

"Now, now," Lucy soothed. "Let's just get

this done."

Darby unlocked the office and gathered chairs around the conference table. The five sat down and Darby began to go through the documents.

"Here is the deed we agreed upon," she said, giving a copy to Arthur Toussaint. He grunted, showed it to Peyton, and placed it in a file.

"This is a sketch of the boundaries," Darby explained, handing Peyton's lawyer another piece of paper. "And here is the list of personal property which is also conveying with the house."

Arthur Toussaint waved his hands in the air and gave an exasperated look. "We don't have all day, Ms. Farr. May I present the settlement statement, or do you have a few more pieces of paper you'd like to push my way?"

Darby made a show of looking through her file as she stalled for time. Where was Ed Landis? When would he arrive to arrest Peyton?

She pulled out a property disclosure form. "Actually, I do need a signature on this document," she said, giving the paper to Peyton.

"Where do I sign?" Her voice was flat with boredom.

"Right here — after you've read it, of course."

Peyton shot a murderous look in Darby's direction and began to read the three-page disclosure.

Arthur Toussaint placed a form on the table in front of Lucy and Mark. "While my client is signing that, here is what you will be signing. There's the purchase price of the property, $5.2 million, minus the commission and other fees. I have a check for Near & Farr Realty right here, and the remainder in a nice big cashier's check." He pulled papers out of an envelope and glanced at Darby.

Peyton Mayerson looked up from the papers. "Don't spoil my fun, Arthur. I want to be the one to give Darby the check." She handed the papers to her and signed the settlement statement. "After all, I'm the one who's the new owner of Fairview."

"Not quite," said Ed Landis, bursting through the door, his gun pointed at Peyton. He grabbed her by the arm, "You're both under arrest." Another man, Landis' partner, grabbed a startled Arthur Toussaint, who looked as if he was about to vomit.

"Emilio?" Peyton shrieked. "What's going on?"

"FBI." Landis read the two their rights

and signaled for his partner to handcuff them.

Peyton's shocked expression turned quickly to disdain. "You," she spat, shaking her head at Ed Landis. "You're a Fed?" She smirked and gave a bitter chuckle. "Unbelievable. I slept with a federal agent. That will be something for my memoir."

Ed Landis lifted his eyebrows and pulled her toward the door. "Good idea, Penelope. You'll certainly have lots of time to write."

Landis and his partner shuffled Peyton and Arthur Toussaint out the door and into a waiting unmarked car, leaving Darby, Mark, and Lucy in their wake.

"Wow," said Lucy. "What just happened?"

Darby turned to them both. "Peyton is actually Penelope Mancuzzi, and she's wanted by the government for her connections to organized crime." She saw the disbelief on their faces and felt sick. Would her next plan even work?

"So what you're saying," began Mark slowly, "is that we do not have a sale of Fairview . . ."

"Oh, I don't know about that," Darby said lightly. She looked out the window to the parking lot and signaled to someone. Moments later, Ryan Oakes strode into the room, papers in hand and a smile on his face.

"I'm here to make an offer on Fairview," he said, brandishing a purchase and sale agreement. He turned to Mark and Lucy. "I believe your property is available, and I'm ready — on behalf of the Island Association — to buy it."

Mark reached out for the contract and looked it over. A moment later he was laughing and handing the paper to Lucy.

"What do you say?" prompted Ryan.

"It looks like we have a deal," quipped Lucy. Darby watched as Ryan Oakes pulled a crisp, one dollar bill out of his wallet and presented it, with a flourish, to Lucy Trimble.

Mark gave an apologetic look. "Donating Fairview is fine with me, Darby, but I'm afraid there isn't much in the way of commission for you. Other than the highly coveted lifetime membership in the Island Association."

"Some deals can't be measured in dollars and cents," smiled Darby. "I'm glad to know that Fairview will be put to good use."

Ryan Oakes was grinning. "It's a dream come true for us. We plan to have a gallery, a small restaurant, offices, and, of course, a great room to entertain our wonderful donors." He smiled at Lucy and Mark

Trimble.

"Speaking of dreams," said Mark. "There's one more piece of business to attend to. Come with us, Darby."

Dusk was falling as they drove to Jane Farr's house. Darby was surprised to see several cars in the driveway, and she entered to find a small cocktail party in full swing in her aunt's living room. Once again, a crackling fire blazed in the hearth.

Glasses were raised as she entered, and Tina hastily handed her one. "We can't have a toast without champagne," she explained, smiling.

She made sure that Ryan, Mark, and Lucy each had a glass.

"Here's to Fairview and its new life as the Maine Island Association Center," said Mark, "and to Darby Farr, for making it all possible."

While the firelight danced on her glossy black hair, Darby smiled and lifted a champagne glass. "To Fairview," she said, looking around the room. Miles Porter gave her a grin and Chief Dupont nodded in her direction.

"Thank goodness it has finally sold!" exclaimed Tina.

Ryan Oakes chuckled. "Did you think

you'd sell it on the deck of a tug during a tropical storm, Darby?"

"No," she admitted. "But I'm sure it's something my Aunt Jane would have approved of."

Chief Dupont nodded. "You're right about that. She was a firm believer that real estate trumped everything, that's for sure. And she loved happy endings."

Lucy poured some water into her champagne glass and lifted it again as a toast. "Here's to more happy endings," she said. "For instance, I believe there's someone here with something special for you, Miss Darby Farr."

Darby watched as Lucy looked around the room and smiled at the elegantly dressed older woman with whom Darby had spoken that morning.

Claire Doyle moved through the crowd. In her hand she carried a letter-sized white envelope which she handed to Darby.

"Go ahead, see what it is," urged Tina.

Darby took the envelope and opened it up. Inside was a key chain with two keys and an address.

"Two-twenty Cove Road," she read. She looked up, incredulous. "That's my old house. What's this all about?"

"A final surprise from Jane Farr," said

Lucy. "You tell her, Claire."

Claire Doyle fixed her gray eyes on Darby and smiled kindly. "Your aunt told me on numerous occasions that she had one regret: selling your childhood home. She always said that it was the one deal she should never have made." She paused. "When the property came on the market a few years ago, she gritted her teeth and bought it back, even though she had to pay triple what she sold it for! Since then, it has been rented to a young mother and her daughter, but the deed is in your name."

Darby remembered seeing the small blonde girl sitting at the kitchen table with her crayons. She smiled. "I don't believe it. I wish she had told me."

"Oh, your aunt was like that," Tina said. "Liked to have a few tricks up her sleeve." Tina downed her champagne and looked around for the bottle. "When it comes down to it, everyone likes to have their little surprises, I guess."

"Or big ones," said Mark.

Lucy Trimble handed Darby a large canvas wrapped in tissue paper. "We wanted to give you something to show our appreciation for everything you've done, Darby," she said. "I hope you'll be able to bring it on the plane."

Darby unwrapped the canvas. Lucy had

painted a vibrant sky with an island surrounded by a tranquil azure sea.

"It's beautiful!" she exclaimed. She read the title of the painting. "New Beginnings." She smiled at Lucy. "Thank you. It's very appropriate."

Miles Porter stepped forward to admire the scene and give Darby a secret squeeze on the waist. "It's brilliant, Lucy, absolutely brilliant."

"I feel like we all have a fresh start," said Lucy with feeling. "I'm going to see if I can find that baby boy I gave up years ago, and if he wants to see me, I'm going to try."

Mark Trimble glanced at Ryan Oakes. "I know I'm charting a new course."

Darby Farr looked around the room at the faces she had come to love. "Here's to new beginnings," she said, "and happy endings, too."

ACKNOWLEDGMENTS

I owe a debt of gratitude to many people who have helped me on my journey.

First, to my parents — thank you for teaching me to love books and mysteries. To my friends in Camden and beyond, especially Elaine, Patty, Nancy, Cindy, Becky, Lynda, Valerie, Marya, and Trish — thanks for your friendship and support. To fellow members of the Mt. Battie Book Club. I'm grateful for our insightful discussions of all kinds of books. And to my hiking group, "Twelve Wild Women" — you keep me moving! Thanks for the enthusiasm over the years.

I appreciate the skill of my manuscript readers: Becky Ford, Lynda Chilton, Lucy Morgan, Gloria Guiduli, Valerie Alex, and Ed Doudera. A big thanks to Alexandra Doudera for her design talent, and Erika Doudera for her insight into Darby's heritage.

For specialized assistance when I needed it, thank you to Attorney Linda Gifford of the Maine Association of REALTORS®; William J. Albany, Chief of Police, Limerick Township, Pennsylvania; Patricia McGee Albany, R.N.; and Public Affairs Specialist Philip Edney, Federal Bureau of Investigation.

Thank you to my literary agent, Tris Coburn, and to all the good people at Midnight Ink, including Marissa Pederson, Connie Hill, Brian Farrey, and Terri Bischoff. I'm looking forward to our continued partnership.

Much appreciation to my fellow real estate agents in Maine, above all the team at Camden Real Estate, and to Tess Gerritsen, a friend who has taught me so much over the years.

Finally, this book would not have been possible without the support, love, and encouragement of my family. Thank you Mom, Will, and Lucia — as well as Matt, Nate, Lexi, and especially, Ed.

ABOUT THE AUTHOR

Vicki Doudera never imagined her career as a top selling real estate agent would lead to her dream job: fiction writing. A graduate of Hamilton College and the author of several non-fiction books, she entered real estate in 2003, joining a firm specializing in coastal properties and becoming one of its most successful brokers. Meeting clients, touring luxurious homes, and negotiating deals prompted her to pick up her pen and create Darby Farr, a gutsy agent selling houses — and solving murders. The thrilling result is her brilliantly twisted debut novel, *A House to Die For.*

Vicki has written two nonfiction books, *Moving to Maine* and *Where to Retire in Maine.* Her magazine credits include *Yankee, Parenting, Reader's Digest, The Old Farmer's Almanac, Down East,* and *People, Places & Plants.*

She belongs to the National Association of REALTORS® and is president of her local Habitat for Humanity. She lives with her family on the coast of Maine.

Contact Vicki at www.vickidoudera.com.

We hope you have enjoyed this Large Print book. Other Thorndike, Wheeler, Kennebec, and Chivers Press Large Print books are available at your library or directly from the publishers.

For information about current and upcoming titles, please call or write, without obligation, to:

Publisher
Thorndike Press
295 Kennedy Memorial Drive
Waterville, ME 04901
Tel. (800) 223-1244

or visit our Web site at:

http://gale.cengage.com/thorndike

OR

Chivers Large Print
published by BBC Audiobooks Ltd
St James House, The Square
Lower Bristol Road
Bath BA2 3SB
England
Tel. +44(0) 800 136919
email: bbcaudiobooks@bbc.co.uk
www.bbcaudiobooks.co.uk

All our Large Print titles are designed for easy reading, and all our books are made to last.